T0171698

"Guten Tag, Mr. Churchill"
Mr. Churchill"
and
Other Tales

"Guten Tag, Mr. Churchill"

and

Other Tales

MICHAEL J. MERRY

To order additional copies of this book, contact:
Palibrio
1663 Liberty Drive
Suite 200
Bloomington, IN 47403
Toll Free from the U.S.A 877.407.5847
Toll Free from Mexico 01.800.288.2243
Toll Free from Spain 900.866.949
From other International locations +1.812.671.9757
Fax: 01.812.355.1576
orders@palibrio.com
734374

Contents

These stories are dedicated to my wife and grandsons

Mariela Esther Merry

James Michael Merry

Jason Patrick Merry

Ryan Elizabeth Little-Merry

'El lobo siempre será malo si sólo escuchamos a caperucita.'

(Old Spanish saying)

'GUTEN TAG, MR. CHURCHILL.'

Chapter 1 – *'Caligula's Horse.'*

Things really started in that April of 1936. Winston Churchill M.P., was having a solitary lunch at Simpson's when Walter Monkton entered the dining room and headed straight for his table. Churchill pushed back his chair and stood. They shook hands.

"Hello Winston. Bad news for you I'm afraid. Baldwin just appointed Inskip as Minister for Co-ordination of Defense."

Churchill placed his glass of wine on the table and looked at Monckton.

"Thank you Walter. I appreciate the information. That will change my plans a little but not to worry. Will you sit?" He motioned at an empty chair.

"Sorry old chap. Have to meet with the Duchy people and I'm late." Monckton was referring to the Duchy of Cornwall, of which he was Attorney General. Churchill nodded his head and sat down while Monckton turned to seek his lunch companions.

Churchill was disappointed with the news. Sir Thomas Inskip, England's Attorney General, although he had great knowledge of legal matters, he had little experience in Defense. Churchill had campaigned for such a post to be set up to study how far the Nazi's were ahead of Great Britain in the arms race and had great hopes of being appointed as its head. He had already formulated plans he considered essential to Britain's basic safety in the uncertain times ahead and this appeared to be a setback. Still, he thought, as he sipped his wine, he hadn't lived this long and got this far by giving up on anything. He smiled as he called for another carafe.

A few days later, the historian A. J. P. Taylor, an admirer of Churchill, said of Baldwin's announcement, 'The most extraordinary thing since Caligula made his horse a consul'.

Churchill finished his lunch and returned to the House of Commons where he made a telephone call to Thomas Coke, heir to the Earl of Leicester.

The Earldom of Leicester was re-created for the third time in 1564 for Queen Elizabeth I's favorite and as some historians say, her lover Robert Dudley. Re-created for the seventh time, in 1837, it was from this re-creation that the present Viscount Coke hailed. Born four years earlier than Churchill they had both attended Sandhurst. However, their careers did not bring them together, Freemasonry did that. They met in 1930 at a Lodge meeting in London and finding they shared the same interests regarding England's future, became friends. Churchill had no qualms about calling Thomas Coke.

As a result of the call Churchill returned to Chartwell that afternoon, and after packing his regular clothes, along with some old trousers, a thick sweater, and a pair of hiking boots, he took the train to Norwich where he was picked up and driven to Holkham Hall. There he passed the weekend riding around much of the six thousand acre Estate and engaging in animated conversations with Coke his host, and Jimmy Carr the Head Gamekeeper, before returning to Westminster early on Sunday morning.

Thanks in part to the above events, Great Britain was a little better prepared for the German invasion when it came at the end of 1939.

Chapter 2 – *'A vision.'*

War with Germany was declared after they invaded France in April of 1939. In June England sent an expeditionary force across the channel comprising a hundred thousand men to assist the French Army.

In September, 1939 Winston Churchill, now First Lord of the Admiralty, called Thomas Coke at Holkham Hall and drove secretly to Suffolk along with Hugh Dalton.

Dalton, a bitter enemy of former Prime Minister Neville Chamberlain, became Minister for Economic Warfare in the new government in October 1939. In this position he became responsible for conducting espionage, sabotage and reconnaissance in occupied Europe. Dalton was charged with forming what would become the 'Auxiliary Units', a top secret resistance organization that Churchill had dreamed up that would be activated should an invasion threaten Britain.

Dalton returned to London impressed with what Churchill had envisioned, Coke had financed and Jimmy Carr and a group of trusted men had built. Although he didn't realize it at the time, he would have less than four months before the Germans invaded.

What Churchill had shown Dalton was a prototype of a bunker built to house up to a half-dozen 'Auxiliaries', as Churchill called them. Constructed in secret, the bunkers were intended to be the bases from which trusted men would be able to operate against any invading forces and remain hidden when not actually on operations. Coke agreed to finance and build the model. He imported an engineer, an electrician and a plumber and assigned four laborers from his Estates in Ireland. They constructed the prototype as Jimmy Carr had explained it to them.

Jimmy Carr served with the Sandringham's Territorial Battalion at the Gallipoli Campaign in mid-1915. This Battalion comprised of men from the Royal Estate at

Sandringham where the fourteen year old Carr, born in Dersingham, a village to the north of Sandringham, worked. He tricked the Enlistment Officer regarding his age and was accepted into the Battalion. His comrades said nothing, allowing the youngster to train and then serve with them. On August 12th they attacked the Turks at the village of Anafarta Saga. That is where the myth grew up that they had charged into the mist and vanished. One minute they were being led by their Commanding Officer, Sir Horace Proctor-Beauchamp, and the next they disappeared. Their bodies were never found. There were no survivors. They did not turn up as prisoners of war.

Carr had been shot in the head during the desperate charge. Knocked unconscious, he was found several hours later and carried to an aid post where medics found that a Turkish bullet scored the top of his head but didn't penetrate his skull. However, the rest of the Battalion perished that day and their disappearance has been shrouded in mystery ever since. Carr fought at Gaza in 1918 where once again the Battalion suffered horrendous casualties and he received another wound.

He stayed in hospital in France for six months before being returned home and while recuperating from his injuries he learned German from the POW orderlies who worked there. When he tired of this he talked with another patient, an older Sergeant named Arthur Collins, a Norfolk Regiment veteran, the Chief Gamekeeper at the Holkham Estate.

Collins was one of the first snipers in the Army. An excellent shot, he got plenty of practice before the war on the Estate. Impressed with the young soldier he asked Jimmy if he wanted a job. Carr accepted and after being released in early 1919, started his apprenticeship in game-keeping. As a born and bred country boy Jimmy understood the workings of a big Estate. Allotted a small room above the stables, he slowly learned the trade. In 1920 he married Jean Longbridge, a local girl but she became ill with the Spanish Flu epidemic that ravished England and she died in August of that year. After that Jimmy kept to himself most of the time. He rarely visited a pub and cooked his own meals.

It was hard at the beginning but he persevered. He left his room by five each morning. For the first year he accompanied Collins as the Game Keeper showed him around the Estate and pointed out what he had to take notice of. Fences might need repair. Streams blocked by fallen branches and brush must be cleared. Pheasants and partridges had to be nurtured so that good seasonal shooting prevailed. Vermin such as foxes had to be controlled. The deer needed to be watched and there were a hundred other small tasks which were necessary to maintain the Estate in good shape.

Arthur Collins, wounded at Gaza, found it increasingly difficult to walk the long distances around the Estate and in 1935 he retired. His leg had been operated on several times and he felt that eventually it might have to be amputated. He rented a small cottage at Wells-next-to-the-sea, fitted one room out as a workshop and made it known to the local Estate owners his availability to repair any firearms that might require attention.

His recommendation that Carr be named Head Gamekeeper met with favor from Thomas Coke who had got to know Carr well over the years. Late in 1935 Carr took up his duties. Knowing the Estate's six thousand acres like the back of his hand it was a bold poacher that tried for game or fish at Holkham.

In April 1936 Carr met Winston Churchill. Called to the Great Hall, Coke told him that the conversation they were about to have would remain private and never mentioned unless Coke said otherwise. They sat down that Saturday morning and listened to what Churchill had to say.

Starting off, Churchill referred to the military service of both men, telling them he knew of their experience. He mentioned that the 3rd Earl now in his 80's, was semi-retired and for all intents and purposes, the Viscount Coke was the man in charge of Holkham. Then he told them why he had come that day.

He wanted, said Churchill, bases where groups of patriots might shelter when Germany invaded England. There was no doubt in his mind that this would happen within the next few years. He had been laughed at when he expressed this theory in London. Neither Carr nor Coke showed any sign of amusement as he spoke and this encouraged him with his talk. The bases, he said, must be well hidden and have access to water. They would need generated electricity. There would be room for six to ten persons to sleep and work and storage space would be required. Equipment such as weapons, explosives, food and other supplies would be delivered when the time came. What he wanted now was a commitment from Coke to build the first base and from Carr to keep it maintained until needed. Both men pledged their help.

That afternoon, dressed in old clothes and carrying flashlights, they climbed aboard a small cart pulled by two horses and rode out to examine the Estate and see sites which Jimmy Carr thought might be suitable. They passed the well-known limestone obelisk and headed through the deer park, leaving all tracks and trails behind, climbing gently as they entered the pine forest. Leaving the cart with its horses tethered they turned due east, finding themselves in a silent wonderland of nature. It seemed no one had ever ridden or even walked through these pine trees. Box, broom and hawthorn bushes starting to flower abounded, and everywhere underfoot, green ferns, large and small grew.

Jimmy Carr knew where he was going and after about an hour they crossed a small stream and he pointed ahead at a low hill. They pushed through the heavy undergrowth eventually arriving at the bottom of the rise. At ground level the limestone rocks were interspersed with bushes and stunted pines. Then the hill rose up a hundred feet to form a ridge line. Thick stands of pines, with heavy shrub at their base, grew there. The ridge meandered down as it turned in a north-easterly direction. Several hundred yards on it flattened out and disappeared into the pine forests again.

Carr pushed forward, separating plants so they could get through. Finally he paused at a huge hawthorn bush and walking round to one side of it, pulled back a flowering branch. The men slipped past the thorny limb he held back and ducked low to enter the cave it revealed. Inside it was dim, and they switched on their flashlights. The roof loomed twelve feet above them. After a narrow entrance of about ten feet it became bigger.

The rock floor was uneven, and the walls looked to be thirty feet apart. They walked in further and the ceiling became lower and the cave narrower and eventually they came to what seemed to be a dead end. Turning, they saw light filtering through the back of the hawthorn bush at the entrance about a hundred feet behind them. Carr pointed ahead and when they focused their torches they saw that before ending, the cave made a right-hand turn. They followed him along and as they turned they came to another, much smaller grotto. Six feet high, a stream ran through it and before the water vanished beneath an outcrop of limestone, a small pool had formed. Carr told them that this exit tunnel gradually became narrower. He had followed it for some two hundred yards and seen where it exited from the rocks, well covered by bushes. He had not left that way but later walked around the hill and seen where the watercourse appeared below. The textbook escape hole. Churchill smiled and nodded his head. Perfect. Just what he had in mind.

Returning the Hall in the waning light Carr went to his room to clean up and then joined the other two in Coke's study where they were bought a supper of bread and cheese as well as cider to drink. The three talked into the early hours of the morning, making several drawings and sketches, all of which were locked in Coke's safe when they retired.

That evening they agreed Coke would finance and build the base they had designed. An engineer, an electrician, a plumber, two carpenters and four laborers from the family Estates in Ireland would construct the prototype with the refinements needed before the men were sent home again. Payment over and above their usual wages would be provided, and all had to sign an oath of secrecy. Jimmy Carr would supervise the overall construction.

The eight men would be housed for two to three weeks in an unused cottage on the grounds and have everything they needed. Their breakfast and supper would be taken care of but they must not go out unless it was to be transported to the base sight. The men would all agreed that for the wages they were being paid, the terms did not seem too difficult to put up with.

After Jimmy Carr left Coke and Churchill that Sunday evening the great man asked Coke what the cost would be to complete the work. He told Churchill that he shouldn't worry about that, he understood that if he ever required help he could call on him. Churchill thanked him for his faith and that part of the conversation appeared to be forgotten. Churchill however forgot nothing. In 1944, Prime Minister Churchill, when asked by the King for his recommendation for the post of Lord Lieutenant of Norfolk, endorsed Coke who His Majesty then appointed.

Germany never invaded Britain. Operation Sea Lion, Hitler's plan to cross the Channel was postponed indefinitely in September 1940. However, it was (to quote the Duke of Wellington, after Waterloo) "The nearest run thing you ever saw in your life".

Supposing the invasion had occurred? What would have happened to Britain? The possibilities are explored here.

Chapter 3 – *'Early days.'*

Work started at the end of October, 1936. Autumn was beautiful that year. The job proceeded at a fast pace, and by the time the Irishmen arrived Carr had all the required components that the engineer, plumber and carpenters said they would want. These were stored in the empty cottage which the men would occupy during the build-out. They transported the materials to the cave over two nights using horses to pull one of the large carts used during the harvest.

Once the materials were in the cave the build started from Carr's diagrams. The engineer made changes to facilitate the construction, but the finished base was basically as Coke, Churchill and Carr had envisioned months earlier. After a few days Carr, carrying a letter that Churchill supplied, made a trip to Norwich and picked up four heavy wooden cases from a Territorial Army base there and drove them back to Holkham.

Carr took care with the cave entrance as to cause a minimum of disturbance to the surrounding grounds. The installation work would be done at night and the first thing that had to go in was a generator from one of the Norwich boxes. This they temporarily set up near the stream in the rear of the cave, and wires were run to small low voltage bulbs around the working area. Once the men arrived each evening they stayed within until they left the next day. It took two weeks for them to complete the base and when finished Thomas Coke expressed his satisfaction with the work and thanked the men before they returned home.

The entrance, camouflaged by the hawthorn bush, they left alone. However, once inside, the first of three thick walls of lumber and sandbags were constructed routing any visitor to the right where they would be obliged to turn after six feet and then make a left. After a further six feet came a heavy wooden door with a lock. They cast concrete columns at the end of the second wall, to support this. A small periscope gave a limited view outside the door. The carpenters also installed a battery bell. Unlike a normal door where this would be very accessible, they put it in the uppermost corner of the jamb. Unless you had business here you would have no need for a bell. A simple model, it sounded inside the cave when the button was pushed.

The carpenters and laborers lined the interior of the cave with wood until it resembled a regular hut with an inverted 'V' shaped roof. There was an attic for storage. They insulated the timber construction by covering the outside of both roof and walls with heavy tar paper which would contain any leakage through the limestone and prevent water penetrating the wood. After completing the basic structure the uneven floor they leveled by pouring fast setting concrete and once firm, covered again with canvas which they nailed in place. While the cement hardened shelves, several cupboards and two built in tables, along with six bunks in three tiers of two, were installed.

The other boxes from Norwich were opened and their contents removed. Then the small generator was permanently installed on a concrete base in the rear grotto and the packing case it came in was lined with thick blankets to muffle its sound and nailed back together around it. The exhaust ran through a rubber hose into the stream. Permanent wiring for lights was strung into the main space. Three, fifty-gallon drums, set into wooden bases, supplied the fuel. A table supported the radio which came out of another of the boxes. Once installed, an antenna was strung back to the door frame. There a four-foot hole, drilled through the rock, emerged over the entrance. Hidden by the brush and ferns, they buried it six inches underground inside a rubber pipe and ran it fifty feet up to the ridge, painted it in a camouflage pattern and strung it to the top of one of the pine trees. It became invisible after the first five feet as the branches hid it. They had another small radio similar to those sold in any electronics store, for entertainment. When they switched the antenna over from the main set they would hear regular BBC broadcasts.

The final work consisted of storing the weapons that Carr had picked up. There were six Enfield .303 rifles, two Thompson sub-machine guns with 100 round drum magazines plus four Colt .45 automatics, which used the same ammunition as the Thompson's. A case of Mills bombs and another of 808 explosives were put on shelves. Six complete Army webbing harnesses, camouflage uniforms and boots were unpacked and stored along with two pairs of night binoculars. Heavy duffle coats, insulated underwear and woolen sweaters completed the clothing inventory.

Mattresses, blankets, pillows, towels, toothpaste, brushes soap and saucepans were stockpiled and a primitive shower, using the stream as a water source, was constructed. Basic medical supplies were included. At Thomas Coke's suggestion a bookshelf was built and stacked with a few popular volumes. They sorted spare parts and crystals for the Type 'A' Mark III radio, the diminutive 'spy' set used by agents overseas and tested the simple apparatus, by turning it on and off to ensure it functioned. Lamps were filled and wicks checked. A small tank of oil was put on blocks. They had a Primus stove for cooking and a large can of methylated spirit for fuel. The cave had natural cross ventilation through the entrance and exit of the stream. Because of the weather they were likely to be cold and two electric heaters were installed.

When the job was finished the tools were packed and stored. The surplus lumber they lifted into the attic and the remaining bags of concrete stacked behind the entrance buttress. Carr estimated that the small disturbances to the terrain close to the cave would disappear in a week and this proved to be correct. When he went by ten days later all looked normal and untouched. It remained that way, occasionally visited by Carr, until the end of the year.

By December 31st, 1939 Carr felt sure the base would be activated momentarily. In early January he received a message at his cottage requiring him to be at the Hall the following morning to meet with Coke. The Viscount informed him that Churchill had said the Germans were attacking towards London and their *Panzers* advancing on a broad front. They were driving the badly mauled remnants of the British Army before them. The German Me-262 aircraft, although they could stay for only a short time over the battlefield from their French bases, were shooting the few remaining RAF fighters out of the sky and Churchill prayed the promised Canadian Divisions, and later the Australians and New Zealander's, would arrive to establish a holding line within the next sixty to ninety days.

Few people were aware that the RAF, working with the Canadian branch of Pratt & Whitney, were test flying their own jet aircraft, the 'Meteor'. Churchill was told that it would be in production by May and that it could be delivered to England in late June providing they cut testing to a minimum. Churchill immediately agreed to the gamble. He understood that if England could hold fast until the end of April then they might drive the Germans back across the Channel later in the year.

Chapter 4 – *'Reconnaissance.'*

Dalton had almost no time to act on Churchill's plans for an Auxiliary Force. The invasion came in late December and it was all the government and military could do to organize a retreat and try to stabilize a front. However, he decided to make Holkham the first of the bases. In early January Jimmy Carr met with Coke who told him of a message from Dalton asking if he was able a nucleus of 'trusted men' in his area to be the first Auxiliaries and activate the base immediately. Carr thought of who he could recruit on the Holkham Estate and the Burnham and Wells next-to-the-sea villages close by.

He then advised Thomas Coke what he would be doing and after receiving his blessing, contacted the first person, Arthur Collins. Collins, now a popular gunsmith, could maintain his marksmanship skills testing weapons bought into him. His cottage at Wells-by-the-sea was close to Holkham Hall. The leg wound had long healed, but he walked with a cane and sported a pronounced limp. However, his military service and weapons skills made him an ideal candidate. He and Carr stayed close over the years and were good friends, which made the offer easy to present. Collins readily agreed to Carr's request and was told about the base. As the former Head Gamekeeper, he knew about the cave in its original state but he would be amazed to see the changes done to it.

The following morning the two men met two hundred yards from the base. They hid their bicycles in the brush and walked forward up the slope towards the entrance. It seemed unchanged outside. Inside things were different. After showing Collins how to start the generator, the two men sat down while Carr filled Collins in on what they must do. The first thing discussed was a method of communication. The two men decided it was too dangerous to meet openly, so the base should be their rendezvous. If they were to be at their respective houses a flower pot on the front porch would be on the right side of the front door. If they needed to communicate the flower pot would be moved to the left of the door. Carr went daily to Wells-next-to-the-sea to get the post and this would be his chance to ride by Collins' cottage.

Also in January, Dalton instructed his assistants to contact several dozen more 'trusted men' in other areas and arrange for additional bases to be constructed. They should make themselves available to anyone who expressed an interest in helping resist the Germans. Then it could be decided if the person was suitable and if they thought that training may be required. After reporting the details to Dalton's people, they would make arrangements. Most volunteers they informed him, would not be active service material but people in normal walks of life who might be willing to help out on specific missions. These people had to be registered, their special skills noted, and kept under deep cover

Hugh Dalton sent word to Thomas Coke that he would be at Holkham Hall January 31st and to have Carr on hand. At the meeting Carr received instructions about starting operations as soon as he received the appropriate radio message. Dalton's Friday visit to Holkham coincided with the arrival of an Army truck filled with provisions for the base. These were loaded onto a harvest cart and taken to the cave next morning and unloaded there by Carr and Collins later on that day.

Dalton also explained to Carr that the Germans had limited resources for administration in England. They were using locals in many key positions until they could be replaced by German's. He, Dalton, received a constant stream of information from inside the German Military Headquarters from these undercover people. Carr was told he would be contacted by a radio operator to operate the set during the following months, enabling them to keep in touch with Dalton's Headquarters.

The Germans intended to pass through Peterborough, then after establishing a front line twenty-five miles to the north starting at Boston, in Lincolnshire bordering The Wash, they would refit the *Panzers* in Peterborough before their next push.

Dalton told him he learned through his spy network that five wings of Me-262 fighter-bombers, about two hundred aircraft, were due to be moved over the next few months from their bases in France to an airfield in England, allowing them more time at the front to support their *Panzers*. All the aircraft needed to be repaired and refitted in France first and Dalton felt sure the attack could not start again until both aircraft and *Panzers* came to operational readiness again after the initial heavy fighting.

The chosen air base for the Me-262's, said Dalton was Horsham St Faith north of Norwich. It had the required long concrete runway and space for a great deal of aircraft to park. It also adjoined Norwich Airport for additional capacity. Dalton asked Carr to reconnoiter the airfield as soon as possible, before the Germans increased their security, and then, after submitting his report, wait for orders. Carr learned that upon his arrival in St. Faith he should contact the local Justice of the Peace, Albert Berrins, a well-known farmer in the area who supplied fresh vegetables and eggs to the air base. Berrins and Carr should meet at the Kings Head pub around 11am. Berrins would say something about Horsham's famous Church, a natural introduction. Carr should reply he understood it dated from the 13th century. They could then talk about getting into the airfield.

Early on Monday, February 3rd, 1941 Jimmy Carr set off on his bicycle for Horsham St. Faith. He carried a small backpack that contained repair kit for any punctures he might pick up, a flashlight, a bottle of water and a pair of work gloves. Also in the pack was a book listing old Norfolk Churches and a blanket. If questioned he would say he wanted to examine the painted saints on the 1528 rood screen at the well-known St. Mary and St. Andrew Church at St. Horsham St. Faith. In his jacket pocket he had a pencil for making notes and a comic book.

He noticed a great deal of military activity as the German's moved north, he stood for a little watching them, however this didn't affect him. The weather was cold but there was no frost. It would be a twenty-five mile ride and he expected to arrive close to 11am. His journey, apart from the various troop conveys he encountered, proved uneventful. At Fakenham he took time to ride around the town and check the roads where, in an emergency the road block he could see in the distance, could be avoided. There seemed to be a path along the Wensom, the River outside town that ran west. That might be of use. He made a mental note. Returning he went through the block at Wells Road manned by German Army troops. He showed his ID, and they waved him through.

At Foxley there was an even smaller block manned by two uninterested soldiers who barely glanced at his identification. He arrived at St Faith at 11.10am. Cycling down Church Street he saw the large church on the left. Following instructions he made a right turn into Back Street and stopped outside the Kings Head. He noticed no rack for cycles so he secured his machine with lock and chain to a convenient drainpipe. Pushing open the door of the Private Bar he walked through. It was quiet inside with a few comfortable arm-chairs and a sofa arranged around a low wooden table. Four cushioned stools stood in front of a small bar behind which stood an elderly, man in deep conversation with a well-dressed customer. Carr strolled over.

"Bitter, please. A half pint."

The man turned and removed a glass from a shelf and drew the beer. Placing it in front of Carr he wiped the counter, smiled, and without speaking, walked back through the narrow entrance that seemed to connect to the Public Bar.

The well-dressed man turned to Carr.

"There's a wonderful Church here in Horsham if you're interested?"

"Yes, I've been told it dates from the 13th century."

They smiled at each other and the man held out his hand.

"Berrins. Albert Berrins. I understand I'm not to ask who you are. Let's sit over there." He pointed to a pair of arm-chairs in a corner and they walked over.

"I know why you're here. The airfield eh? Well it's been quiet for the last two months once the RAF moved out. My farm has always had an arrangement to supply vegetables and eggs. When the Jerries moved in two weeks back, they wanted to continue the deliveries. I have a man ride up there twice a week on a grocery bike, you know, one of those with a big wicker basket on front. He goes through the main gate and delivers the stuff to the NCO at the kitchen. Right now there can't be more than a couple of dozen men stationed there but last week the NCO told my man that starting in February they wanted a lot more stuff. That tells me they will increase personnel there soon. A few days back a whole fleet of concrete mixers went to the base and yesterday there was a convoy going up Church Street. Six lorries. Four carried bulldozers. Make what you like out of that!"

Carr digested the information. This was critical and Dalton would want to hear about the developments as soon as possible.

"When is the next delivery due." he asked Berrins.

"Tomorrow about 10am my man takes the stuff up there."

"Can I take his place without causing problems?"

Berrins smiled. "Tom, my man, is not what you call 'all there' He's always been backward. The Germans realize this and they don't bother him too much. We can say you're his brother and you can act the same way he does. I've got some old clothes that will fit you so it shouldn't be a problem. Not many Jerries' around at the moment but that will change I imagine. I'll go back to the farm now. Relax for a little here and then take a look at the Church, it's well worth it! From the belfry you'll be able to see the airfield. Then take the road outside the pub down to Blind Lane and about half a mile along there's a side street with a sign saying 'Berrins Farm' on it. Follow that. Come up to the main house and we'll fix you up."

They shook hands and Berrins left. Carr spent two hours at St. Mary's and St. Andrew's Church marveling at the rood screen paintings and afterwards, the view of the airfield from the belfry. He then rode his bicycle to Berrins Farm, took a nap in the spare bedroom that had been prepared for him and later enjoyed an excellent dinner with Berrins who gave him more information about the base. Before he went to bed, Berrins gave him an ID Card. It was in the name of Alfred Grizzle and stated he worked as a deliveryman. He went upstairs at eight o'clock and slept the clock round.

Berrins woke him next morning, and he enjoyed a good breakfast. The clothes he received were old and had seen better days but were what he needed for his role as a simple farm worker. They loaded the wicker basket with six dozen eggs packed in a box of newspaper shavings and put them on top of a ten pound sack of potatoes and a smaller one of turnips. He also showed Carr a half bottle of whiskey.

"That's for Werner, the Mess Corporal. Keeps him sweet. There's also a sandwich for your lunch here." He smiled at Carr as he carefully put the bottle and sandwich into the potato sack.

Carr turned out of the farmyard and cycled to the airfield. Stopping his bike at the checkpoint hut he noted that a wire fence extended out both sides of the open gate and vanished into the distance. There were two cement mixers behind the hut and piles of sand at their sides. It looked like they were almost read to pour. He took of his cloth cap and clutching it with one hand, rang the bell on the handlebars. He allowed spittle to escape from the corner of his mouth. Two soldiers, one a Sergeant, came out from the hut. Carr greeted them, removing a piece of notepaper from his pocket and holding it out to the Sergeant.

"Good morning Sir's. I be Tom's brother from Berrins Farm. I come with the groceries for you. It say that in the note 'ere." He grinned lopsidedly at the men. The Sergeant grinned at the other soldier.

The Sergeant whispered in German to the soldier, "This must be the village idiot. Look at him dribble." Then, in English he said "Well village idiot show me your ID Card, I don't have all day to stand here and watch you slobber." Both soldiers laughed, and the Sergeant held out his hand for the pass.

Carr, understanding their language, dribbled more, causing the soldiers to laugh again. He fumbled in his jacket, first producing a filthy handkerchief and then a torn comic book before digging out the ID Card. He held it out for inspection.

"Can you read that comic book fool?" Asked the Sergeant. Carr smiled.

"Not good Sir. But I like the pictures!" The Sergeant looked at his companion and shook his head. He lifted the top of the egg box and took out four large brown eggs.

"These will do for our breakfast! Now, get your stupid backside up to the Mess Corporal!" He pointed up the road and Carr mounted his bike and pedaled off. The soldiers laughed again at his unsteady progress as he wobbled from side to side up the path. He disappeared over a slight rise and they returned to the comfort of their hut.

Carr cycled along the road observing everything around him. He came to a crossroads and deliberately turned away from the buildings he could see about half a mile ahead. The dirt road took him towards the perimeter of the airfield and followed a waist-high fence surrounding it. There were coils of barbed wire and bundles of iron stakes had been dumped every hundred yards along the fence waiting to be installed and increase the security of the airfield. Then he came upon the first of the square concrete foundations, still showing the damp surface of newly poured cement. Piles of lumber which he assumed would be for construction of elevated sentry towers were randomly strewn around.

Pulling out his comic book he used it to record distances from the gate to where the towers would be started. Cycling two miles north he saw a *Kubelwagon* coming from the opposite direction. He kept pedaling with his head down until it roared up and stopped in front of him. An NCO holding a sub-machine pistol climbed out of the passenger side. A roving patrol thought Carr.

"Where do you think you're going?" He gestured at Carr with the gun. Carr smiled at him, allowing spittle to dribble from the corner of his mouth. He reached into his jacket and pulled out the note, offering it to the soldier.

"Good morning Sir's. I is Alfie, Tom's brother from Berrins Farm. I come with the groceries for you." The lopsided grin seemed to amuse them. "It say that in the note 'ere" he offered.

"You idiot!" shouted the man in heavily accented English. "The Mess is over there." He pointed back along the track. "Get your stupid groceries over there now. What have you got there anyway?" He opened the egg box and removed a half-dozen eggs, holding one up so the wagon driver could see it.

The soldier returned to the wagon grumbling to the driver. After making a turn the vehicle headed back the way it had come with Carr wobbling along behind in the dust. He noted more advanced construction on the way. Emplacements for what he assumed would be anti-aircraft guns and other, smaller enclosures, facing outwards, gave protection against any air or ground attack. Cement mixers seemed to be everywhere and piles of sand, bricks and iron rods were stacked near the buildings they were approaching. Close by he could see more concrete foundations that were laid out. Once dry these were to support more structures, admin huts probably as the barracks for personnel were already finished and located about fifty yards away. Several men entering and leaving carrying furniture caused him to draw this conclusion.

The *Kubelwagon* stopped, and the driver pointed to a large hut.

"Der Mess," he shouted, and the vehicle drove off. Carr pulled the bike onto its stand and walked up to the open door.

A man in an apron with Corporal's stripes on his sleeve stood in the doorway, hands on hips. This must be Werner thought Carr.

"Where have you been? The gate said you were on your way 20 minutes ago!" Carr went through his note routine, and the Corporal shook his head after reading it.

"Unload the bicycle idiot. Bring it all in here and put it on the table. I hope they remembered my gift!"

He walked back inside leaving Carr to carry in the sacks and eggs. Once everything was unpacked and Werner had his bottle, he seemed more condescending towards Carr. "Those thieves have stolen eggs I see. If you come back you must refuse to let them taken any. You understand?" Carr nodded. "I will require more supplies from Mr. Berrins starting in two days. Can you tell him that from me? Here, I have written what I need, take it to Berrins." He handed a piece of paper to Carr who managed to look confused. Werner sighed.

"More supplies! I have almost a hundred new men arriving this weekend to take care of the airfield security. They have to eat. I will need many goods. I think you get Berrins to come here. Then we will have no confusion. Give me the note, I will write it." Werner took the note and added his demand that Berrins visit him.

"A hundred at the weekend and then next weekend all the new administrative people and then in a month the mechanics. More than two hundred people. I need help here! I cannot feed all these men without at least six more men." He looked at Carr. "You would not understand. Now go back to Berrins and do not get lost!" He waved Carr out of the hut.

The bicycle, unloaded became easier to ride. Carr deliberately took a wrong turn and headed to the other side of the airfield.

It appeared that on this side, construction was far more advanced. Barbed wire was laid down and secured to the iron stakes and at least three towers stood ready in place. Men still worked around the wire. About two miles along Carr stopped and updated his notes in the comic book while he sat by the roadside and ate his sandwich. He heard a motorcycle in the distance and quickly mounted his bike, riding off wobbling from side to side as the engine noise of the cycle coming up behind sounded.

Judging when it was close he fell off and landed in the roadside ditch. The motorcycle stopped, and he heard laughter. Turning he saw the cycle, with a sidecar attached, above him. Both passenger and driver were pointing at him and giggling. It was muddy, and he was covered in slimy water on one side of his jacket and trousers. Finally the men stopped laughing. The driver dismounted and walked round to the ditch.

Looking back, he said to the driver in German, "This must be the idiot Werner said to expect. Look at him! He really looks the part of the village fool!" He shook his head. "You! Idiot! Get out of there. It's not a swimming pool."

Both driver and passenger howled with laughter.

"Werner swore you would lose yourself and here you are." Looking down and seeing the ever present dribble coming from Carr's mouth and the strange grin, he realized that this was a mentally ill person. Bending over he pulled the bicycle from the ditch. Reaching out his hand he helped Carr up. "Follow us to the gate. I do not want you wandering again, idiot or not!"

He remounted the motorcycle and drove slowly so that Carr could keep pace. It took ten minutes to arrive at the gate. The same Sergeant opened it and Carr cycled back towards St. Faith pleased with what he had accomplished.

Carr gave Berrins the note and explained that Werner and the rest of the soldiers he had met, were convinced he was an idiot. Berrins laughed. "As long as they think that then we're safe. What next?"

"I need to get out tonight. There's a curfew so I have to be careful. About eight o'clock I'll go to the airfield. By ten o'clock I'll be finished. If all goes well I can have a rest until the curfew lifts at five o'clock and then cycle back. Should be back at Holkham by about nine tomorrow morning."

Berrins nodded. "Fine. Rest this afternoon and leave when you're ready. I'll be asleep by the time you go. I wish you luck!" He held out his hand and Carr shook it. "Thanks for your help. Will you be back here anytime soon?"

"I can't say. If so I'm sure you will be advised. I had better keep the ID until I get clear."

Berrins agreed and told him to tear it up when he arrived back where he had come from. Turning, he went to his room to re-read his notes.

Shortly before eight he left the farm and cycled as close to the airfield as he could get. Hiding the bicycle in some brush he removed a small compass stuffed into the padded bike seat and headed off to reconnoiter. The gate was lighted ahead, and he slipped off the road and into the trees.

Heading north, he soon saw the fence to his right glinting in the moonlight. Making notes he paced out distances. Walking slowly, in and out of trees at the edge of the heath, he checked each stretch of land before moving on. After about two hundred yards he peered out from behind a tree and saw between where he stood and the fence, what appeared to be a dark shadow on the grass. There were no trees near it so he knew that it was something man made. He stayed still for five minutes and when nothing moved, he walked forward. What he found was a slit trench. He noted that it was fifty yards from the fence and had been carefully prepared to cover the approach of anyone coming from the tree-line. Noting its position he moved on.

Over the next mile he found a dozen more trenches, all within sight of the wire. The fence started a right turn to the east, and he continued following it, encountering more slit trenches as he did so. After a thousand more steps the fence turned almost due south. There were trenches every hundred yards. Now he saw he had reached the end of the airfield and was heading back. Some of the construction he had noted in the morning came into sight. Another month and all the security would be in place.

There was the sound of an engine and he noticed a single high beam pierce the sky as a motorcycle went over a small rise on the airfield perimeter path. Carr saw it through the fence and noted the time it had passed. It didn't slow down at all.

Giving the illuminated gate a wide berth he found the road and the bushes where he had hidden his bicycle. As he came closer there was a noise, and he ducked behind a bush. A group of men were walking down the street singing. They had probably been into St. Faith drinking and were now on their way back. Carr kept silent and soon he could hear the gate being opened as the men arrived back at the airfield. He stayed very still. The blanket came out of his pack and was wrapped round his shoulders. It was cold, but he had been far colder in France in 1917.

Chapter 5 – *'Knowing thine enemy.'*

He shivered through the night, standing up several times to swing his arms, jump and stamp his feet. At five by his watch he mounted the bike and rode through the village and down Church Street, the way he had entered the day before.

This morning it was different. A fair sized checkpoint had been established. There were two farm carts waiting to go through and four or five laborers on their way to work, standing in a line. He saw prefabricated hut and a pole barrier. Two soldiers were moving it up and down to allow the carts though. Carr's turn came.

"Your Identification card."

Carr took his ID Card in the name of Alfred Grizzle from his jacket and handed it to the Corporal.

"*Wo arbeiten Sie*"

"Oh, where do I work? I work delivering things to the airfield." He pointed back the way he had come from.

"Ah, you have a little German eh Alfred? That's good. To where you are leaving now?" The sentry asked.

"Have to meet the milk truck down the road in five minutes." Replied Carr.

"Ah! milch. Very good, very good." He sounded friendly and as there was no one behind him Carr asked.

"This checkpoint is new. It wasn't here yesterday."

"Correct. We have inaugurated more security at all entrances and exits to the village. It is now necessary. Do you come this way often?" He smiled invitingly at Carr.

"Rarely Corporal but sometimes. Why all the new security?"

"I cannot reveal that. Would you like to meet me for a beer this evening if you live close?" Again the simpering smile.

"Well, if my work at the farm allows I will be at the pub there." He pointed back to the Kings Head.

"I hope I will see you. Now you may go." He waved Carr through.

He mounted his bike and rode off. It seemed like Dalton's information about the village was correct. He was stopped again at the check points in Foxley and Fakenham but his ID was scarcely glanced at and he continued his journey. Before leaving Fakenham he bought himself a bottle of Tizer and a bag of Salt'n' Shake crisps.

He cycled slowly through Well-next-to-the-sea past the small cottage where Arthur Collins lived noting that the flower pot was on the left of the door. His watch showed almost nine o'clock. Early for this kind of activity. When he came for the mail it was usually around noon. He increased his speed and twenty minutes later climbed off his bike about a quarter of a mile before the base.

Putting the bike on the stand, he took the blanket, bottle and the crisps from his backpack and squatted down to eat. As he did, he looked around. All was as it should be, quiet and undisturbed. Walking and pushing the bike he came to the shrubs and then the trees. Making sure the bike was out of sight he walked up towards the cave.

Moving aside the bush he entered and reached up and pushed the bell. A key grated in the lock and the door opened to reveal Arthur Collins. He looked relieved to see Carr as they shook hands.

"Christ Jimmy, thank God you're back! I was worried!"

Carr walked in and Collins shut and locked the door. He heard the soft hum of the generator supplying the exposed light bulbs with a low source of power. It was pleasantly warm.

"Arthur. Remember what I told you. The less you know the less you could give up if something happens. Everything's fine. What's been going on here?"

Collins ushered him in and he saw another man present.

"Jimmy. This is Havildar Deoman Prahdan, previously with the 8th Gurkha Rifles. He's our wireless operator."

A small, brown man walked forward. He had a Gurkha pillbox hat on his head and was dressed in a loud green check jacket, a yellow open-neck shirt and baggy blue check trousers. He held out his hand and a big smile lit up his face. Carr saw he had a bad wound that had removed part of his lower jaw.

"Hello Jimmy. They said you needed a wireless man and I'm it! Don't mind my clothes. This is what most of us Gurkha's wear off-duty."

The disfiguration affected his speech, but it was still perfectly understandable.

"Pleased to meet you. Do I call you Sergeant or what?"

Pradhan smiled. "Whatever is easier for you Jimmy? I prefer De. I got used to that in France."

"OK De. Where was the 8th over there?" Carr asked him.

"Well, I joined in 1912. Went to France end of '14. In '15 I got sent to Loos. We lost 750 out of 800. Reformed and went to Mesopotamia until the end of the war. Garrison duty India until '35 and then came the earthquakes, and we went north to help out."

"I got hurt there and spent four months in hospital here in England. They tried that new reconstructive surgery but I suppose it was asking too much. That finished it. I got invalided out and stayed in Manchester. Got offered a job at the hospital helping other blokes like myself. Seeing the wounds would have upset most people but being a survivor, it didn't bother me."

"A few weeks my boss, Mr. Thapa asked if I would help out now England's got problems and here I am. Got in yesterday and went to see Albert. He brought me here. Nice place!" He smiled.

"That's fine, De, welcome to the Auxiliaries. We are getting started so everyone is feeling his way so to speak."

"Understood. Shall I make tea? Albert told me where everything was?"

Everyone laughed. But tea was what they needed in a time like this.

After they drank their tea, Collins continued to explain the details of the base to De who listened intently. When he finished De told him when he was ready he would check the transmitter and try out the regular radio using the antenna. Then Carr sat at the crude desk, took out his comic book and a message pad and recorded the details of his trip to St. Faith.

Starting with the bicycle journey to the airfield he told them of the checks at Fakenham and Foxley. Type of barrier, number of guards, state of alertness. The meeting with Berrins and his observations when he had visited the base, both during the day and then again in the night hours. Every detail was set down and his final report covered four pages of block capitals. It had taken him over an hour to finish. He called De over.

"Here we are De. Can you fire up the Mark III and get this out? I suppose you have a list of frequencies?"

"Yes I do Jimmy. Let's make sure everything is working and I'll get going. They said they will stand by from nine to ten each morning and again six to ten each evening so I hope we will be OK. I spent two days working with a similar model before coming here."

He took the message over to the radio table and sat down. He put on headphones and took out a small notepad covered with neatly recorded letters and figures. As he turned on the power switch the set hummed as it warmed up. Within minutes De was ready. The Mark III was a Morse only set and De tapped out what Carr assumed was the call sign. A reply came back immediately.

"All good. Their reply checks out. I've got a go-ahead." He started to transmit and Carr was amazed at his speed on the Morse key. The four pages were sent in under five minutes.

De transmitted his sign off call and then sat back and listened to a short reply. He noted the transmission on a message pad and handed it to Carr. It said briefly that the message had been received and understood. He was told to stand by on the assigned frequencies at the hours agreed upon.

Carr was satisfied. He had completed his first mission and now the fatigue set in.

"I'm going to sleep. I'm sure you both have a lot to do so wake me at about 3 o'clock please." He walked over to a bunk and took off his boots, stripped off his jacket and trousers and laid down. He was asleep in minutes and stayed in the bunk until Collins called him at three.

They agreed that De should remain permanently at the base but that they themselves must continue their regular daily routines. Carr doing his game-keeping rounds and Collins working at his gunsmiths business. All stayed quiet for the next two months. De manned the wireless and a twice a week reported what Carr wrote out on the message sheets. Despite the invasion, East Anglia was away from the main fighting front which was more to the north-west towards Oxford and then on to Coventry. There was not much to report.

On 9 o'clock on Friday morning April 19th, De received a message for Collins. He knew he was accustomed to coming to the base each Monday, Wednesday and Friday. Carr, if he saw no movement of the flowerpot at Collins cottage, might drop in occasionally while on his rounds but would always be there Friday morning and both Saturday and Sunday afternoons. At 930a the bell rang and Collins arrived. De gave him the message. Fifteen minutes later Carr turned up and was shown what Dalton had sent.

It was an execution order for one SS *Obergrupen Führer* Reinhard Tristan Eugen Heydrich. Collins, would travel to London the next day. He should go by bus to Norwich and take the 9.15a train to Liverpool Street Station in London's east end. When he arrived at 11.05a he must buy a copy of the Daily Telegraph and carrying it his left hand, wait outside the Great Eastern Hotel.

Someone would meet him there and Collins should go with that person after giving and receiving a password. His contact would call him 'Dad'. He should reply that his train arrived late. If no one met him he was to take the 3.15p train back to Norwich and report to the base. If met, then he would be told what to do to accomplish his mission. When completed he should return to Norwich and take a bus to his home at Wells-next-to-the-sea. He must take nothing except some money and his Identity Card with him. The message finished with a detailed schedule for Heydrich's movements for that Monday.

"Well, that seems easy enough," said Collins. "Go to London. Kill the Protector of England and come home for tea. No problem at all. Oh! I forgot, do I beat him to death with my walking stick or will they give me a weapon?" He laughed.

Then he spoke seriously. "How the hell does Dalton know the schedule? He must have someone at Heydrich's Headquarters I suppose." He scratched his head and looked at Carr.

"Arthur. The less you learn the better. Just memorize this and do what it says. Dalton and his people know what they're doing. It's been worked out and shouldn't be a problem. Follow instructions and things will be fine." He smiled at Collins but inside he had his doubts. It wouldn't do any good to let Collins hear that though.

"You're right Jimmy. I believe they know what they're up to. I'll just have to be careful."

De kept silent and went to make tea. Afterwards Collins told him to reply and say he would carry out his instructions.

Chapter 6 – *'Invitation to an assassination.'*

The train pulled into Liverpool Street at 11.20a after being stopped in the station approaches for a few minutes. There were a lot of people around and after handing in his ticket he went to a newsstand to buy a copy of the 'Telegraph'. The early morning rush hour had passed, but the station appeared very busy even so. German uniforms were everywhere. Field green for the Army, the Air Force in light blue and the Navy in blue. There were many Nazi Party members in brown. SS troops in their black uniforms guarded the entrances and with them, hard looking men in long leather coats, probably Gestapo, looking at everyone who passed.

Collins walked out, avoiding eye contact with anyone. The Great Eastern was to the right and holding his Telegraph in his left hand he casually walked by the entrance. No one accosted him. Walking back again he turned and stood for as minute. A pretty girl walked towards him and he thought this might be his contact but she ignored him and walked on. He returned to the Hotel again. Feeling exposed he tapped his walking stick in frustration before starting out again. As he did, he felt someone take his arm.

"Hello Dad." Said a feminine voice. He looked sideways and saw the pretty girl he had looked at a few minutes before. He recovered quickly.

"Sorry I'm late dear. The trains you know!" She nodded her approval.

"Come on then. Let's catch the bus!" she led him down the street to a bus stop with a short queue.

"Won't be long! Should be home in half hour. I'll get tea ready."

"That's will be nice I'm sure," replied Collins.

The number 133 bus pulled up. He saw the word Kennington on the front. The girl pushed him in and they found two seats downstairs.

"Fares, please!" It was the conductor. A woman.

"I'll get them Dad." She turned to the clippie. "Kennington Church, two please." She passed over half a crown.

"ain't you got nuffin' smaller?" The woman asked.

"Sorry. That's all the change I've got."

The clippie mumbled under her breath but punched two tickets and fumbled in her satchel for change.

"'ere yer go love." She poured coins into the girl's hands and walked forward.

"Christ! All pennies," said the girl. Then she laughed. "Well I suppose we can use 'em for the gas meter."

They got off the bus at Kennington Church. The girl lead Collins to a side street with the name 'St. Agnes Place' displayed high on a wall at the corner.

"I live here in a flat," said the girl. "Let's get in and have tea and then we can talk."

They went through an entrance and up two flights of stairs. The girl stopped in front of a door, produced a key and unlocked it. They walked in to a small hallway. There were two closed doors and then an open space revealing a small kitchen. At the end of the hall was a sitting room with two arm-chairs and sofa. He noticed a large radio on a table. Its windows, curtains drawn back, showed a blank wall and below he could see a small courtyard.

"Make yourself at home. I'll put the kettle on." She closed the curtains and walked out. He heard water running. When she returned she sat opposite him.

"Look. I don't want to know who you are or what you're here for. My instructions were to meet you, bring you home, open the door when your next contact arrives to get you and then close the door when you leave and forget I ever saw you.

I'll bring tea in a minute and then I have to go out. I'll be back with food about five. You stay here. Don't move."

"The sofa is your bed. I'll bring pillows and a blanket in a moment. Use the radio if you like. I'll be going to bed for a few hours. My work is at Buckingham Palace and my shift this week is from 10pm until six in the morning. At nine fifteen I'll leave and will be back at six thirty Sunday morning. Then I'll be getting my head down. I'll put sandwiches in the kitchen. Your contact will be over to talk to you at noon. Don't answer the door. I'll let him in and then I'm off to see my mum in Wandsworth. When he leaves make sure the door is locked." She looked at her watch.

"Sunday at six I'll be back. When I get here you can tell me when you're leaving, it'll be Sunday night or Monday morning. Lots of people from the Palace live around here so don't be surprised if you hear doors opening and closing at all hours. They work different times. We'll learn more tomorrow. Anything else you want to know?"

Collins shook his head. His tea arrived along with pillows and blankets and he sat sipping it. It was warm in the room and putting the cup and saucer to one side, he dropped off. He didn't hear the girl leave, and it wasn't until five when she came back with fish and chips he awoke. The radio kept him occupied for an hour then he arranged the sofa with the pillows and he slept. Perhaps it was the stress, but he did not awake until the doorbell rang on Sunday. He took his legs from under the covers and sat upright. The door opened and a bearded man wearing a long overcoat entered.

"Good mornin'. I'm Nathan. I don't want to know yer name. Elsie will bring tea in a minute so let's wait before we talk."

The tea came and Elsie said she had to leave. They heard the front door close.

"Right. We can talk now. First up. Do you know who 'eydrich, the Protector is and what 'e looks like?"

"Of course. His face is everywhere."

"Good. Now, you know yer way round weapons, right?" Collins nodded.

"What about the 03 Springfield sniper rifle?"

"I used it in the last war. Started with an Enfield but when the Yanks came I picked up a Springfield. Liked it a lot."

"Great. That's what you'll be using. Now. I'll fill yer in. Make sure yer pay attention. You'll stay 'ere until five tomorrow morning. At five yer need to be downstairs waiting. A bloke will be there to meet yer. You'll go by bus to Westminster. There, you'll be taken to a ware'ouse and along with three others, you'll load up a barrer and push it to Big Ben. Someone will be waiting to let you in. The barrer will have four rolled swastika banners to be 'anged from below the clock face, you and the other fellows will do that. By that time the German guards will 'ave changed and won't remember if three or four persons went in early. In one roll will be the Springfield. Take it to up to the gallery above the clock face. Yer will be overlooking Parliament Square. No one will be there. The others will 'ave left." He sipped his tea.

"At four o'clock yer kill 'eydrich. Leave the rifle and descend as fast as yer can. You knock on the entrance door and someone will open it from the outside and re-lock it. Yer walk away and catch a bus to Liverpool Street. Should be in time for the five fifteen back to Norwich. From there yer to go 'ome. Tuesday morning go to yer base." He paused for moment. "Yer know what they're saying around 'ere lately? If 'itler, 'immler and 'eydrich was in a room locked up and someone gave yer a gun with two bullets and sent yer in, what would yer do?"

"I've no idea," said Collins.

"Nathan laughed. "Well, they say yer shoots 'eydrich twice just to make sure the bugger's dead like!" He chuckled. "He's a nasty bit of work that one!" He continued.

"At the ware'ouse they will 'ave a work order for the delivery and installation of the banners. Yer will also be given an Identification Card at that time. Yer don't 'ave to say much to anyone. They will understand. That's it."

Collins sat back on the sofa digesting what he had been told. It sounded simple but he could imagine the work that had gone into getting the information and making arrangements. The resistance networks must be good!

He looked at Nathan. "I understand,"

"Right! Now repeat it back please?" Collins obliged, three times.

He stood up. "Best of luck!" They shook hands and Nathan left.

Sleeping through the afternoon he woke at six when Elsie came home. He said he would be out at five in the morning. She made him a cheese sandwich and some tea and left him alone. He played with the radio. A weather forecast was being broadcast. Then came ringing voices singing the 'Horst Wessel lied';

"Raise the flag! The ranks tightly closed! The SA marches with silent solid steps.'

After one verse the music ceased and an announcer speaking in English said mockingly

'Guten Tag, Mr. Churchill.'

Goebbels' radio broadcast to the population was beginning. Collins turned the set off and dozed until midnight. After that he stayed awake. Elsie bought tea at four thirty and shortly before five, opened the door for him, kissed his cheek and he went downstairs.

A man stood outside.

"Hello Dad. Ready to go?" He asked.

Collins nodded, and they caught an early bus to Westminster. Neither spoke until the bus arrived.

"Let's get a cuppa'. Warehouse won't be open for another ten minutes."

There was a mobile Café parked near the bus stop. A converted van with open sides selling tea and bacon sandwiches. Hand painted below the counter was a sign proclaiming "Sonny's Refreshment's". They ordered two cups and the other man pulled out a pack of cigarettes, offering it to Collins who told the man he didn't smoke.

"Wait here a minute. I'll walk to the corner and take a look if they're open yet."

Collins put the cups on the counter. "Thanks mate. Nice cuppa you make."

The man laughed. "Yeah. This time in the morning the only thing better would be a tot of scotch!"

"I'd walk a mile for that!" said Collins.

"Never seen you round here before. You local?"

"No I'm from Wells." As he spoke the words he realized he shouldn't be talking to anyone. He turned away and waved a hand, limped towards the corner. His contact was walking back. "OK it seems they're open. Let's go." They walked down, around the corner and saw a pair of large double doors opening a few yards along the street.

"Here we are! This is where I leave you. Go right in, they'll be expecting you. Don't forget, your name is just 'Dad', that's all. Good luck!" He shook Collins hand.

Collins walked through the doors and three men turned to look at him.

"Dad?"

"That's me."

"Good. My name is Don. Come in and we'll go over everything again. I know Nathan gave you the outline but there's more." He pulled the doors together. "Here, take this Identity Pass."

He handed over a dog-eared Pass with the name William Hanson printed on it.

"That takes care of the most important thing. Give me your own Pass. I'll be the one opening the door of the tower when we're finished. I'll give it to you then."

"Right. Now we have to load…" He stopped as the doors were pushed opened and a three-man German patrol walked in. A Sergeant and two privates. The Sergeant carried a machine pistol and the other two, rifles. He gestured with his weapon.

"*Was ist das?* Why are you at this place? It is very early. You are ten minutes before the curfew is lifted. Show me your ID Cards." He held out his hand and looked quizzically at them.

"Yes Sergeant. We have cards and I have papers here." He pulled an envelope from his overcoat pocket. "We are to deliver your flags to the clock tower to be hanged for the visit of Mr. Hess today."

The Sergeant studied the papers and nodded his head. "*Sehr gut.* Now the ID please."

They gave him the passes and the Sergeant scanned through them. He nodded and returned them.

"What time do you leave this place?"

"We will leave in a short while. Is that OK?"

"*Gut.* There will be no curfew. You may go then." He held out the envelope and stepped back.

"*Heil Hitler!*"

The patrol turned and left and Don closed the doors again and looked at Collins. "Well that was the first test, and we passed. When we leave here this morning we won't be back so it doesn't matter. These premises have been closed for months so there won't be any trace of anyone or anything. Let's get the banners loaded and off we go."

"What about the gun?" Collins asked.

"It's in the middle of one of the rolls don't worry!" The man smiled and they all helped load the barrow. The rolls were heavy. Turning off the light and locking doors, they pushed the cart down the road. It was six fifteen and just getting light.

They pushed the cart to the main entrance of Portcullis House on the Victoria Embankment facing the river and then approached the door. Two bored looking soldiers stepped out of the shadows.

One spoke to the other after checking a clipboard.

"Ah! These will be the banner people with the flags to hang for Hess."

Then, turning back to the men he demanded their work order and passes. They were handed over and the guard read through them he turned to the door and opened it, standing aside so the men could enter.

"Leave the cart here. Take the flags with you. It is a long climb to the top. I hope you enjoy the view!" He laughed and stepped back. "We will be here until noon. When you come down knock on the door and either this patrol or our replacement will open it."

They each took a roll and shouldered it. Then came the long climb. By the time they reached the top Collins felt exhausted. His leg bothered him and he sat down to rest. As he did so, the clock started its striking routine. The seven final strokes were loud in the small space.

The Springfield came out from the center of one roll and was given to Collins. He spent almost an hour taking it down and re-assembling it again. Don came over to him.

"I'm to tell you the scope is sighted for two hundred yards. I don't know anything else." He returned to his hanging duties. Collins finished up, satisfied the rifle was ready to do its job. Then he helped the others until the job was complete and the banners decorated all four of the sides of the tower. The bell chimed twelve times for midday, temporarily deafening the men. Don came over to Collins.

"We'll wait a bit and then go out. You stay and do what you have to do. I'll be outside just before four o'clock. I'll tell the guards I'm waiting for you. You will be bringing the tool kit we left. Knock three times and I'll open up. Then we scarper."

Ten minutes later the men left and Collins was alone. All he had to do now was wait. At three thirty he positioned himself behind one of the miter shaped, glassless windows above the clock face. He had a perfect view of Parliament Square about two hundred yards away. A cloth- covered table had been set up and several waiters busted around a bench which supported cups, saucers plates and sandwiches. Standing back from the window he peered down the scope and was treated to a close up view of a waiter preparing tea. Everything was in order.

The clock struck four. Collins saw Heydrich and Hess exchange the Nazi salute and then they were led to the table by a waiter. Collins sighted carefully lining up Heydrich's cap badge in the cross hairs of the scope. As he raised his hand to remove the cap he paused and Collins pulled the trigger.

Chapter 7 –
'Oh! To be in England now that April's there.'

The guide droned on. "Robert Browning wrote 'Home thoughts from abroad' in 1845. It contains the famous poem whose first line is, 'Oh! To be in England now that April's there.' He was actually in Italy at the time." He let out a small, but hopeful laugh, however, receiving no acknowledgement of his bon mot, he continued.

"Now, ninety-six years later this is his memorial." The guide looked up at SS *Obergrupen Führer* Reinhard Tristan Eugen Heydrich as he stood, holding the hands of Klaus and Helder, two of his children, at Poets Corner in Westminster Abbey. It was Monday, April 22nd, 1941.

Heydrich nodded at the guide and waved him away. Enough English culture for today. He had other important matters to attend to. He had dominated the population of Bohemia and Moravia and Hitler, well pleased, called him "The man with an iron heart".

After this success he received the same mandate for ruling England. He enjoyed the task and all the perks that went with it.

Looking at his watch, he saw the hands showing almost four o'clock. He spoke briefly to an accompanying aide who beckoned to the children's nanny. She stepped forward to take them into her charge. Heydrich bent and kissed their foreheads and waved as they left for the Savoy Hotel which Heydrich had requisitioned upon his arrival to take up the position of Protector of Britain some two weeks earlier.

The SS bodyguards closed round Heydrich as he walked out of the Abbey. Looking around, he noted that few people met his eye as he walked to his Mercedes limousine. Once inside, his motorcycle escort roared off with the Mercedes following behind. They didn't go far. At Parliament Square the vehicle stopped and Heydrich alighted. He searched the docile crowd standing on the boundaries of the Square. There were SS troopers on foot everywhere and several armored vehicles, their anti-aircraft guns pointed at the sky seeking non-existent RAF aircraft. All these were in the background. A small table was set up on the green and several waiters bustled around it. Here Rudolph Hess and Heydrich would take afternoon tea.

When Hitler had planned Hess's visit two weeks earlier, he had sent him to speak with *Reich* Propaganda chief, Joseph Goebbels who told Hess that instead of a parade they might ingrate themselves with the people by observing that so very English tradition of taking afternoon tea. It could be taken in a public place and would show that the Germans observed traditions.

Hess found Goebbels writing his daily vitriolic message to be translated, and broadcast in English over the BBC network which covered England. It was called *'Guten tag,* Mr. Churchill' and contained news of the previous day's victories along with stories of how the residents of Little Whiton or South Grinley had welcomed their German 'rescuers'. It dripped with sarcasm and insulted Churchill and other English leaders. Hitler had told Goebbels it was a masterpiece. Goebbels tended to agree.

"Come in Hess. I believe I have found another way that will encourage these English to make us welcome. Tea, Hess! The English love tea! Yes, tea I think. Tea and cucumber sandwiches. Make sure you set up a public afternoon tea where you and Heydrich can be see drinking tea! You must have cucumber sandwiches. Specify that! The English are very skilled making cucumber sandwiches. Very thin and dainty. They taste horrible but we must all make sacrifices for the *Reich*! Ah yes! Tea has to be at four o'clock." Goebbels smiled and patted Hess on the shoulder. He rarely made jokes. Goebbels continued.

"Now, Heydrich can help out here. I have been studying and he should make a well-publicized visit to Westminster Abbey. When he leaves the Abbey you can both meet at

Parliament Square. There is a large green where the tea can be held. The English public can be held back around the Square so they can see but not get too close. I have spoken to the *Fuhrer*, he agrees,"

Goebbels picked up a letter from his desk and handed it to Hess.

"Here is the *Führer-order* with the dates and times. Himmler knows about it so there will be no problems."

Hess readily agreed. Heydrich in England, was advised to get things ready. News of the event was broadcast to the public so they could see the two great men together.

Heydrich walked forward along the pavement and as he did so a tall, dark haired man, stepped out of another limousine ahead. The two raised their right arms in the Nazi salute and exchanged greetings. This was Rudolph Hess, the Deputy *Führer,* third in the *Reich* after Hitler and Herman Göering. Hess wore a Nazi party badge in the lapel of his civilian suit. In the center of the badge was the number sixteen. He was a very senior member of the party. His fanatical loyalty to Hitler had earned him his post, but it was well known that his principal task was to introduce Hitler at the numerous Party rallies. He had been an infantry officer during the first world-war but held no military rank with the Nazi Party. Heydrich thought him a fool but was obliged to entertain him during his visit. This he would do, reporting everything back to his own master, *Reichsführer* Heinrich Luitpold Himmler, the Minister of the Interior. Big Ben struck four o'clock.

The two men, wary of each other, were led to the table by a white coated waited and seated. As Heydrich raised his hand to remove his cap he looked up towards the Big Ben clock tower. Something glinted above the clock face. Heydrich frowned. Almost immediately a small hole appeared between his eyes and the back of his head exploded. His body catapulted backwards off his chair. He had been shot with a

30.06 bullet fired from the Big Ben clock tower by a 1903 Springfield sniper rifle.

Hess kneeling on spilled cucumber sandwiches, groveled for cover as the sound of the shot echoed around the Square. Many spectators also fell to the ground as they heard the noise. However, lots of them got pictures of Hess cowering beneath the table. The bodyguards ran from the limousines where they had been assembled and surrounded the sprawled corpse of Heydrich. Hess's men got him to his feet and covered his retreat to his vehicle which roared off proceeded by his motorcycle escort.

The SS Captain in charge of Heydrich's men stood and looked back at the Square. He turned his head and realized the only vantage point from which the shots could have come was the iconic bell tower. He shouted to the NCO and crew of a four barreled *Flakvierling* to open fire high up on the Big Ben tower and right away the shells shattered the upper windows and the clock face, hosing downwards stripping the façade of the tower and exposing its stairway within. The Captain moved behind the gun and told the NCO to keep firing.

Hit by dozens of shells, parts of the interior of the tower could be seen. The Captain, realizing that anyone in the upper half of the tower would now be immobilized, told them to cease fire and after confirming that Heydrich was beyond help, directed his Deputy, a Lieutenant, to get the body to a hospital. He then commandeered all the troops he could muster and told them to proceed to the tower building and surround it. The motorcycle escort, followed by an ambulance carrying Heydrich's body, left at a high rate of speed. Troops tried to confiscate cameras from the crowd but with such a throng of people, many were smuggled away. Within twenty-four hours pictures of Hess, groveling under the flimsy table surrounded by teacups and cucumber sandwiches made the front page of the newspapers of the free world.

The Captain arrived at the damaged tower and gave instructions to surround it and get engineers and equipment to the scene. Thirty minutes later a man was pulled down from just below the clock face. A Springfield rifle and a walking stick were beneath his body. In a jacket pocket was an Identification Card in the name of William Hansen. This later proved to be a forgery. In the trousers were six pound notes and four and three pence in coins. The man was dead, but there again, so was the Protector of Britain, *SS Obergrupen Führer* Reinhard Tristan Eugen Heydrich. The sandwiches in the grass were snapped up by the ever-present pigeons.

Chapter 8 – *'Invasion.'*

Germany's successful invasion of Britain in late December 1939 was due to two main facts. The first was that after the British Army's retreat from France across the Channel they had little artillery to combat the inevitable *Panzer* attacks from the landing force. The second was that Messerschmitt's Me-262 jet fighter could out-fly anything the Royal Air Force could put into the sky.

Rudolph Hess, the Deputy *Führer* and Herman Göering, second only to Hitler, had supported Willi Messerschmitt's Me-262 new jet fighter over Ernst Heinkel's He 2800 and despite opposition from Erhart Milch at the Reich Aviation Ministry, Messerschmitt was awarded the contract to build the aircraft in 1933. A top secret prototype was flying as early as 1937 and the aircraft went into full production in late 1938. By the time WWII started Germany had over 200 Me-262's ready for action and the pilots trained to fly them. Of course, true to his growing reputation, Göering did not back Messerschmitt out of patriotism. A consummate thief and a violent morphine addict to boot, he shook him down. Willie Messerschmitt, to win the contract, went to *Kerinhalle,* Göering's Estate fifty miles north of Berlin, with an initial payment of 2.5 million marks. He was to provide Göering an additional fifty thousand marks for each Me-262 delivered.

Starting In 1934 Göering demanded kickbacks from anyone who had business with the Reich government. A favorite of Hitler he had marched in the Beer Hall Putsch in 1923. In that same year Hitler placed him at the head of the S.A. In November he marched with the *Fuehrer* to the War Ministry and was shot in the leg, further enhancing his reputation for loyalty. Then in February 1933 Göering was responsible for the *Reichstag* fire and later that year received his reward when Hitler became Chancellor. He appointed

Göering, Minister without portfolio, Minister of the Interior for Prussia, and Reich Commissioner of Aviation.

Not satisfied with these appointments, Göering wanted to increase his power even further. Meeting in secret with Heinrich Himmler he felt Himmler out regarding his future ambitions. Göering offered his support providing Himmler would back him in his bid for additional influence in military affairs. Göering was convinced that Hitler was losing interest in police matters and was concentrating more and more on building military might. He wanted to command the Luftwaffe in this upcoming militarized regime. Knowing that Himmler had allied himself with Wilhelm Frick, the Reich Interior Minister, he had weighed his options and decided on the military side of things instead of the civilian. He offered to support Himmler's aim to head the *Gestapo,* and an uneasy truce began.

The Royal Air Force was destroyed by the end of the first week of January, 1940. The ME-262 Swallow had a short engine life of about four hours. However, this proved adequate to conquer the RAF. It flew at six hundred miles an hour and its 4, 30mm cannon were more than a match for any British fighter, as was shown during the opening weeks of the war as it commanded the Channel.

It could also carry rockets and bombs and once the Spitfires and Hurricanes of Fighter Command were downed, the ME-262's were refitted and sank or heavily damaged thirty warships of the Home Fleet before it steamed back to Scotland to lick its wounds. Of the 400 English operational fighters available in June of 1939, almost 300 were destroyed by mid-January 1940. Coupled with the disastrous retreat from France, where all but thirty thousand men were lost along with most of the Army's artillery, England appeared doomed. Germany had declared war on France in April 1939 and entered Paris on June 14th. Six months later, at the end of December its airborne armies landed at Dover, moving inland and setting up strongpoints along a line from Margate to Southampton.

With the ME-262's controlling the air over the Channel, reinforcements consisting of troops and armor, came ashore and drove through the line and headed north to London. Nothing stopped the German tanks and by mid-January the Capital had fallen. By the third week of January the *Panzer* armies had run out of steam on a course extending from Boston, north of The Wash, along the River Witham to the Fosdyke Canal and along to the River Trent. From there the front meandered down the Trent and Mersey Canal and on to the Manchester Ship Canal connecting to the Mersey. Along this line the British, reinforced by the Canadians who had just arrived, held the Germans, who had exhausted their ready supplies.

Neither side seemed willing to attack the other as February drew to a close. All was quiet through March and then April started with its usual showers. After the first week it changed to a beautiful month, matching Browning's description. The elm trees were in leaf and the swallows nesting. Meanwhile, Germans faced Canadians and Englishmen and many realized that within a few weeks, there would be other colonial troops arriving from Australia and New Zealand.

The south of England remained quiet. There were isolated acts of sabotage after the Heydrich shooting but the sheer viciousness of the reprisals left most people struggling to believe how unhuman the Nazi's could be.

That evening, following the killing, Heinrich Luitpold Himmler, the German Minister of the Interior, after speaking with Hitler, sent *SS-Gruppenführer* Richard Glücks immediately to England to replace Heydrich and, as Himmler instructed. "Use any methods to bring the English to their knees". Glücks, who had vast experience setting up concentration camps in Germany was an ideal candidate for the task.

He had the SS deployed in Westminster before dawn the next morning and as people arrived to work, over a hundred were randomly arrested. All were taken to the Tower of London and one by one, brutally interrogated regarding the previous day's events. Glücks reasoned that someone who worked in the area must have seen something. The ruins of the clock tower had been searched but nothing was found other than a body, a false I.D. card, a rifle and a walking stick.

None of the arrested people had any knowledge about the killing. However, the next morning they were lined up against the walls in groups of twenty on Tower Hill and executed by squads of troopers with machine guns just as people were arriving for work. No one seemed to know a thing and so additional eighty were arrested and tortured for the information that Glücks was sure they were hiding.

The following week, in an act condemned by the free world, eleven were taken out to Tower Hill and publicly beheaded using the block and axe from the Tower armory. The inexperienced executioner made a mess of the first victims. Having no experience, the huge SS trooper who had volunteered for the job, swung the weapon and cut through the scull of the first man on the block. The second he sliced through the shoulder, amputating an arm. After that he became more skilled, taking one stroke on all but two of the remaining victims. Many of the horrified crowd who had been rounded up to witness the killings were physically sick and even two of the SS men left ranks to vomit.

One man remained in custody. He had been slow in denying knowing the person in the photograph he had been shown. They isolated him and the work of extracting every possible shred of information began.

The public was unaware of who caused Heydrich's death. However, to Dalton and Churchill, at the new seat of government in Manchester, and Harry Carr and Havildar Deoman Prahdan in Suffolk, it was no mystery. They were aware who the man was, and that he had done an almost faultless job.

Chapter 9 – *'Manhunt.'*

Sonny Solomon was surprised. On Tuesday April 23nd, the day following the assassination, his tea wagon was visited in the afternoon by two Gestapo agents who showed him a photograph. They had been visiting every business throughout the area asking if anyone knew the person in the picture. Sonny hesitated just a little too long before replying that he didn't know the face. That delay triggered suspicions, and the agents took him to the Tower and handed him over to the SS interrogators.

He was placed in a small room containing two hairs and a table, searched and left alone. An hour later a man in civilian clothes came through the door.

"Mr. Solomon?" He asked. Sonny nodded.

"My Name is Nebel. This picture." He held up a photograph of Arthur Collins that had been taken when they removed him from the clock tower. The face had been cleaned up.

"I believe you can tell us who this man is?" Sonny shook his head. "I've never set eyes on him before."

The man nodded and turned towards the door. "*Komm!*" he called out. The door opened and in walked a brutish looking SS Squad Leader.

"*Heil Hitler*" he gave the Nazi salute and came to attention. He stared at Sonny.

Nebel spoke. "Mr. Solomon. This is *Oberscharführer Benstutz*. He is a nasty man. He works for me, and although I dislike him I find him efficient. I can leave you two alone to talk or you can talk with me. If you choose the latter you will be well treated. You will be held for a few days and released. We will have your mobile Café guarded. It will be safe. However, I require the information you have. Do I make myself clear?"

Sonny didn't have to think. "Yes sir. I'll talk to you."

Nebel turned to the trooper. "Leave us here," he said, and the SA man saluted again and left.

"Let's talk, Mr. Solomon". He pulled out a chair indicating Sonny should take the other one. Sonny sat.

"Well, who is it?" asked Nebel.

"I don't know his name sir. He stopped by the Café early Monday morning. He was with another man and they ordered tea. Then he left. That's all I know."

"Ah! I understand. What you mean is that you remember nothing else. Right?"

"Right" said Sonny.

"Then I will assist you Mr. Solomon."

It was then that the interrogation really started.

Nebel was a policeman and a very skilled operator. He talked quietly to Sonny in order not to frighten him any more than he was already. He avoided the identification of the picture and talked about the mobile Cafe and how Sonny did business. After ten minutes a guard entered with tea and biscuits. After that Sonny's memory improved.

The man, Sonny told Nebel, said he came from Wells. Nebel was aware that Wells was a cathedral City in Somerset. He also knew that Tunbridge Wells was a City in Kent. He discarded the second. It would not be called 'Wells' but Tunbridge Wells by any Englishman.

Sonny recalled the face and the fact that the man used a walking stick. Nebel, an experienced interrogator, knew that there was an urgent need for the information and pushing Sonny any further wouldn't help. He had him taken to a cell, given an excellent dinner with two glasses of wine. He was told to relax until morning.

Upon leaving Sonny, Nebel sent agents to Wells with copies of the photograph. They arrived that evening, and the search started. It was the smallest City in England and Nebel was hopeful of results. He was to be disappointed. At eight the next morning, despite showing the picture to over a thousand people, no one could identify the man. Nebel called for Sonny to be given breakfast and then taken to his office at nine o'clock. Punctually at nine his door opened and Sonny entered.

"Mr. Solomon. I hope you slept well. I have bad news I'm afraid. We didn't find the man in Wells. I'm afraid you will have to stay with us a little longer. Now, let's go back to those words you exchanged with him. Tell me again, how did the conversation start?"

Sonny thought back and repeated everything he recalled to Nebel.

"That was it. He waved and then walked down to the corner, meeting his friend on the way and then they both turned the corner and vanished."

"You are certain it was Wells he said? Wells in Somerset?"

"He didn't say Somerset. Just Wells." Then he remembered and blurted out "He didn't have a Somerset accent at all. Not a west country accent, more East Anglia."

Nebel nodded and from as desk draw took a folded map of England. He found Wells-next-to-the-sea in seconds. East Anglia, not far from Norwich. He picked the telephone on his desk and spoke into it. Smiling at Sonny he thanked him and had him returned to his cell.

Gestapo agents in Norwich were dispatched to Wells-next-to-the-sea with the picture. In an hour Collins had been identified by three different merchants in the small town. Nebel called *SS-Gruppenführer* Richard Glücks and gave him the news. He was instructed to obtain information on Collins immediately. In an hour he had learned that Collins repaired the guns of some of the local Estate owners and farmers. He had been the Chief Gamekeeper at Holkham Hall and was a sniper in the first world-war. Glücks was informed and Nebel received further instructions.

Calling the agents in Wells, now established in the local police station, he told them to secure the cottage where Collins had lived. Then ordering his car, he and two SS agents motored to Wells, arriving at three in the afternoon. Nebel learned Collins had left Holkham, and could not be found. It was a dead end. He returned to London but had his agents remain to seek further information, including anyone that Collins might have known.

Wednesday midday at the base, De received a message that the SS was on its way to Wells. When Carr arrived early afternoon he was told of the developments. Knowing they would find nothing connecting Collins to the Auxiliaries but ever careful, he stayed at the base to await any further news from Dalton's people. At six o'clock a message came through. The SS had been to Holkham Hall looking for Carr. They had learned that he had worked under Collins and the two appeared to be friends. He should remain hidden at the base.

The searchers were not expected to stay long. A message arrived to the effect that on Thursday morning, May 2nd, at 8am Carr should meet a man outside the Victoria Inn on the Estate. He was to greet the man with the words, 'it's a lovely day' and receive the reply 'yes but windy'. Carr would get detailed instructions from him regarding their next move. He dictated a message confirming he understood and De sent it out immediately. At the same time he wondered how the intelligence was received by Dalton's group so quickly. They must have people inside the SS he reasoned.

Chapter 10 – *'Attack.'*

It was a blustery morning as Carr exited the base and made the long walk back towards the Hall. The Victoria Inn was located on Park Road and as he approached he saw someone sitting on one of the wooden benches outside. As he walked past he greeted the man "It's a lovely day". The reply came, "Yes, but windy". They shook hands.

"I'm Smith. You are Jimmy Carr?"

"Right. Let's get to the base. We can talk there. I'll walk ahead about fifty yards, you follow. When I beckon, close up and we'll get into the trees and brush. I don't think we will see any patrols. They are very rare around here. If we do, the terrain is flat and we should have plenty of warning. There's good cover so hide until they pass. There's been activity in Wells looking for me but they won't stay long if I'm not found. Now, do you have an ID Card?"

"Yes. I'm listed as a Medical Case. Recovering from TB. I have a Doctor's note saying I need plenty of fresh air."

Smith nodded, and they set off. Carr's own I.D. card listed him as a wounded WWI casualty now retired. They passed two laborers walking to work but saw no one else as they left the road and started across the heath. The walk took forty minutes and then Carr raised his arm and waved Smith up to join him.

"I'll move into the tree line now. Keep your eyes open. It's quite thick brush. We'll stop again in about a quarter of a mile. Stay back until I advise then move quickly."

Smith did as he was told and in fifteen minutes they were behind the hawthorn bush. Carr rang the doorbell and De opened it. He introduced Smith, and they sat down.

De went to make tea and Smith started his instructions.

"Well, I'll cover everything first then we can go back and take the notes we need. I'll be staying here with you."

De came with three mugs of tea. Smith took out a notebook and continued.

"Back in February you took a look round the St. Faith airfield. We have reliable intelligence that last Friday the 26th of April, 262's started to arrive at the field. They were to be prepared for bombing and strafing missions to the north. The Germans are intending to bring up their armor from Peterborough and to break out of their bridgehead along the Boston front. Air support would enable them to do this. They expect over 200 aircraft."

"Teams of fitters will arrive to refit and re-arm them. The attack will start using the 262's on Saturday, May 4th. That's what we know and our source is impeccable. Now, what can we do to throw a spanner in the works? Well, this is the plan we have and after I tell you about it I'll explain what happens when it's complete. After that I'd like comments."

He paused and sipped his tea. Carr again wondered where they got this incredible information from but he didn't ask. Smith continued.

"Holkham Bay Jimmy. I'm sure you know it well?" Carr nodded. "Yes, it's part of the Estate."

"At 1130pm on the night of May 3rd an LCT Mark 1 will land four specially equipped Bedford petrol bowsers and two light *Flakvierling* wagons fitted with twin MG42 machine guns at Holkham Bay. The bowsers carry about 300 gallons of petrol each. Well, three of the four will anyway. The fourth will carry inside, eight men. Of these, six will be flamethrower operators, and two weapons experts carrying Bren guns and thermite grenades. All bowsers will have two-man crews, one will be a German speaker. The *Flak's* will carry a German speaking officer and three men." He lifted his cup and drained it.

"Once landed these vehicles will go in convey via Branthill, Edgemere, and Fakenham down to Foxley and on to St. Faith. A *Flakvierling* will lead, then the bowsers and another *Flak* in the rear. The convoy will enter the airfield and deploy on the concrete pad where the ME-262's will be parked. Then the *Flak's* will peel off and attack the administration buildings and suppress fire from the airfield defenses."

"Our bowsers will extend their special equipment, which consists of an apparatus which allows them to spray their petrol up and behind them as they cross the pad. They look similar to those agricultural things that spray the fields with manure! The 262's will be, with typical German efficiency, deployed in straight lines, west to east. They are to be arranged in this manner because *Reichsmarschall* Hermann Wilhelm Göring is scheduled to inspect them early on May 4th before they take off in support of the *Panzer* offensive."

Smith paused as the other two looked at him in disbelief. He nodded his head. "In addition, there will be pilots and mechanics staying in tents. Killing them is a priority!"

"So, we also have Göering himself to take care of. On arrival at the field the special teams deploy from the fourth bowser. They mount the other three bowsers in teams of two. Everyone else goes with the *Flaks*. Once the bowsers have spread their load amongst the aircraft the flamethrower men will do their part. This ignites the petrol and destroy the 262's."

"The worst-case scenario is that the special tires those jet aircraft use will be destroyed. They are valuable because replacements would be impossible to find and install for at least two months." He paused to look at his notes.

"Once the petrol is ignited the bowsers will be turned back towards the aircraft and bricks placed on their accelerators as the driver and the special teams jump clear. Flamethrower crews use any remaining fuel on the administration buildings. They get be picked up by the two *Flak's*. Rendezvous is at the eastern end of the parking pad. They exit the field and attempt to return to Holkham Bay."

"An MTB will be waiting to pick them up where they went ashore originally. It will have muffled engines to keep the noise down. The recall signal from a flashlight is dot dash dot, letter 'R', every five minutes. It should arrive at 245am but under no circumstances wait after 3am. That means the 25 miles to St Faith must be covered in about 40 minutes so the raiders must leave the airfield absolute latest 2am." He checked his notes again.

"Now. When we get back here Jimmy goes back to the base if all is well. If not, he comes with us on the MTB. Let's see about the details and then your questions. Firstly the bowsers are to be English but with all necessary German markings. The Germans are used to seeing captured English lorry's and stuff so no problem." He looked up expectantly but they remained quiet.

"Secondly, all personnel will be provided with German identification papers. The officer in charge will be a Major, he will carry the movement orders. Because the German's have been storing fuel in Kings Lynn, next week there should be numerous convoys from there to St. Faith. Therefore it's our belief that any checkpoints will be used to seeing the same type of columns."

"They expect different routes to be used to avoid congestion so our Fakenham route should not create any suspicion. The LCT will come from the north down to the Bay. When it leaves Grimsby it heads out to sea for about fifty miles and then turn south and then west. We know the Germans are bringing in fuel on barges from The Hague so the LCT will not be noticed in that traffic, light as it is, and can peel off we hope, without a problem." Again he checked his notes.

"The first *Flak* to come ashore will have German uniforms for Jimmy and myself. Jimmy knows the way and rides in the first *Flak*. I ride in the rear. There will be security but our plan should get us to the airfield. After my *Flak* goes through the gate then it will be a race to get to the parking area and do the job. We expect Göering to spend the night at the field so he will have his personal guards. There is to be a dinner for all wing commanders and senior staff that evening."

"I have a map of the field drawn from Jimmy's report and some updates that the local man Berrins, contributed after his visit about supplying more food to the camp. This map shows where Göering's quarters should be. If, and I say if, there is an opportunity to hit this hut then one of the *Flak's* will do so. We start today with a reconnaissance to the Bay and come back to report." He flipped a page in his book.

"Now, you should know that very early on May 4th, while we attack at St. Faith, another group like ours, using local people for guides, will attack the *Panzer* parks in Peterborough at four in the morning. The men will carry hundreds of small explosive charges and thermite grenades to place in the *Panzer* vehicle tracks. They have to destroy the park defenses, especially anti-aircraft guns. Withdrawal will be at 04:45am. There are estimated to be about six hundred vehicles in the depot. Canadian forces using Bristol Blenheim light bombers which have been flown in stages from Newfoundland to Iceland and down to Scotland, will hit the German *Panzer* forces from a very low level at five o'clock, before their scheduled departure from Peterborough. Their bombs should set off the charges and grenades. We will destroy their armor before their attack can start. Because the German's believe their superior air power can knock anything out of the sky, once the ME-262's are destroyed the *Panzers* are vulnerable." He sat back for a moment recalling the final items.

"There should be no German aircraft flying early that morning we hope. Also, we now have three divisions of Canadians and one each of Australian and New Zealander's, about seventy thousand men with equipment, including tanks and artillery, ready to attack south, so your mission must be successful! On May 7th, three days' time, two further divisions from India will land at Harwich."

"Their approach will be covered by ships of the Home Fleet. They must advance west the seventy-eight miles to London, meeting the attacking troops which should be arriving from the north on the 8th and 9th. We believe that the Germans will be in full retreat by then. Half of the Home Fleet has sailed and went north between the Orkneys and the Scottish coast. They have already refueled in Belfast and will arrive off Portsmouth on the 8th of May." Smith had one further item.

"The other half of the Fleet is coming down the east coast and has a rendezvous at Dover on the same day. This will force a German surrender when no cross channel evacuation is possible. The first forty of our new Meteor jet aircraft from Canada arrived yesterday at Barrow in Furnace and are being assembled as we speak. They will be flying in two days and this gives us the air power we need. More will arrive within 15 days." He paused as De bought more tea.

"I suppose you have questions so go ahead and I'll answer all I can. What I don't know or what the planners hadn't thought about and needs to be fixed, then we will use the radio and get answers. Now, everything I've told you may well be known to the Germans within a few days. It can't remain secret. All depends on how fast we can move, and above all your success on the morning of the 4th."

They talked for an hour and at the end of that time there was a list of items that needed clarification. After lunch of tea and sandwiches Carr and Smith set off to walk to the Bay. They crossed Station Road and then followed Lady Anne's Road to the sands. There were a few people walking, but the men kept well clear of them. They could see the two hooks of land right and left that marked the entrance to the Bay. Smith said that's where the LCT would come in. He'd flash the letter 'D' with a torch every five minutes starting at 11 o'clock. The LCT should head for the tiny light. That was high tide, and after dropping the ramp at the beginning of the inlet they would drive across the hard sand to Lady Anne's Road. The

LCT must depart on the high tide which was 12:05am on the 4th of May. The MTB would arrive at 02:45am for the pickup. They turned to walk back and Smith spoke.

"On the way back we will have to shoot our way through any checkpoints but the *Flak's* have plenty of firepower and will be stuffed with spare ammunition. From what you say there shouldn't be much of a German presence in the area?"

"I hope not. It appears they are concentrating in the towns and cities. They haven't had time to set up a proper civilian administration yet this far out. I know you mentioned German uniforms for us. What about sizes?"

"You're right! I'm fine but we will have to add your size to the message when we get back. Let's think about anything else we've missed as we walk."

Their return journey was uneventful, and they came upon the base around two in the afternoon. Sitting down, they prepared a long transmission and when it was finished, De sent it out. That night after dark they climbed to the top of the ridge and used field glasses to search through 360 degrees. It was cold and overcast. There were lights at the Hall and to the south, in Wells. Out to sea they could see nothing and after half an hour they went back in and slept.

On Saturday they stayed busy with the radio messages arriving and requesting weather updates or signs of activity in the area. Finally, at 10 o'clock Saturday evening they left the base after saying goodbye to De and headed for the Bay. There was no moon, and it was only because of Carr's knowledge of the territory they could navigate.

Visibility was poor and patches of fog were everywhere. They arrived at 10:45pm and searched the beach using the night glasses. There was absolutely nothing to be seen. At 11:00pm Smith, at the head of the inlet, flashed his signal. Immediately they heard engines and within minutes the LCT had dropped its ramp and was unloading its cargo.

The Major commanding the force greeted them as the first *Flak* drove down the ramp and onto the sand.

"Good evening. I'm Major Keith Donaldson. I'm in charge of the raid. Which of you is Carr?" Jimmy stepped forward. "That's me."

"Good." He shook hands and turned to Smith.

"Mr. Smith? Nice to meet you at last. We really don't need to do all round introductions. Would take too long and time is of the essence so to speak. By the way, Lieutenant Bentley is the officer in the rear *Flak*. Once this lot is ready we can move out right away. I know we're early but it's fine to have a bit of time in hand. Any problems with that?"

Both Carr and Smith shook their heads. "Very well. Here are the uniforms." He handed over two German uniforms with *Hauptmann* insignia on them along with two garrison caps. They put them on and hid their own clothes in a clump of bushes nearby.

Ten minutes later they were on their way. Donaldson in the front of the *Flak* with the driver and Carr in the rear sitting with two soldiers. Smith went to the back of the file.

"This is Lady Anne's Road." Said Carr. "We take this across Station Road and head down to Fakenham. There will certainly be a checkpoint there." Donaldson nodded. "Ok. Leave the talking to me. You keep make sure we go the right way."

The vehicles all had slit headlights which didn't help much at first. However, as they drove inland the fog cleared and visibility improved. Carr leaned forward and touched Donaldson's shoulder.

"About a mile further on the town starts. That's where the checkpoint will be." Donaldson nodded and stood up in the *Flak* gripping the top of the windshield. The checkpoint loomed ahead, and the convoy slowed down. Donaldson jumped out and walked to the pole barrier. Several soldiers stood around a small fire set in an oil drum. A sentry walked forward and saluted. Donaldson returned the salute and said:

"Fuel convoy for St. Faith. Here's the movement order". The sentry looked at the paper, counted the vehicles and came to attention.

"Yes Major. Please continue."

The sentry handed back the papers and leaned on the pole raising the barrier.

Donaldson climbed back into the *Flak* and called out. *"Danke."*

The convoy moved on. It was 12:15am. As soon as they were clear, Donaldson turned to Carr. "Let's hope the rest of the trip is as easy!" Carr didn't reply, he was busy watching the road for any familiar signs. Guist was silent as they drove through.

Next would be Foxley, and Carr kept scanning the road remembering the checkpoint had been smaller than the one at Fakenham the last time he had come this way. There appeared to be no changes. A wooden barrier was pulled aside as soon as the movement order was presented and with a minimum delay they were through and gathering speed. Donaldson turned and held a thumb up to Carr. He nodded.

"That should be it until Horsham St. Faith. They will have increased security. The checkpoint is outside the village on the airfield road. We'll arrive in about ten minutes."

They drove on and after a few minutes Carr spoke to Donaldson. "About three hundred yards" He warned. Donaldson stood as the *Flak* slowed. Carr peered ahead and saw a Corporal walk to the middle of the road and hold up his hand. In the light from the prefabricated hut he saw it was the same Corporal who had tried to pick him up on his last visit. He pulled his garrison cap down low over his eyes and slumped in his seat.

Donaldson presented the movement order, and the Corporal walked to the hut, exiting a few seconds later with a Sergeant. Donaldson climbed out of the *Flak*.

"What's the delay? This fuel is urgent." The man stepped back.

"I apologize, Major. Please continue."

He pushed down on the counterweight and as he and the Corporal leaned on it, the pole went up. The time was 12:45am. Donaldson waved the convoy forward, and they drove towards the airfield. In two minutes they were at the gates. These were thin logs covered with barbed wire, guarded by two sentries, one on each side of the road.

Donaldson stood up. "Good evening. I'm Stein, 4th Air Force supply. I have an urgent delivery for tomorrow's mission."

The sentry saluted took the movement order and asked him to wait. He went into the small blockhouse and returned with a *Luftwaffe* Captain. The Captain didn't speak but walked through the access gate and down the length of the convoy. He returned and stood in front of Donaldson tapping the papers on the side of his leg.

"*Vielen Dank Major. Bitte um Gottes willen nicht machen keinen Lärm, wie Marshall Göring schläft und wird böse, wenn geweckr.*"

He handed Donaldson the papers and indicated that the sentry's should open the gates. In moments they were through. "He seemed scared that Captain. What was wrong?" Carr asked. Donaldson laughed. "He said Göering was asleep and if we made a noise and woke him there would be a problem! Right, everyone knows what to do so let's stop here and get ready."

They stopped on the approach road to the aircraft park and in the pitch blackness the bowser without fuel was unloaded and the men mounted the other vehicles as they had been directed. Donaldson ran past each vehicle and giving final instructions. The convoy re-started minutes later and passed the first of the security towers on the left that were being built when Carr had last visited.

Safely through they arrived at the edge of the park. Dim lights shone from where mechanics worked on some of the aircraft. They could see the rows and rows of camouflaged painted ME-262's, scores of them, nose to tail in four columns facing to the east. It was 1am.

A sentry, rifle on shoulder, approached the lead *Flak*. He spoke briefly to the driver.

"You need the tank farm. Turn right and follow me to the road, please. I will go with you."

Donaldson got down from the vehicle and walked round, papers in hand.

"*Guten Abend.*" The sentry, seeing he was an officer, saluted. Donaldson didn't hesitate. He pulled the sentry towards him and stabbed upwards with his Fairbairn knife. The man died instantly. Donaldson remounted. He called to Carr, "He wanted to show us the way to the fuel tanks. Now the cat is out of the bag". He waved his hand and the bowsers and *Flaks* started to move.

The empty bowser was abandoned but the other three, their sprayers out and ready, started down the columns of aircraft, petrol gushing freely upwards coating them and leaving small streams of fuel running around their landing gear. No alarm had sounded. They went slowly, allowing the petrol to spread down over the tarmac and onto the airframes. To traverse the entire fifty planes in each column took them five minutes.

Meanwhile the *Flaks* took off on the left flank headed for the administration building. At first nothing happened and then their MG's opened fire. It was devastating. The wooden walls of the buildings were shredded by the gunfire. As the *Flaks* passed the flamethrowers made sure everything was alight. It was 1:15am.

The bowsers had reached the end of the parked aircraft. The men with the flamethrowers fired on the lakes of fuel. It was terrible to see. The gasoline had run all round the jets and as it ignited, so did the planes. What made it worse was that they had been fueled and armed the previous evening and munitions and jet fuel made the conflagration even worse.

Finally the German defenses reacted. The security towers fired on the *Flak's* and they took hits. Two men fell into the road, hit by the hail of bullets. Three bowsers, stationary at the park's end were hit and two exploded killing their crews and three flamethrower men. AA guns on the perimeter looked for targets and engaged the *Flaks* as they came out from the rows of administration buildings and headed for the tents they could see ahead. The pintle mounted MG42's hosed the tents and men came running out, unaware of what was happening except that they were being shot at. Then the flamethrowers opened fire and the smell of burning flesh made the gun-wagon crews gag.

Carr was a very frightened passenger, but he helped feed the MG belts when two of the men were wounded. He had been in the trenches in the first world war but this was very different. Everything was happening so fast! He kept loading.

The perimeter AA guns added to the carnage. Their shells, fired at the *Flaks* and bowsers, hit huts and the already flaming aircraft. The *Flaks* turned at the end of the tents right under the guns, and a small-arms fight broke out between their crews and the men from the gun wagons. Three more men went down dead or wounded. Finally the firing stopped as the perimeter gun crews ran out of ammunition and tried to surrender. The *Flaks* didn't hesitate, they fired and then started back down the rows of tents shooting at anything that moved and burning anything that wasn't already alight. It was 1:30am.

Reaching the eastern end of the parking pad the *Flaks* stopped but there was no one to pick up alive from the bowsers. They turned towards the administration huts again and found one position heavily defended and firing at them with what sounded like MG31 machine guns.

Donaldson shouted "That has to be Göering! Hit that hut with everything you have. Flamethrowers, I'm going closer, make sure you wipe that target out!"

Carr fell sideways as the *Flak* turned sharply to attack the hut. At that moment one of flamethrower men was hit and fell from the wagon, his fuel tank exploding as he hit the ground. The second man didn't miss and hosed the hut as the *Flak* passed by. As he did so a burst from an MG-31burst knocked him and another gunner from the wagon.

A counter attack to trap the invaders was being organized. They could see a line of lights coming along the perimeter road from the main gate. There seemed to be at least a dozen vehicles.

"Where's the other *Flak?*" asked Donaldson. Carr looked round and saw the second wagon arriving.

"Behind us," he said. "We need to get through the perimeter fence here to the right. It's suicide to go back to the main gate. We can crash through the wire to Holt Road and take that to Horsford. We carry on through Lenwade to Foxley and home. One thing, there are slit trenches beyond the wire. Keep clear of them at all costs!"

Donaldson nodded and signaled the other vehicle to follow. The driver turned onto the perimeter road and headed towards the fence. The barbed wire loomed up and the first *Flak* fired, blowing the supporting posts from the ground and creating a gap. As Carr had predicted a light machine gun stuttered from about fifty yards ahead. It was in one of the slit trenches. The driver of the *Flak* was hit, and the vehicle swerved. Again Carr was flung sideways, but he grabbed the seat and climbed over to take the wheel beside Donaldson who fired with a Sten gun at the slit trench. He straightened the vehicle and pushing the driver too one side, hit the accelerator and drove past the trench. He dodged trees and ran through another fence and across a field. There was a wooden farm gate illuminated by the burning aircraft and he went crashing through this to reach the road.

He swung the *Flak* north-west towards Horsford and accelerated. They gathered speed. The second *Flak* was close behind. Carr turned west at the first junction and after a few miles came upon the Fakenham Road. Looking back he could see no pursuit. They went through Lenwade and up to Foxley, crashing the barrier there without stopping and firing at the sentry's as they ran into the road behind them. Twelve minutes took them through Guist which was quiet in the early morning with nobody about. A short while later they reached the outskirts of Fakenham.

Carr slowed down. It was here that any an attempt to block them would occur. They must have received news of the raid via radio and told that the escape vehicles were heading that way. He spoke to Donaldson.

"I think I know a way round the town to miss the block. If it's clear and they haven't closed the road we might make it through."

"We'll do it." Donaldson waved the second *Flak* forward and called out to the officer in the front.

"Lieutenant Bentley. What's your situation?"

"Two wounded Sir including myself. Two others, a flamethrower bloke and the driver are OK. The vehicle took hits, but it's holding up so far. Mr. Smith was killed as we exited the field."

"Where are you hit Bentley?"

"Right hand and left foot Sir. I did some first aid, and the bleeding stopped. I'll be OK."

"The others?"

"Not good sir. Both have chest wounds. One is really bad and spitting up a lot of blood. Don't think he can last long under these circumstances. What about you?"

"We have three here, one slightly wounded. Mr. Carr here and myself doing fine. Do what you can. We have to get through. Carr knows a way that might avoid the block but keep alert, we can get hit any time." Bentley saluted and Donaldson moved off.

Carr turned to Donaldson. "I'm going to turn here. There's a path along the River Wensom that avoids the town.

It will let us turn west later and pick up the Fakenham Road we need to get back to Wells."

"OK. Let's go!" The *Flak* went slowly towards the town and then turned left across the fields. They bumped across several, pushing through the hedges, until they saw the glint of the Wensom in the moonlight. It was 02:10am.

Carr followed the river for about two miles. It headed away from Fakenham. He went slowly as the path was very narrow and twisted and turned as it followed the Wensom's contours. A bridge loomed. They drove up the grassy bank and right onto the street to Barsham. They had avoided contact in Fakenham and had plenty of time to get to Wells.

Driving carefully to avoid the casualties moving too much they scanned the road and the skies but saw nothing. East Barsham was only three miles from Fakenham, and as they approached, noticed an Inn on the left-hand side. They pulled over into the car park and stopped.

"The village is ahead on the right. No need to go through. It's very small and only has a couple of shops. We're only two miles from Wells and then Holkham Bay. Think about what you have to do when we arrive." It was 2:30am.

They walked over to the second *Flak*. Bentley turned towards them.

"The gunner's dead. He was hit in the chest. Nothing we could do for him. What do we do about the body?"

Donaldson rubbed his chin. "Leave him in the wagon. We'll see when we get to the rendezvous." He turned to Carr "Let's get going. Better early than late!" The exited the inn car park and headed west. Through Wells all looked good and then as they reached the Holkham Road they noted it was blocked ahead by several wagons across the street. As they slowed the second *Flak* pulled up.

Machine guns firing tracers hit in front of the *Flak's*, the bullets ricocheting off the tarmac and hitting the light armor. Carr steered to the side of the road. Donaldson turned, but the gunner was already firing with the MG42. It raked the wagons and the machine gun fire ceased. Donaldson, now in the back seat put another belt into the gun and it barked again, cutting down two men seen running from the vehicles. The second *Flak* also opened up from the other side of the road and no further fire came from the barricade.

"Push through! Keep going!" shouted Donaldson and Carr sped up. They pushed past the carts and saw four men, dead or wounded, besides an upturned light machine gun. They were wearing SS uniforms. Two more were sprawled twenty yards further on.

Donaldson climbed back to the front seat as the *Flaks* stopped.

"Let's get to the Bay. I don't think we will see more but we can't take a chance. Bentley are you Ok?"

"He's hit bad Sir," came a voice.

"Bugger it! Follow us. We've got to move fast."

"Right behind you Sir!" came the answer, and the wagons started forward again.

A minute later they reached the landing spot. Donaldson jumped out and pointed his flashlight out towards the Bay. He flashed the letter 'R'. The time was 0240am.

"Well Jimmy? Coming with us or staying?"

"I'll stay. We have to hide the *Flak's* though. Let's just run them into the sea. Tide's coming in and they will be covered in ten minutes. That gives you plenty of time to get out of the Bay and head north. At the speed those MTB's fly at, you should be back at your base in about three hours. We had better get these two buried as well."

Taking the two bodies from the *Flak's* and using an entrenching tool, they dug shallow graves and covered them with scrub and grass.

The *Flak's* were started and driven into the waves. They had to drive out almost a hundred yards before the motors stalled. As they did they heard the heavier beat of the MTB motors as it slipped closer to shore. Donaldson flashed the signal again and two minutes later it loomed up by their side. Those who could walk climbed aboard after handing the wounded up the side. Donaldson leaned over and shook hands with Carr who stood on the hood of one of the *Flak's*.

"I'll say *adios* Jimmy. Just six of us out of the twenty-four. Still, I'd like to hear the damage report from St. Faith! See you after we finish up these Germans. Good luck!" The MTB reversed in a circle and then accelerated and headed out west.

Carr waded back inshore, found the bushes where he had left his civilian clothes, and dressed. He buried his uniform and Smith's clothes in a hastily scraped hole hidden by scrub a little way inland and walked back to the base.

Forty minutes later he was ringing the doorbell. De had the door opened in seconds and shook Carr's hand as he came in. "I have a million questions Jimmy but you take your time while I put the kettle on."

He walked back to the small stove while Carr sat down on a bunk and rubbed his eyes. He called out to De. "It's all right De. I'm fine. Must you send a report immediately?"

"Yes, as soon as you arrive back I have to flash that. They'll wait a bit for details."

"OK, send the flash and then come sit down." De went to the radio, made contact and was back two minutes later. "That's done. They acknowledge. How was it?"

Carr told him the basics first and then De took a pad and recorded the whole story.

"Jimmy. This must be sent right away. Why not take a nap? It's going to be awhile." When he finally turned from the radio, Carr was already sleeping.

De woke him at seven o'clock with a cup of tea and a bacon sandwich.

"Thanks De. First I've had since yesterday afternoon! Any messages?"

"MTB got back OK. Arrived at Grimsby about six this morning. No problems. Manchester is sending out a Spitfire recon aircraft with cameras to see the damage but our man on the ground has already reported that fires were still blazing at five in the morning at the airfield. Damage is 'very heavy'. Nothing else. We are to stand by at ten o'clock to receive what is termed 'a very important message'."

"What about here? Any news?"

"They say all leads regarding Heydrichs' killing have dried up. The investigation is still open but after last night's disaster everyone will be run ragged! We've also learned that *Gruppenführer Glücks* has been recalled, and Hitler is blaming Himmler for not knowing about the Heydrich assassination or your raid. Go back to sleep. I'll let you know when they are due to transmit."

Chapter 11 – *'Retrospect.'*

Carr slept again and woke without being called. De sat before the set as it squeaked and the fast Morse came through. It was a long message. When De finally stood up he had four sheets that he passed to Carr. "Take a read Jimmy. It's fantastic!"

Carr took the papers and read.

'Recon aircraft confirm one hundred seventy-eight ME-262's destroyed in attack. Additional twenty damaged. Local intelligence advised one hundred thirty-two aircrew killed, forty-eight seriously wounded. Hundred thirty plus aircraft maintenance personnel killed, forty- two wounded. Göering alive but has lost a leg below the knee, an arm and is said to be badly burned. He is being evacuated immediately to Berlin. German attack canceled after bombers hit *Panzer* parks unopposed early today causing heavy damage. Stay at base until further advice. Advancing forces will be in your area shortly. We will advise how to contact.'

They kept inside for two days. A message early Sunday told them that all was going well, and the advance had reached Northampton, about seventy miles from London. Troops would be at Holkham late Tuesday. Next day, they were told that on Tuesday evening at five there would be a meeting at Holkham Hall. Carr should make himself available.

That afternoon Carr picked up his field glasses and called De to come with him as he walked to the door and opened it. Beyond the hawthorn bush it was warmer. May was doing its best. Leaving De, he climbed the ridge and scanned the surrounding countryside. Nothing significant could be seen. In the Bay the tide had receded, and he picked out the two abandoned *Flak's*. As he swung the glasses to the horizon he noticed gray shadows steaming south. That would be the Fleet. Turning to come down he heard a whining noise which gradually got louder. He looked north-east over the sea through the binoculars and silhouetted against the clouds he made out a dozen or so small specs. They were moving so fast it was hard to keep them in focus. They came closer and he could see the streamlined shapes. These must be the new Meteors that Smith had talked about. They roared above him and vanished into the growing overcast as the noise subsided.

He climbed down from the ridge and saw De still looking in wonder to the south.

"Never seen anything like that Jimmy! What a thrill!"

They went inside. Carr dressed to get ready for the meeting at the Hall and just before five o'clock, he approached the driveway. It was congested with vehicles. Armored cars and Jeeps prevailed. Two command trailers dominated the scene. There were MP's everywhere. He was stopped at the gates and asked to provide identification. A Jeep drove him to the Hall entrance where Donaldson was waiting for him.

"Hello Jimmy, come in." They shook hands "A few people want to meet you. Go ahead, you know the way." Jimmy was certain where they would be and walked in front through the reception hall and across to the Garden Room. Sure enough, Coke came forward to greet them.

"Come in gentlemen. Jimmy, you know the Prime Minister." Churchill in RAF uniform, cigar in hand, stepped forward and shook his hand.

"Mr. Carr. We must thank you. I'm happy to say that the Germans are retreating. However, they have nowhere to go!" He laughed, "The roads out of London to the south are packed with them and soon, when they find out there is no transportation whatsoever on the coast, we expect a surrender. They are finished! The pride of their armed forces destroyed. We shall make sure they will never rise up again. An approach has already been made by two of their senior military commanders asking for terms."

"We have told them that terms will be unconditional. Hitler is still in power but we expect the military to depose him any day now. He had his chance and lost it. He's finished! The game is over and we have won." He beamed and shook his cigar at the men in front of him.

"Now. I have to tell you that we won't need your help any more. The professionals will take over. I want you to close up the base tomorrow. Donaldson here will tell you what to take and what to leave and provide transportation. I want the base to remain as is. Who knows? We hope in the future it will never be needed again. You, Mr. Carr may return to your work with Viscount Coke here once you finish at the base. When we take care of these invaders I will have the Viscount send you to me in London. Once there I want to speak with you at length. The people will show their gratitude at that time also! Goodbye Jimmy, again our thanks." He held out his hand and Carr shook it. A wave of the cigar and Carr was dismissed.

He nodded politely to Coke and walked out of the room with Donaldson. "I'll walk to the cottage. It's not far. Do we meet in the morning?"

"Yes, show me your place and I'll be there early, about seven. I'll have a Jeep and we can use that to ride to the base. We can sort out what to take and what to leave and in a couple of days I'll have a lorry here that you and De can load. He'll be returning home afterwards."

"Fine. One thing though, who was Smith? He seemed remarkably well informed."

Donaldson pulled a wry smile. "You might say that. I knew about him but until the raid I didn't know him personally. His name was actually Schmidt and, he was German. Worked in military intelligence in the 1930's and then went to America to spy on them. He was rather upset with Hitler and his doings so he got in touch with our embassy in Washington. They had him 'killed' in a traffic accident and the news leaked back to Berlin. His wife was Himmler's Personal Assistant."

"She went on vacation, and a meeting took place in France. He told her about his worries and doubts about the Nazi's and how he had made arrangements with the British. She loved him and told him she would help. A small transmitter changed hands and then she went back to Germany. She was familiar with everything that passed through Himmler's office and because Himmler's job was state security, that meant he saw most military plans and operations. Himmler worshipped her but as her husband had sacrificed his life for the Reich so to speak, his worshipping had to come from afar. Nevertheless, he trusted her and each night when she went home she took out her little radio and broadcast on a prearranged frequency. Her information was recorded, and I hear it went straight to Churchill! So, we had a lot of information! That's the story."

"I see. Well, he's gone now so I wonder what will happen to her."

"We are taking care of that. Don't worry."

Carr asked no more questions. He went to bed and the next morning traveled with Donaldson to the base. They explained things to De and then inventoried everything, deciding what to keep and what would be picked up. The job took several hours but at last the lists were completed. They went back to Holkham and dropped Carr off at his cottage. De stayed at the base. Two days later Germany surrendered.

Carr went to the base the next afternoon. De said a message had arrived and they should expect to be picked up in the morning. The following day before noon, everything had been packed, and they closed up for the last time. De said goodbye at Holkham and stayed with the truck. It would drop him off in Manchester. Carr would never see him again. He decided to return to Nepal, the country of his birth in 1944 and died there in 1950.

Donaldson stayed in touch over the years, writing every six months or so, but they met only twice. Once was when Carr went to London to meet Churchill in 1943. The King decorated him personally with the George Cross at Buckingham Palace. The second was thirty-five years later.

It was not until January 1978 that Arthur Collins received his medal. Before November 1977, posthumous awards were not allowed. Donaldson was by then a retired Major General but when Carr contacted him that year he called friends who remembered what Collins had contributed. Carr, then 81 years old and retired from the Holkham Estate, accepted the medal in Collins' name. It was a very private ceremony at the Home Office. After all, assassination is a word seldom mentioned in Government circles. Donaldson attended, and they had lunch before Carr returned home.

Two days Carr died in his small cottage. Most of the Estate employees came to the funeral and the son of Lord Coke, also named Thomas, was the Chief Mourner. Jimmy Carr had no family. He bequeathed the two George Crosses to the Royal Norfolk Regiment. They are displayed to this day at the Regiment's Museum in Norwich castle.

What of the others mentioned herein? Well, Sonny Solomon got out of jail when London was re-taken. He went back to selling tea and bacon sandwiches from his van. His narration of the events he became involved in were somewhat different to what actually happened. Sonny told how he valiantly held out when questioned and refused to say a word. He regaled many of his clients with this tale and was considered a hero in the area where he parked his café.

Albert Berrins went to the airfield several times after Carr had done his reconnaissance. He reported what he had seen to his cut-out in the Auxiliaries. When it was all over he received an official letter from the War Office thanking him for his assistance.

Elsie the girl who had sheltered Collins, worked at the Palace until she was sixty and then retired. She lived in the same apartment in St. Agnes Place until she passed away in 1981.

Don, and his friends at the warehouse continued their efforts to disrupt the German occupation. They received no recognition for this and they themselves always brushed off any questions, preferring to remain anonymous.

Upon his return to Germany *Gruppenführer Glücks* was shot, on Himmler's orders, for his failure to protect the Reich's interests. Later, Himmler, Goebbels and Hitler committed suicide as Allied troops entered Berlin in July of 1941. Göering eventually died from his injuries in 1942 before he was well enough to face trial. Hess was tried and imprisoned for war crimes. Nebel went back to police work in Hamburg.

In 1944, work started to rebuild the Clock Tower. It was finished in 1946.

The base still sits at the bottom of the pine-covered hill. These days' no one remembers it. It's hidden and never likely to be found. Unless of course another Hitler comes along!

'FINDING JIMMY.'

Chapter 1 – *'An accident.'*

You must have come across that old chestnut of an expression 'It's who you know' I had heard it for years and never thought much about it, until that June day anyway.

Last June, on the way to a job interview, I stopped at a red light five blocks from where I intended to park. From there I'd walk to my destination. It was a warm June morning. The dashboard clock said twenty to ten. On the odometer, 57,698 miles showed. A sticker in the top left hand of the windshield advised me that the car needed an oil change at fifty-eight thousand. I was doing what most people do when obliged to sit in their vehicle and wait for a few minutes. Just passing the time. Opposite me, on the other side of the intersection, I saw a white Jaguar, an older XJ model, in the middle lane. An indicator flashed for a left turn.

As I checked the light above me two things happened. A green arrow appeared to the left of the red. Glancing into my right door mirror I saw a low-slung dark vehicle approaching in the inside lane. I looked down as the car passed. The driver wasn't going fast, but he wasn't concentrating on the road. From my truck, which was much higher than his vehicle, I watched him peering at something in his lap through his half-spectacles. He made it half-way across the intersection but then he 'T' boned the Jag as it turned left. There was an almighty crunch, and what looked like a Ferrari, pushed the Jaguar across the street, leaving bits and pieces strewn everywhere.

Silence. The light changed to green but not one vehicle moved. Exiting my car, I ran across to the crash. The driver of the black vehicle was entangled in his airbags which had deployed. However, he was moving. I went to the other side of the Jag. The driver, seat belt tight, leaned back in her seat. Pulling open the door I noticed blood on her head. She had a small cut over one eye that was bleeding profusely. Taking out a handkerchief I placed it over the cut and put the girl's left hand over it to hold it in place.

"Are you hurt anywhere else?"

"No, it think it's my eye that's cut."

"Sit still. Someone has probably called 911 but I'll make sure." I dialed on my cell phone and an operator said the accident had been reported. Police and an ambulance were on the way. Sure enough, as I closed the phone sirens blared and two cruisers arrived. An officer bundled me aside but asked me to stay on the scene. He told the girl to keep still, help would arrive momentarily. The other policeman assisted the driver of the Ferrari out of his vehicle. I looked at my watch, there were still had seventeen minutes before my interview.

The ambulance came, and the paramedics were soon checking both drivers. A pair of tow trucks arrived simultaneously. Like sharks, they could smell blood in the water a mile away!

One policeman came over, notebook in hand, and asked if I had seen the accident.

"Yes, I was stopped, waiting for the red light, and saw the whole thing."

He took down the details, and I provided my name, address and telephone number. They said I could go but might be called upon to give evidence or be deposed if the case went to trial.

By this time my watch indicated ten. I eventually arrived at my destination at ten fifteen. The receptionist said that the interview had been for ten o'clock. Unfortunately, I had not met the basic rule for meeting with the HR Manager. Punctuality was very important and I should... At this point I turned and walked out. The last thing I needed was a lecture from a receptionist!

Chapter 2 – *'The deposition.'*

Two weeks later, on June 21st, I got hired. When I arrived, early on this occasion, I learned the HR person doing the interview had graduated from the same Community College as myself. This gave me confidence. I realized providing I didn't pick my nose or scratch below the belt, the job should be mine. There would be an aptitude test but I could handle that! Sure enough, an hour later Jay Valley was welcomed as the newest employee of the Antique Auto Parts Company. The job involved finding parts for clients that owned or restored old cars.

After a few days I became absorbed in the job. A client would call and say he was restoring a 1939 Oldsmobile. He wanted two rear fold- away seats for a Club Coupe. My job? Find them for him. I had lists of people and companies who might have what we needed. My days were spent calling around to get these special parts.

I hadn't thought about the crash I had seen a few weeks earlier. The new job kept me very busy, so it didn't cross my mind. Then one morning my cell phone rang. It was an Attorney for the Jaguar driver requesting that I be deposed about the accident. I agreed to go to their offices that coming Saturday.

Downtown as usual, had no traffic on weekends. My appointment had been made for eleven. The offices of Blake, Mortensen, Fletcher and Gonzalez was in a low, modern building with its own parking lot. That told me they were a successful firm. With office space at a premium, to have your own parking meant you were doing very well.

I waited in a luxurious reception area and drank a cup of excellent coffee. Five minutes later a lady arrived and explained that I would be asked formally to provide a deposition in a traffic accident case. It involved Judy Niven, represented by Blake, Mortensen, and Fletcher.

The defendant, Mr. Charles Langtree, was represented by Donahue and Smith, Attorneys at Law. Mr. Fletcher would conduct the morning's events. She turned and led me to the inner sanctum. We went into a conference room and a white-haired gentleman stepped forward to meet me.

"Mr. Valley. Good morning. I'm Victor Fletcher."

He extended his hand, and I took it.

"This won't take long I'm sure. In a moment the court reporter," He pointed a finger at a lady sitting at the long table, "That's her there, will ask you to take the oath. She will then record of all that is said during the deposition. You will be asked questions about the accident. Providing things go well, you will not be required after today. Are you ready to go ahead?"

"I'm ready." I replied.

The deposition started, and the Attorney asked about where I had been when the accident took place, what I had seen and what I did after the occurrence. It seemed simple. The only comment I made was that when the other driver passed me he wasn't looking forward across the intersection, but downwards. Asked to expand on this comment I explained that I looked down to my right and saw the car as it slowly passed by. The driver was looking down and not forwards. I was sure of this because his eyeglasses were on the end of his nose. Being stopped at the time I had nothing to do other than watch events going on around me. The deposition finished on this note and I after thanking me the Attorney said I could leave. I had a quiet weekend reading through a collection of antique auto collectors magazines.

Chapter 3 – *'The Call.'*

The job kept me busy every day. I now knew the most common items that people wanted. I could find for instance, a 1923 Ford gas cap, an original, not a copy, with one or two calls. A 1946 would take a little longer!

On Monday morning, a week after I had gone to the Attorney's office. I received a call. I didn't immediately recognize the caller name, J. Niven, then I realized this was the driver of the Jaguar involved in the accident. She wanted to tell me that thanks for my deposition, she had won her civil case for damages. The other driver had admitted he was using his phone to answer a text message and had not seen the red light.

"So Mr. Valley. I wanted to say thank you for being so alert. It saved me a huge repair bill."

"It's no problem Ms. Niven. I think that the cellular companies should have a button you push when you got into your car that advised any caller you were driving and weren't available. Leave a message. When you stop, you re-activate by pushing the button again. I believe that would prevent a whole slew of accidents!"

"Mr. Valley, will you repeat that please?" She sounded surprised. I did what she asked.

"That's a great idea! I work for a cellular company as a matter of fact. No one has ever suggested that!"

"Pleased to help." I answered, expecting her to say goodbye. She didn't. "Mr. Valley. I'm near the stadium in the north of the city. Are you anywhere near there?"

"Believe it or not, my building is at the end of the north parking lot."

"Wonderful, I'm two minutes away. Do you think we might get together? I'd like to talk about what you mentioned earlier. You know. The button you push?"

"Sure. When do you want to meet?"

"You must know Charlie's Grill, on the corner of Delancy and Grayvine? Is noon good for you?"

"How will I know you Ms. Niven?"

"I'll be standing by my Jag in the parking lot! See you there."

The Jag looked better than the last time I had seen it. Whoever had done the repairs was very good at their job. Julie Niven seemed to be in her mid-twenties, well dressed in a smart business suit, and looking very competent.

"Well, Ms. Niven we meet under improved circumstances today."

She smiled. "It's Julie. May I call you Jay?"

"Of course!" We walked to the door and entered. It was early, but a table was set for us in minutes. Sitting down I waited for her to start the conversation.

"Jimmy. You mentioned something this morning that my Company would be interested in exploring further. Are you an engineer or involved with any kind of telephone organization? I ask this before we go any further because today's intellectual property laws are so strict that it's necessary to be clear before we talk."

"No. I find old automobile parts for restoration enthusiasts. No engineering or telephone companies."

"Good. I'm the Vice President of Impro Cellular. It's a software company. I'm an engineer and I run the development side. The Company isn't huge or anything but what we do is develop applications for the big companies to use on their own models. I'm an MIT graduate." Having impressed me with her credentials she continued.

"After we talked this morning I spoke to Gatik Chopra, our President. He couldn't believe that such a simple idea might be turned into an app and not only make money but make us innovators in cellphone safety."

"I'm pleased he liked it. I hope it works out."

"Jimmy, it will work out. Gatik already assigned two engineers to have something ready by tomorrow. There can't be delays in our business. If we agree today I'll have this sold by Friday!"

"Friday this week?"

"Yes. We buy your idea. You sign all rights to that idea over to Impro in exchange for an agreed upon sum."

"Sounds great! It must be worth a few hundred bucks I guess?"

"Jimmy. There can be one of two deals. The first is a straight sum of money. You sign and get paid. That's that. The other is doing a royalty deal. Impro gets paid by the people we supply. There's a down payment to you and then a royalty per unit sold. It's your choice."

"Well. I understand the first one. That's easy. What about the second?"

"Let's start with the first. Impro can offer you fifty thousand cash. I have the papers right here,"

She touched the large handbag she carried. "The second is five thousand cash and ten percent of any royalties Impro receives from customers." She looked carefully at me.

"They report their sales to us and enclose 'X' dollars for each sale of the app. For an app like this we would normally expect to get a royalty of about five cents. However, the safety factor is an enormous sales point and I think in this case, six cents wouldn't be out of the question." She looked up at him.

"We expect to receive royalties on at least ten million sales of the app. Impro can offer you 10% of any royalty we receive if you take the deal. Royalties are paid after we get paid. It could be a year. One other thing if we sell the app it will be 'live' for only twelve months. The industry considers that's the maximum life of an app, something will be developed to replace it by then."

Having a good head for math I figured this might amount to sixty thousand for the second deal. I didn't hesitate.

"I'll open box number two please!"

Julie smiled. "How did I know that? I have a contract here. It's simple. Read it and sign. I will have Gatik counter-sign, and we will notarize it this afternoon and put a copy in the mail to you if you give me an address?"

"How about you get it signed and I pick you up for a celebratory dinner this evening? You could hand it over then."

That's how I started dating Julie Niven.

Chapter 4 – *'Wally.'*

We were very different Julie and I. Raised in Wisconsin, her parents died when she was sixteen. She went to live with her grandfather for two years before going on to MIT. Being independent she had her job because her boss, Gatik Chopra, an MIT grad himself, received help with his recruiting from faculty friends. They informed him of students likely to fit in at Impro. He heard about Julie and asked if she would do a three-month internship before her final year. She accepted. Nothing exceptional came from her work during that summer but Chopra recognized a gem when he saw one and offered her a job upon graduation. The next year she moved to Atlanta and started work. That was three years ago, and she had done very well.

I, on the other hand, joined the Coast Guard after high school and served four years. Then I attended Community College and after graduation started applying for jobs. Antique Auto Parts happened to be my first employment. Despite our differences we got along well. Atlanta was a pleasant town, there was plenty to do there.

The five thousand dollars appeared in my account. After a week Julie told me that her company sold the app to two major cell phone manufacturers. The estimate for sales came out to ten million over twelve months.

Both Julie and myself were busy during the week but usually met on a Friday night along the Beltline, walked for two miles and then found a restaurant. One evening I asked her where she got her '76 Jag.

"Oh! It was a gift from my grandfather, Wally. You know I lived with him for two years after my parents died. He's a car enthusiast and over ninety now. Heaven knows where he got the Jag from but he said when it arrived at Solon Springs it was a mess. Wally lives outside Solon, it's in Wisconsin where

I grew up. Anyway he told me he read everything he could about the car and when he was ready he started to restore it."

"After sitting around so long rust had set in. Another problem happened to be the twin gas caps which sat on top of the trunk, an invitation for the rain to trickle down the filler tubes. He relocated a tank cap to the side of the rear fender, making one opening. He eliminated the two on top and plugged the original holes. After a year he had it ready. It was my graduation present. He had been a machinist in the Navy during the war that's where he learned to put things together and take them apart. What a wonderful gift. Wasn't that sweet of him?"

"It certainly was!"

"Would you like to meet him?"

"Of course! How do we do that?"

"Oh! It's easy. Fly to Duluth via Chicago. A five-hour trip. Pick up a rental car at Duluth and drive to Solon Spring. It's forty miles. I do it three or four times a year. He has ten acres of land there called The Pines. We go fishing on St. Croix Lake and generally have a good time. These days he's getting on, but he's still as sharp as a blade. Plays checkers like a pro. Said he learned in the Navy!"

"The Navy eh? Well we should have a few things in common, me being ex-Coast-Guard."

"I bet you will. He was in for twenty years. Then a guy he had served with got him a job with the Teamsters Union and he worked there for a long time and finally resigned. He was only fifty and said he wanted an outdoor life somewhere quiet. Finished up with The Pines. Still gets a pension check from the Teamsters each month so he has plenty to live on and enjoy himself."

We both took three days off and I made the reservations for next Wednesday. Julie called her grandfather who said he would be waiting for us.

The following Wednesday, after a five-hour flight, we picked up a rental car at Duluth and drove down to Solon

Springs. It was all farmland and forest along the way. There weren't too many houses to be seen. Julie told me the whole population comprised of six hundred persons, a small, quiet corner of America.

Wally Niven waited at the gates of The Pines. For a fellow of ninety he looked good! He still had all of his hair and stood straight with no slouch. Dressed casually he wore jeans and a sweater. He gave us a big smile. Julie got out and ran over to him. They hugged, very happy to see each other. I gave them a minute and then walked over to them.

"Wally, this is Jimmy."

Wally and I shook hands. He had a good grip!

"Hello Jimmy. Pleased to have you with us." Turning, he spread his arms. "This is The Pines. You'll like it here. It's quiet, but that's the way I prefer things. Now, let's go up to the house. I've prepared lunch for us and afterwards we can take a look round the Estate. I've got an old pickup that still runs so we'll take that. Perhaps get a rabbit or two for dinner."

We had tuna sandwiches for lunch and they were very good. The bread was fresh and Wally used some horseradish in the mayonnaise to give it a kick. We talked about going to sea and to places Wally had served. After lunch finished we agreed to meet in an hour and Wally would show us everything. It wasn't a big house, but it had two bedrooms and two separate bathrooms on the top floor and a kitchen plus a living room on the ground floor. The furnishings were plain with plenty of pillows and throws on the comfortable chairs. A huge fireplace dominated the downstairs area. There was no TV, but he did possess a radio set which could pick up stations from all over the world. He showed us the antenna that ran up through the roof and protruded upwards on a long rod attached to the side of the chimney.

We met downstairs at four o'clock and walked over to the garage ten yards from the main house. Wally unlocked the doors and there was a Chevy Silverado, about fifteen years old. We sat in the front seat as Wally drove. The only road on the property led from the gates to the house. However, the ground didn't have many bumps. As we drove away I saw there were two other structures close by. Wally stopped at the first one and we got out. There was a padlock on the door and he used a key from the ring he had on his belt to open it and swung one of the double doors aside.

"Come on in here. This is my workshop. Got used to working with my hands in the Navy. I was a machinist."

He turned on a light switch inside the doors and bright neon overhead lights illuminated the area. Light coming through two large windows also helped. Along both sides of the building were benches. There were a lot of tools, all neatly stored in racks and seemingly in great condition. There were two lathes, a Baileigh wood and a Baileigh metal. I walked over to them.

"Nice eh? The metal is a PL-1860E. She's got an 18' swing and 60" between centers and operates on 220 volt three phase power. Does everything I need!" He obviously understood his tools. I'd seen the machinists in the Coast Guard shops when we were ashore and this was what they used.

In the middle of the floor, a tarp covered a large object. Wally walked over and pulled the tarp aside. A Ford Model T came into view. It didn't have a motor and only two of the four wheels were attached.

"This is my project. It's one of the last T's produced in 1927. Missing a few parts but I'm getting them slowly. I don't work on this every day, just twice a week I come over and do a little. Been at it for two years now. Before this I had an Austin 7 from '35. That took me about four years to finish!"

They admired the Model T and asked a few more questions. Then Wally drove them around the rest of the Estate. In a far corner near a stand of trees he stopped the truck and pulled a shotgun from a rack over the back seat.

"Here's a good place for rabbits. Let's see if we can get a couple."

Wally knew a lot about his land because ten minutes later we were back at the house with a brace of cottontails for dinner. It was very enjoyable. Wally insisted in cooking the meal and he did those rabbits justice! He told us he brazed them first and then cooked them in a closed saucepan with wine, celery, onions, butter and parsley. He said that took an hour and then he added flour to the cooking liquid and used it as a sauce on top of the rabbits. With baked potatoes it was delicious.

We slept well that night and the next morning drove down to the lake where we fished for largemouth bass. We were lucky, or rather Wally and Julie were! They both caught two bass, and we cleaned these and Wally promised them for dinner.

Over the next two days we drove all around the area. The lake was exciting with lots of little bays and inlets. We fished for crappies on the Saturday and had a lot of fun pulling them out of the water.

Sunday morning came all too soon, and we were on our way. On the long flight back to Atlanta, we both sat quietly while going over our memories of the past four days.

Things were soon back to normal upon our return. I was busy with a collector who needed everything I could find to restore a Vauxhall Cadet VY. I felt sure he just bought the chassis and bodywork because he seemed to want everything else!

Julie had a lot to do with her own job and it wasn't until the following Friday we got together. She didn't seem very happy, and I asked her why.

"It's Wally. He's not doing well. Two days ago he saw the doctor because he hadn't been feeling good. They say he has pneumonia. So he's in hospital at Hayward. That's thirty miles south of Solon. I've spoken to the doctor who is treating him and he said at ninety anything might happen. I have to call back tomorrow morning to check." Our date was a somber one. We had dinner and returned to Julies. About half an hour later the telephone rang, and we learned that Wally had died. It was a shock for both of us. We had seen him a week ago, and he had been fine.

After the first tears Julie pulled herself together. Then we sat down to decide what had to be done and how to do it. Julie was the only relative, so the burden fell on her. The first order of business would be to make funeral arrangements. She pulled out an old satchel and inside were all the relevant documents she had kept. There was a local news-sheet with addresses of companies and professionals. She found the undertaker. They were used to receiving late night calls. Provisions to collect the body at the Hayward hospital were made. Funeral arrangements would be approved by Julie the next day.

She called the local Attorney that Wally used and he confirmed he had a copy of Wally's will on hand. They agreed to talk when the funeral had been arranged. There were a million things to do. Julie got permission to take the week off and I did the same. Then I made arrangements to fly up with her the following day, Saturday. By the time we finished the clock said one fifteen, so I slept over at Julie's.

Leaving early the next morning we stopped by my place to pick up a bag. By two o'clock The Pines loomed up ahead on the track. We called the Attorney and the funeral director as we drove from the Airport at Duluth.

Wally was buried the next day. There were no mourners apart from myself, Julie and Davies the lawyer. Wally had been a solitary person and didn't have friends locally.

Back at the house Mr. Davies the Attorney, read the will. Everything was to go to Julie. Davies would take care of filing the necessary papers with the authorities and he felt sure things might be wrapped up within a week. He told us that the house and land might bring in $100 thousand at auction. If we worked on making up an inventory, he would appreciate it. When we finished we only had to call. After expressing his regrets again, he left us there alone.

Sunday afternoon we started an inventory of Wally's belongings. We tried to estimate what everything was worth and as there wasn't a lot, it didn't take too long. However, an examination of Wally's financial and personal records turned up a few surprises. He had two accounts at the Commercial Savings Bank in town. The checking account showed that every month Walter Niven received from the National Bank of Detroit, three thousand dollars, described as 'Teamsters Pension deposit'.

He also received transfers from the US Navy and the Social Security Administration. Wally used about a thousand of this to pay his water and electricity bills plus groceries. There were checks made out to various automobile parts suppliers, and donations to the local Church. The remaining amount was transferred to his saving account the day after the five thousand Detroit deposit arrived. He always left two hundred dollars available. The records went back for twenty years. In the savings account he had seven hundred thousand dollars. A big surprise to both of us.

That was nothing compared to when we uncovered the documents for The Pines. The deed showed that the Estate had been paid for by a Teamsters check. We stared at each other in disbelief.

"That's a lot of money for a Navy vet for a start. Secondly, why did the Teamsters pay for The Pines?"

"I don't know. A farewell gift perhaps? What about the Teamsters check every month? You said he worked in Detroit for them but three thousand every month is a lot of retirement money."

"Wally kept in touch with the guy that got him the job I remember! His name was Alfonse Antoni. He'd also been a machinist in the Navy. Let's see his address book and try to find his number."

Five minutes later they had Antoni's telephone number in Detroit. Julie made the call and Jimmy listened in on the extension.

"Mr. Antoni? My name is Julie Niven, Wally's granddaughter. I wanted to tell you Wally passed away a couple of days ago. This is the first time I've had an opportunity to call."

"Julie! Yes I know of you. You lived with Wally for some years. He told me this. I am so sorry my friend has gone. That was a good man!"

"Thank you Mr. Antoni. I appreciate that."

"Please. Call me Alfonse. I last heard from Wally about six weeks back so it's a big surprise for me. We served on a cruiser, the William Thomas, from nineteen sixty until he got out in nineteen sixty two."

"Thank you Alfonse. You are very kind. I wonder if you might help me. Wally worked with the Teamsters. He retired in nineteen seventy- six. He said you were the one that got him that position and I wonder if you might tell me more about it?"

"Sure, sure. I was with the Teamsters. My father got me the job. Those were good times. As Chief of Maintenance I worked at the Marble Palace in Washington, the Headquarters. Wally became my assistant. We got on good together. You know, he was only two years older than me. Makes you think doesn't it?"

"Yes Alfonse it does. I have a question. Why did Wally get a check for three thousand dollars every month? Back in seventy six when he retired that kind of money was far greater than Wally may have made in six months!"

"Julie. Listen. I'm sorry about Wally. I liked him but let me tell you this. There are mysteries in this world that need to stay mysteries. Just forget it. Tell the bank that Wally is deceased. They will let the issuers of the check know and payments will cease. Leave it at that. Please!"

Julie remained for a moment. She glanced across, and I nodded my head.

"Alfonse. Thank you. I'll do as you say. No further questions."

"That's good Julie. Leave it be. I'm an old man so I have to rest. So, if there's nothing else I will say goodbye."

"Bye Alfonse!" She hung up the telephone and the two of us sat shaking our heads.

"Well that's a mystery I guess we'll never find out about."

"I agree. Let sleeping dogs lie."

The next day, just like the 'Baha Men's' song, we were asking ourselves, 'Who let the dogs out?'

Chapter 5 – *'The back seat.'*

We awoke early on the Monday morning. An inventory had to be done of the outbuildings for Mr. Davies, the Attorney.

I picked up Wally's large keyring, and we went outside to the workshop. We opened the doors and switched on the lights. Nothing had changed since our last visit. I called out names and numbers, Julie wrote the information into a school notebook she bought along. When we were finished we summed up values and were sure there was another fifty thousand dollars, including the unfinished Model T, to be added to the Estate.

Picking up the keyring, I called to Julie. "Let's check that barn building over the way there. Wally never mentioned that one."

We walked the twenty yards across to the other structure. It was smaller than Wally's workshop and had no windows at all. There were three separate padlocks on the single wide door. All were rusty and seemed like they hadn't been opened for years.

"Three padlocks? That's excessive isn't it?"

"I guess so. I've never been in here. Wally said it held a bunch of junk from his time in the Navy. He didn't mention it and I didn't see him visit it. I had so much to do in those days."

We tried opening the locks, but the keyring didn't have a key that would fit any of them.

I was mystified. "There has to be keys for these locks. Where would he keep them?"

"Let's go back inside and search through his room again. We might have missed them first time."

Back in the house Wally's bedroom door remained open. I walked in to look around. Julie went downstairs to make us some sandwiches.

We had been here earlier and removed a few boxes from the wardrobe with Wally's papers. There didn't seem to be much else. I stood still and concentrated. Where would I myself put something that I wasn't intending to use in the near future? In a closed container I reasoned. Whatever I kept mustn't get lost and needed to be there when I wanted it. Where might the container be? The bathroom perhaps?

I went in and opened the cabinet over the hand sink. There were deodorants, talcum powder, razors and blades, toothpaste and a box of Band Aids. I saw a small, round plastic container with a screw top. A faded label reading 'Aspirin' written by hand, stuck on the side with tape. Inside it was a ring with five keys and a tag. Three looked like they were for a padlock, the others, a car. The tag had a label that spelled out 'BARN'.

Jubilant, I ran downstairs to show Julie who was as excited as me!

Taking a ham sandwich each we munched as we walked over to the locked barn. The first key wouldn't turn. I went back to Wally's workshop and found a can of 3-in-1 oil in a spray can. I grabbed a flashlight and a box-cutter knife while I was there. The other building I recalled, had no windows. I squirted quite a lot into each padlock and finished my sandwich. Then I tried again. After a little maneuvering I opened all of them.

The door had heavy hasps, and I hung the locks on these. The keys I put back in my pocket. It took the combined strength of each of us to get it fully opened. Inside it had a musty smell and the dust which was everywhere, made us sneeze. It was much smaller than the workshop and most of the floor space was taken up by what must be a car covered by a tightly tied nylon tarp.

"Well? Want to take a look?" I asked.

"I bet it's another of those antiques he planned to work on."

"Might be. There's light enough from the doorway but we'll need more." I handed the flashlight to her, and she shone it upwards as I slowly peeled back the tarp. Underneath we saw a dark-colored saloon supported by jack-stands. Leaning forward, I took a closer look.

I recognized a maroon Mercury Marquis Brougham. A '74 or '75 two-door model. The once shiny paintwork was covered with dust and cobwebs. A nest of some kind protruded from the front grill. I pulled the tarp back further exposing the windshield. The wiper blades showed rotting rubber. With a last effort I removed the tarp completely and there she stood. Dirty and filthy with the grime of years but even in this condition she still appeared elegant.

"Well. Wally's next project doesn't seem to need anything more than a polish! Let's see what the inside looks like. These must be the keys." I showed her the ring.

Smarter now I squirted oil into the lock on the driver's side door. The key slid in and as I pulled on the handle it opened, creaking loudly. A musty and unpleasant smell wafted up, so I walked to the other side and opened the passenger door. The smell dissipated. Reaching in I released the recline lever and pushed the front seat forwards.

Julie pointed the flashlight inside the vehicle. The roof and door coverings were sagging. Everything else appeared pristine, no damage to the upholstery except age cracks. I looked into the rear seat. That's when my scalp started to tingle. I stepped back. Something or somebody seemed to be slumped there.

Julie stood there with her hand over her mouth. She was just as surprised as me.

"Is that what I think it is?"

"I'm afraid so."

"Let's take a good look."

She lowered the flashlight, and we could now partially see the skeletal remains of a person dressed in a blue suit, the material mostly intact. Tattered pieces of a shirt were underneath and a tie still hung round the neck. Above that rested a skull with hair attached. The 'hands' that protruded from the sleeves were only bones. A gray blanket covered the legs and feet.

I looked at Julie, my question unasked. She nodded. I moved the blue suit slightly and there in the inside pocket I saw a wallet. Taking it out, I walked to the front of the Caddy and put it on the hood.

"Shall we take a look?"

Julie seemed dubious. "Shouldn't we call the police before we do that?"

"Well, in a minute. I'd like to find out just who's been camping here all these years." She nodded her approval.

I opened it. The first thing to emerge was a piece of paper, loose between the folds. A receipt. On the top the wording 'Machus Red Fox Restaurant' and beneath, an address '6676, Telegraph Road, Bloomfield Township, Detroit'. Machine printed, it recorded the sale of two cups of coffee at 230pm, July 30th, 1975.

Inside the wallet I found a Michigan Driver's License issued to James Riddle Hoffa. Date of birth February 13th 1913 in Indiana.

I passed it to Julie.

She took out her cell phone. "Operator, may I have the number of the FBI office nearest to Solon Springs, Wisconsin, please?"

Jimmy had been found, at last.

'JACK.'

Chapter 1 – '*Beginnings.*'

Have you ever loved a person so much they are constantly in your thoughts? Have you ever owned a wild animal? A creature you see every day, and which you pet and love? But, deep inside, you know any minute this animal, your pet, might revert to its basic instincts and bite or lash out at you with a paw. You will have no advanced notice.

If you have experienced these emotions then you will realize how terrible that deep down inside sensation is. The stomach turning feeling whenever you hear anyone mention 'their' name while you stand waiting for the bad news. For bad news it usually is. It goes together with the gut acid. In the end waiting might kill you. But first, it will kill them.

Jack was like that. Someone I loved, someone I cared for, someone who meant everything to me. Someone I wanted to see every day, someone for whom I wept. Someone with a great sense of humor, who laughed at my feeble jokes and whom I thought, one day could be an enormous success, if he would give himself a chance. Someone that loved me back and showed it, not in the way I wanted, but in his own way, the way he understood and hoped that I would too.

It's not a long story. How could it be? My Jack was only on this earth for a little more than sixteen years. How long is that? It's a story that I think should be told though. Perhaps, if we put it on a billboard in huge red letters to be seen by passersby, many would notice it. Perhaps it might help some people. Here though, in small black and white print, it may do no good at all. But I will try. Remember, you can never love too much!

Where do I start? Kids, that's where. At first we are all kids and crawl, walk and then run. For parents, time fly's, and before we realize it the kinder garden is gone and school starts. Some go on to academic or sporting greatness, but in 1915, many joined the armed services. There was a World War going on. My Jack went into the Royal Navy.

Chapter 2 – 'Separation.'

Jack came into this world in January of 1900. He left school at 14 and became a grocery clerk. A wild boy, our Jack. Always up to some kind of mischief. Strange, you never could be sure when he would come off the rails. It would be quiet for a week and then a knock on the front door and there stood a police constable holding Jack by the scruff of the neck. He'd been caught smoking, or he'd taken an apple from the grocers without paying for it. He always had an excuse and always knew more than I did. All small stuff, but it kept me on edge constantly.

I think everyone felt glad when Jack volunteered for the Navy in 1915 and went to Plymouth for training. Early in 1916 he joined the light cruiser 'Exeter' as a boy sailor and was assigned to the forward 5.5 inch gun as a sight setter. He came home to see me before he went up to Scotland to join his ship. One evening, as I sat watching him eat dinner, I asked myself 'What's a fifteen year old boy doing in a War?' As if he had heard me he said, "Dad's fighting and so is Charlie. Why not me?"

He was right. His father and brother, both volunteers, were already abroad, Jack felt he had to do the same.

I believed, deep inside, that my worst fears would be realized. I would lose Jack. God had spoken and you couldn't change his words. So, for a week, I loved him as much as possible, and when he left that day in January something vanished from me as well. I felt empty inside.

Jack wrote of course. He told me he was doing well and was with a great bunch of lads. He was the youngest but wrote that they all looked out for him. Some had children of his age at home. He seemed happy, and that said I shouldn't worry.

The last letter I received was dated Wednesday, May 24th, 1916. It came in the late post. As usual, Jack said everything was fine. Nice weather, lots of sunshine but no shore leave. They expected to be at sea soon and he and everyone was looking forward to it. The lads were still mothering him but he was used to it. It was nice that someone cared. I must not worry and he would see me soon.

Chapter 3 – 'Goodbye Jack!'

It wasn't until June 2nd that I got the telegram. Jack was in Hull Hospital wounded. Would it be possible to come at once? It's a long train ride from the east end of London, nearly 200 miles. I arrived that evening, but it was too late. Jack had succumbed to his wounds earlier that day.

We bought him home and buried him. The funeral, a military one, had soldiers, sailors and flowers, a really swell occasion.

In September a nice officer came to the house. September 15th, a Friday I recall. He said that Jack had been awarded the Victoria Cross for his bravery on the 'Exeter'. Jack had remained at his post even although his gun was out of action and all the gun crew members wounded or killed. The officer bought me a copy of a poem, 'For the Fallen' published earlier in the War and written by a gentleman called Laurence Binyon, He said I may like to read it. I did, but it wasn't very clear to me at that time. He also gave me a cutting from the London Gazette with the citation:

'His Majesty The King has been graciously pleased to approve the grant of the Victoria Cross to Boy, First Class, John Bryan Devon, (died 2 June 1916), for the conspicuous act of bravery specified below. Mortally wounded early in the action, Devon remained standing alone at a most exposed post, quietly awaiting orders, until the end of the action, with the gun's crew dead and wounded all round him. Devon was under sixteen and a half years.'

Imagine that! His Majesty King George approved our Jack's medal! A taxi took me to the Palace in November. I was presented with Jack's Cross by the King. Everyone was so nice! It was the most exciting thing that ever happened to me. That finished it though.

Jack's father, Samuel died in October of that year and then Charlie, Jack's brother got killed in France, August 1918. I mourned them both, but it was Jack that hurt the most.

A year later, I died. I hadn't seen Jack for three years but he was waiting when I got there. At last, I understood that line in Mr. Binyon's poem, 'They shall not grow old'*.

It was my same old Jack. He had not aged a day since I had last seen him, three years before.

They shall grow not old, as we that are left grow old:
Age shall not weary them, nor the years condemn.
At the going down of the sun and in the morning,
We will remember them.

'SECOND CHANCE.'

Chapter 1 – *'The Cell.'*

It was almost dawn in the mountains. At this time of year no wind blew into the many cracks and crevices of the buildings to create the madman's orchestra. Everything was silent. Not even the cypress trees shed their cones to bounce on the flagstones of the courtyard. This was the quietest hour in a very quiet place.

He lay awake, eyes open, waiting as the darkness lessened. Slowly came the pre-dawn, a slight graying in the small window high on the wall. As the ceiling became illuminated, the cross came into view.

At least, he thought of it as a cross, put there to ease his waking each day and to prepare him for whatever may come. In his head he knew that his cross only consisted of two brush strokes which crossed to form ridges. However, for now it was his. It would not be visible for long. As dawn progressed the light flattened as it entered the cell and the ridges disappeared. He didn't care because for the next ten minutes he felt safe from everything, protected by his vision.

Gradually, the gray became lighter and revealed the walls supporting the ceiling. They were rough stonework, whitewashed and free of any embellishment. No pictures or adornments. No graffiti, that was unthinkable. Nothing, just a plain wall.

Under the window was a simple wooden table with a shelf. A clock sat on the shelf showing the time as four forty-five. By its side rested a small toiletry bag.

On the table stood a jug, half filled with water. He had washed before going to sleep the evening previously. What remained would be used when he arose this morning. A rough towel hung from a hook on the side. He knew that if he touched it, he would feel its dampness. At this time of year, the nights were cold and misty, inhibiting drying.

Pushing the coarse blankets aside he swung his bare legs from his bed. The straw-filled pillow was straightened and after he stood up he folded his coverings neatly and placed them below the pillow. The bed was a simple one. A wooden frame with woven strips taking the place of a mattress. The floor could be seen through the square openings.

He washed quickly. The water felt cold and the rough, damp towel made him hurry to dry himself. He ran his hands through his cropped hair trying, unsuccessfully, to straighten it. He had no mirror to check his efforts, but he felt it would pass muster.

From a plain wooden chair at the foot of the bed, he lifted the garments hanging there and dressed.

He was ready. In a few moments he would leave the cell and this time he used to reflect on his day ahead. The vaults awaited him today. The bell rang. He walked to the door and opened it. Then, adjusting the cowl of his garment to cover his head he joined the other eighteen Brothers of the Order of Cistercians of the Strict Observance, the Trappist's, on their way to morning prayer.

Chapter 2 – *'The Monastery.'*

This then is James. Three years earlier he had arrived at the Monastery, a frightened nineteen year old boy who knew he needed help and who became determined to find that help in God. He was eventually accepted as a novice and embraced the silence and meditation of the Order. It calmed him and made him came to terms with his previous actions.

After a night which he hardly remembered, he walked into a Bank with a handkerchief over his face, and his hand in his jacket pocket and demanded money from a teller. Minutes later, a plastic shopping bag in his hand, he was running through a parking lot seeking a way to escape before the police arrived. An unlocked bicycle caught his eye. He jumped on it and pedaled as hard as he was able. In half an hour he was close to the Airport. Stopping on a side road, he calmed down and took a minute to think. It was not the best of areas and he realized that leaving the bike here meant it would soon be re-stolen. He had to get away from the City as soon as possible. A BOLO had surely been issued. Every policeman for miles around would be on the lookout for a young robber.

Slowly he strolled to the main road, hailed a passing taxi, and asked to be taken to Terminal 1. The driver grumbled, at the short journey, but agreed to transport him. He paid with a bill from his wallet and got into the cab. At the Airport he knew he needed a bag for the money and a plane ticket. The first presented no problems. He went into a store and purchased a small duffle. Next he found a bathroom and locked himself into a cubicle. There was twenty-two thousand, four hundred dollars into the plastic bag and he transferred twenty-one thousand nine hundred to the new duffle. The remaining five hundred he put it in his wallet.

Leaving the rest room he saw the Delta counter. The departures board showed a flight leaving in forty minutes for San Francisco. He purchased a ticket, passed security and boarded the plane, arriving six and a half hours later. Tired and remorseful, he had no idea what to do next. Walking through the Terminal he saw a small red neon sign spelling 'CHAPEL'. An insignificant door opened easily, and he went inside. It was quiet away from the crowds and he sat on a bench and looked about him. The Chapel had no religious symbols other than a cross on the rear wall and seemed to be for people who wanted a little peace before flying.

On one side stood a table with literature on it and he started to look at the pamphlets. One caught his eye. It described a Monastery near a town called Coloma. Could this be his destination? He decided to take a chance. Catching the bus, he arrived four hours later. The gates were open, and he went through the double doors. There the Administrator welcomed him and asked him to wait. Minutes after, the Father Abbot spoke with him and understanding a troubled soul and the genuine desire to seek God's help, offered him the sanctuary of the Monastery.

After a year of silence and meditation the Father Abbot asked if he would help catalog the many ancient documents that had accumulated. These were stored haphazardly in the vaults below the main building. It was a project the Abbot had dreamed of for years and he believed that finally work could be started.

It was spring and as he worked to keep the old graveyard clean, the pollen made him sneeze. The Father Abbot's request seemed most timely and James agreed to start the following day.

The first documents he looked at showed that an epidemic of cholera had broken out at the Monastery in 1837, more than twenty victims were buried there. Three were identified as Trappist Brothers. Timothy, David and Walter. The rest appeared to be travelers, and the grave-stones recorded their names and their point of origin. He started to read further.

A month later the task had completely absorbed him. He read and read. There were so many documents, letters, receipts and bills to classify. Nearly two hundred years of paperwork. He learned that the Monastery had been built by Spanish priests in the 1820's, and located at the highest point of the road trail. The nearest town to the east, Coloma, stood almost seven miles away.

As the gold rush started in the 1840's, many settlers stopped there to give thanks that their long journey was coming to an end. Coins and other valuables were given to the Monastery. These helped open an orphanage, administered by the Sisters of Charity, two miles along the road. During this period, as the settlers moved west, the Monastery gained a reputation as a refuge for tired travelers. The wagon park by its side still existed, but these days, instead of Conestoga wagons, it housed the stalls for the weekly sale of vegetables and fruits grown by the Brothers.

The visitors left a virtual history in the form of letters, documents and descriptions of their arduous trip. It was these that he found so interesting, and these that would eventually lead him on his pilgrimage.

Chapter 3 – *'Research.'*

Wolenstein. Solomon and Abraham Wolenstein and their wives, Rachel and Sarah. Four grave-stones with the word 'Wolenstein' stood in the plot and he had often tidied them when working. Now he saw the name written in documents left by other settlers passing through on the final leg of their journey west. This seemed unusual at the time.

He didn't know it, but the Wolenstein's came from Poland and landed in Philadelphia in 1820. They carried with them a considerable amount of jewelry and after selling this, set up as bankers. In 1825 after meeting with a jeweler, Mathias Baldwin they agreed to lend him money to start a locomotive works. This proved very successful for the Wolenstein's and Baldwin and both parties prospered. However, in late 1836 the knowledgeable brothers curtailed the line of credit they established for Baldwin and sure enough, the following year, a financial panic started.

In June 1837, for a reason known only to themselves, the Wolenstein's decided to travel the three thousand miles to California and open a Bank there. They converted their assets into gold and traveled in two Conestoga wagon's each pulled by four horses. Drivers were hired for the task and they set off west through Iowa, Nebraska, Wyoming, Utah and Nevada.

At Scottsbluff in Nebraska they joined a party of a dozen other wagons. This arrangement turned out to be unsatisfactory. The Wolenstein's traveled slowly. They left the wagon train and their drivers in Utah and continued their journey alone to Nevada. Some of the references regarding the Wolenstein's slow progress came from letters left in a chest of drawers and abandoned by a family upon arrival at the Monastery. He read all of these. The Wolenstein's were very unhurried travelers. They often joined with other wagons for a day but were so slow that in the end, settlers anxious to get west before winter, went ahead and left them. They spoke to some of these people about 'a trail to the south that would lead to Sacramento', but didn't said if they would try to find it. After he had seen three references to their difficulty in maintaining speed, he wondered why that could have been. He got his answer after two years of reading.

The Wolenstein's met up with and joined another group of settlers led by Ernest DeVille, a well-known guide, west of Humboldt Wells, about three hundred miles from the California border.

In a document dictated by a Wagon Master, Ernesto DeVille to the Father Abbot in late 1837, he stated that the Wolenstein's could not keep up with the normal pace of the columns they joined. No one had mentioned that the Wolenstein wagons were overloaded with goods or anything else. Why was this? He read on.

DeVille stated that after a day of traveling with the Wolenstein's they were already several miles behind the other wagons. He rode back to guide them in and it was then that he saw them changing a wheel that had cracked. There was a spare one, and they partially unloaded the wagon to enable the replacement to be made. They had almost finished and DeVille offered to help them reload.

It was then he that he discovered that the two 'small' chests he had helped lift were 'as if loaded with lead'. He said nothing to the Wolenstein's but his story recorded his amazement at the weight. When they fell behind again, twelve days west of Humboldt Wells, they told him they didn't want to put too much strain on the wagon wheels. DeVille thought the weight of the chests was the reason.

The Wolenstein's told DeVille that they needed to have their damaged wheel repaired and that he should continue on his journey and leave them behind. DeVille, worried about them but eager to move ahead, agreed. He finally recorded that twelve days after reaching the Monastery, a new group of travelers arrived and with them, the Wolenstein's. They seemed to have had no difficult to keeping pace with the new group but he noted there was now only a single wagon and one of the wives was sick. They quickly isolated the family. The Father Abbot thought they had cholera and the Monastery would help them. DeVille left for Sacramento two days later, by that time, three Trappist Brothers had also fallen sick.

His intuition told him to continue looking and so he did. In the Monastery accounts for December 1837, he found a document listing the sale of one horse to Jerome Buckley, Stonemason, in exchange for four headstones engraved with the name Wolenstein.

Two weeks later, immediately after first prayer, he found his next clue. A sealed envelope that had been placed in a bible. The envelope bore the name 'Wolenstein', nothing else.

He opened it carefully. It contained several sheets of paper. One recorded the last will and testament of Abraham and Solomon Wolenstein. It had been written by a Brother who recorded his own name as Walter. He explained he was writing to the dictation of Abraham Wolenstein.

Why had this envelope remained unopened for nearly one hundred and eighty years? That was the question he asked himself. The other pages seemed to be Abraham's notes. He read the first page and suddenly, things became clearer.

He learned that Brother Walter was isolated with the Wolenstein's. Rachel and Sarah had died two days earlier and Abraham felt that he and his brother would soon follow them. After he had finished reading he felt fairly sure as to what had happened.

Abraham dictated his will, not knowing if he would live or die. Solomon passed away the next day. Brother Walter, very sick, knew he would not recover. He comforted Abraham in his last moments. Abraham died that evening. Walter sealed the envelope and put it in his bible. He died the following day.

What happened next was conjecture but seemed very plausible. The Wolenstein's were buried, along with Walter.

Because of the fear of contamination, their belongings had to be burned and the wagon and horses sold. That would explain the headstones. A horse was exchanged for the stonemason's work. However to burn a bible was unthinkable, and it had been sent down to the vaults and there it remained until rediscovered.

He returned to the will, a simple document that bequeathed all the belongings of the Wolenstein's to the Monastery. On the separate pages of faded paper he found Abraham's handwritten notes.

'Three weeks west from Humboldt Wells. No travelers only DeVille party. Must repair broken wheel. Told DeVille go on ahead. Stopped made repairs. Two tall rocks hundred yards north of trail split by a stream. Pine forest half mile north-east. Small lake mile south. Ground flat. Turned south seeking alternate trail. Went west passed lake.' It continued.

'Followed trail for four hours. Not trail but river bed. Finished in a dry bowl below tall rocks. Turned west one hour. Break between flat black stone rocks. Turned south along gulley three hours. Trail getting steeper. Horses tired. Stopped one hour at small stream crossing trail. On far bank of stream pine forest started. West again to get past. Two hours west able turn south to rising rocks. Three hours then lost wheel of second wagon near pine woods close to deep stream. Purple bushes all along banks.' There was more.

'No replacement and unable to repair. Abandoned wagon. Stayed night. Grazing aplenty. Sarah sickly. Myself and Solomon unloaded chests. Walked along stream west unable climb steep banks. Found cave after one half mile. Well-hidden with purple bushes covering. No sign people. Four chests gold opened and carried one by one to cave. Wrapped canvas and buried under rocks to right of entrance. Took one wagon with eight horses back to trail. Able travel faster with less weight. Know where chests are. Can return later if God gives me life. Will dictate my will to Brother Walter this evening.'

He read the document again and again and memorized the contents. Then he removed it from the vaults and took it with him to his cell. Had the Wolenstein's been searching for 'a trail to the south that would lead to Sacramento' and not finding it, turned back? It was a possibility.

Chapter 4 – '*Out into the world.*'

He walked in silence. As a brother of the Order of Cistercians of the Strict Observance, the Trappist's he rarely spoke. They did not have a vow of silence but Trappist monks speak only when necessary, idle talk is strongly discouraged.

Morning Prayer was the first of the seven calls each day. When it finished, he would make his way to the vaults and commence his daily work. He had been with the Order for three years.

When the bell rang for the day's second call he left the vaults but did not go to the Chapel. Instead, he went to the Abbot's office and sat on the wooden bench. When noticed, he would be able to enter.

Finally, the Abbot himself emerged and waved him through. He asked him to sit and looked at him with raised eyebrows.

"Father Abbot. I wish to speak with your permission."

"Of course Brother. What troubles you?"

"Father, I wish to leave the Monastery."

The Abbot smiled at him and nodded his head. "I realized this day would come James. I see it is sooner rather than later. Do you wish to tell me why you wish to go?"

"Father, in your wisdom you knew I would leave here. May I ask how did you know?"

"For twenty years now I have been Abbot. One tends to develop a certain intuition regarding such events. You are restless, despite the peace of our sanctuary. Many might not see this but the Almighty in his wisdom has allowed me in this case to peer into your soul. Of course, I understand your request and am thankful that we were here when you needed to find God. When you arrived I thought of Psalm 18."

He quoted: 'The Lord became my protector. He brought me out to a place of freedom; he saved me because he delighted in me.' "This seems to have been written for you my son, do you agree?"

"Yes, Father Abbot. I found God. He allowed me to start again. Now there are tasks to complete before I am completely free."

"That is understood my son. You have my permission to leave and my blessing. Go in peace. The Administrator will be informed and when you return from the Chapel, all will be ready for your departure." He raised his hand and blessed the kneeling brother.

An hour later James collected the small bag containing the belongings he had brought with him. The lockers in the Administrator's office, held everyone's personal items. Finally he went to the courtyard. The gate opened, and he walked out into the world that he left behind three years earlier. There were no goodbyes.

The Administrator had provided him with clothes and some money. The spring day was warm, and he set off walking down the road, the new boots somewhat stiff but not uncomfortable. In his duffle he had his envelope, the toiletry bag, a folded jacket and a bible, a final gift from the Father Abbot.

Coloma, was almost seven miles away. The road sloped gradually downwards, making walking a pleasure. There was little traffic so early and only two farm trucks passed him as he strode along the highway. After two hours, he followed a slow turn to the left and low buildings could soon be seen in the distance.

It took him a further thirty minutes to reach the outskirts where he found a sidewalk. He felt for the money in his pocket, two twenties and a ten. This would suffice for the moment. The red and gold of a Woolworth's was just ahead and in front, a covered bus shelter with a bench. Resting there he looked about him. The main street had stores for a hundred yards and then houses could be seen. He had read Coloma was small and best known for its ghost town.

He sat for fifteen minutes, the store being closed at this hour. When he finally heard the doors opening he stood and walked in.

Ten minutes later he came out with his purchases. He found a small motel and paid in advance for a room for one night. The clerk told him that a Diner that served good, plain food existed just down the road. A used car lot at the end of the main street was open all day.

He took twenty minutes to remove three years of beard from his face using the scissors and then the razor and shaving cream he had purchased. A haircut would have to wait. The face that looked back at him from the mirror was thinner than he remembered and it seemed the worry lines had vanished. The green eyes much brighter now he lived such a simple life.

On the bed he opened the bag and took out the envelope. He had to guess what he would need so, he separated five thousand dollars into one pile and then three more piles of five hundred each. The bills were all $20's. From the depths of the bag he removed a small transparent pack of elastic bands and used them to hold the bills together. There remained almost sixteen thousand dollars between the piles and the money in his wallet. The large wad of money he returned to the bag. The Wolenstein document he sealed in an envelope. Taking out his wallet he checked his driving license. Good for a year. The bag he left on a chair by the bed. At the Monastery he had become very trusting.

Turning down the main drag he walked until the used car lot appeared. There were mostly pickup trucks and jeeps on display. A man came out from a small cinder block building.

"Hi there stranger. Interested in something here today?"

"Might be. Let me look around and I'll let you know."

"Take all the time you want. We got plenty of that here."

He laughed at his own joke and walked back to the office.

It was obvious that these were older vehicles and had seen their best days. He finally stopped at a Ford pickup. A

1999 model. The faded red color panels sported dings and dents and one fender, obviously a replacement, was black. He looked at the interior. It wasn't much better. The upholstery was cracked and in places the foam was pushing through. Raising his eyes towards the office he raised his hand. Right away the man came walking out.

"Ah! You found her eh? Wonder how you knew? Donny Donaldson owned this here vehicle. I recall the day he drove it back from Sacramento! Shining new this Ford. Donny drives up to the Diner and parks it. Such a hurry to tell everyone about it, he forgets to put the parking brake on! Walks through the door of the Diner and the truck runs backwards into Salty Haw's Dodge! Should have seen it! Took Donny a month to live that down! Some people still remember it! I'll tell you one thing. She looks beat up, but that Donny he's a great mechanic. Does all his own repairs. This one lasted him fifteen years with no trouble. He bought it in last week. Bought a new one in Sacramento. Used the parking brake this time though!" He slapped his knee and bent over laughing. "Here's the key. Take her around the block."

He handed James a key handing from a yellow plastic letter 'R'.

"That's me, Robert. Robert's Motors."

James stepped into the cab and started the vehicle. He was surprised, she ran very smoothly. Moving the stick he drove slowly out of the lot. The gears changed easily, and the brakes were high and didn't need pumping. Around the block he went and came back to the lot. Robert was waiting. "Told you so! Told you so! 'aint she a beauty?"

"Looks ok as far as I can make out. What's the price?"

"Tell you what, Donny want's six, but I told him with that bodywork the high school kids 'aint interested. They want something that looks good and this old bucket's a long ways from that. What say five and a half and we call it a deal?"

"I'll do five two fifty and you throw in the plate and registration. How's that sound?"

"Deal my boy. Deal! Let's go to the office and sort things out."

Half an hour later he paid for the truck and agreed to pick up the registration in a few days upon his return. He received a provisional plate and the temporary paperwork. Robert arranged for insurance, but he had to pay extra for that, in advance.

Driving back towards the Hotel he stopped at the Diner. Three o'clock. The menu said that today's special was 'Baked Ham Sandwich on rye.' It turned out to be surprisingly good with the orange juice he ordered. He sat at a table near the window and thought about what he had to do next.

He had to find a General Store. Everything he wanted would be there. The waitress told him there was one two blocks down towards the Hotel. Finishing his food he left the Diner.

The General Store was quiet. There was no air conditioning and dust particles, stirred up by the ceiling fans, swirled in the warm air. It had all of his needs.

A sleeping bag came first. He decided not to get a tent, this time of year, although cold at night, the weather was clear. The clerk seemed happy to help him as he chose his purchases and stacked them on the long wooden counter.

The boots he had been given fitted well as did the jacket but he wanted some jeans and a heavier shirt. Also, a pair of work gloves and a neckerchief that would help to keep out dust. A nylon money belt caught his eye, and he decided to take it with him. A shovel, and a machete were added. He thought for a moment and picked out a hacksaw, two spare blades, a flashlight and a ball of twine. Still searching he found a couple of small canvas shopping bags and two larger ones. A thick leather belt and some matches and that took care of most of his wants.

He needed food, so he crossed to the grocery section and bought three cans of Spam, baked beans and two large bottles of water. A bag of hard rolls and small frying pan completed his purchases. The bill came to a hundred and forty-eight dollars. He paid in cash. Before leaving he asked if there was a Public Library in the town and was given the address. Loading everything into the cab of the truck he drove to the small Library building on a nearby side street. An uninterested teenager manned the desk, and he paid $5 for two hours access to the Internet on a Library computer. Sitting at the screen, he started his task.

How much gold did the Wolenstein's have with them? DeVille had said that the chests were 'small'. That meant eighteen inches long by twelve inches high. What could fit inside those chests? He researched the size of gold bars and found the average weighed about 400 ounces and measured 7x3 inches. They fitted four into each chest. That meant a hundred pounds, the maximum weight a small chest could hold. He understood now why Ernesto DeVille had commented on their weight saying 'as if loaded with lead'. Two chests on each wagon made it sixteen bars with a total weight of six thousand four hundred ounces. The price of gold in 1840, being close to $20 an ounce, the Wolenstein's fortune was around $128 thousand dollars. A considerable sum back then but at today's prices for gold, a fortune of about seven million dollars!

Now to find out where they went after leaving the trail. Deville had said he left them three weeks west from Humboldt Wells and Abraham had confirmed this. How fast did a wagon travel back then? The average day might see travel up to thirty miles if the trail was good, fifteen if rough. From the letters he had read the trail west from Wells was average. So twelve days travel could have taken travelers over two hundred miles. It would be his task to find 'Two tall rocks hundred yards north of trail split by a stream. Pine forest half mile north-east. Small lake to mile south. Ground flat.' Looking at an on-line map he noted that Winnemuca, two hundred fifty miles from Coloma, would be a good place to start his search.

Returning to the Hotel at six o'clock, he watched the television for a while, put his money into the belt he had purchased and then slept.

As usual, he awoke shortly after four. He repacked his small bag, and as he left the room, raised a hand to the Desk Clerk as he walked out to the truck. It was still dark as he headed north along 49 to reach Interstate 80 and turned east towards Wells. This would have been more or less the trail that they had taken back in the 1830's

He checked the odometer as he pulled out of the parking lot. He figured he would have to get to Winnemuca before turning back west to look for the landmarks Abraham had mentioned. In Reno ninety minutes later he stopped and purchased coffee and a Danish at a quick-stop. He ate in the truck and kept driving.

Two and a half hours later, Winnemuca appeared ahead. In the Library he had read that Butch Cassidy robbed the First National Bank there back in 1900. It didn't seem much else had happened since. He went into a McDonald's and ordered a hamburger and a soda. Not wanting to delay he returned to the truck and returned west, guessing that Interstate 80 pretty much followed the original trail. He hoped he was right.

There wasn't a lot of traffic. It was possible to drive in the nearside lane and check for the landmarks with no hurry. After thirty miles two large rocks loomed up from a small range ahead to the north. He checked his rear mirror. He noticed no traffic behind him. Slowing as he approached he saw a pine forest to the north-east and a lake to the south on the other side of the road. Coming closer to the range he saw the stream that split the two tall rocks. Opposite this the Wolenstein's had left the road.

Pulling off onto the shoulder he drove across the road and exited south over the flat ground. No tracks of any kind could be seen. Passing the lake he noticed what looked like a trail west. It seemed time to put the truck into four- wheel drive. It was uneven, and he drove slowly. The Wolenstein's said this wasn't a trail but a river bed. It was easy to see how they had been deceived. Not all of it was bad but parts were strewn with boulders and he realized this certainly was a river during the wet months of January through March. In the distance loomed foothills and beyond, peaks. Ten miles further on, he was into the low bluffs. There was one large depression blocking the river bed in front of some tall rocks. He surmised that this had been formed by a waterfall. When it rained heavily it would flow over the large boulders, form the pool, and rush north through the channel he had just driven along.

He turned west along the edge of the foothills and about five miles on, noticed the black rocks referred to by Abraham. Here he stopped and got down from the truck. It was very quiet with only the sound of insects to be heard. Nothing seemed to move and he could see no trace of anyone having been there. The gulley ran south between the two rocks. Mounting up, he drove ahead.

After a mile the trail rose slightly. It flattened out eventually and there in front of him flowed a creek. About three feet across, it ran slowly to the north. The bank's sloped gently down to the crystal clear water. On the far side the pine forest started. He drove carefully across and turned west along its edge. After another mile he turned south when the forest thinned. There was no trail, and he drove over and around all sizes of boulders. Then came a stream. This one was much wider than the previous creek. The far bank was covered in purple sage. Behind that half a mile of grass meadow showed before foothills started again. He descended from the truck and stretched his arms and legs. It was beautiful here. The stream seemed to sing as it ran over the different size rocks and looking closely he could see small trout resting in the pools formed by the twisting bank. Overhead an eagle soared, seeking as always, an unaware jack-rabbit or similar pray.

To his left stood a small forest of pines and when he walked beneath the trees he noticed staves of wood spread around. This had to be the Wolenstein's wagon. Just a pile of bleached boards and a collection of rusted iron bands. He kicked the pile, and the wood disintegrated and threw up dust. Walking away, he returned to the sunlight, pulling the neckerchief from a pocket and knotting around his neck.

Thinking of the eagle he realized he was hungry. Time to eat. Two Spam filled rolls gave him the energy to start exploring west. He took the machete and the flashlight and staying close to the stream started walking. The banks became higher and higher and trees growing at their tops interwove their leaves and branches in places, cutting out the bright sun.

Half a mile further on, he began closely examining the banks. Seeing an especially thick growth of purple sage he felt sure the cave was close. He was right. It was as Abraham had described. Climbing along a narrow depression that lead upwards he saw an entrance about five feet high with sage bushes softening its edges. He entered the cave. It was cool and dark but the flashlight, once he switched it on, allowed him to see the rock pile to the right. Moving a few stones, he touched canvas beneath them. It had worn well. Using the machete to make a slit he looked beneath the material and saw the gleam that could only be gold. This was the Wolenstein's treasure.

Standing back he pointed the flashlight around the cave. It was not big, perhaps ten feet deep. On the floor he saw animal droppings and realized this could mean mountain lions. He would have to take care.

Walking back took him twenty minutes. The clock in the truck registered one o'clock. Starting his task he took two small shopping bags and the thick belt and made panniers which he slung round his neck. He felt fairly sure he wouldn't need a shovel but if he did, he could carry it on the next trip to the cave. Then he set off down the stream bank.

It took four trips to carry the sixteen bars back to the truck. They were heavy, and the work wasn't finished until five. By that time he could see the sun going down, and he estimated there was an hour before darkness. He would pass the night in the sleeping bag on the bed of the truck and leave at first light after loading the gold.

The fire blazed up when he lit the sage branches, warming the cool night air. He scraped the extra fat from two cans of Spam into the bottom of the frying pan on the fire and as it spluttered, sliced the Spam with the machete and put it into the pan to heat. Two small cans of beans followed and in five minutes he had a meal, not pretty but something to fill him up. Three rolls and half a bottle of water later he finished with his repast. Working with the hacksaw for an hour and breaking two blades, he finished the other task he wanted to accomplish.

By eight o'clock stars in the night sky twinkled everywhere. A half-moon allowed him to see around his camp site. He built up the fire with some thick pine branches and confident that this would keep any predators away, lay down in the sleeping bag in the bed of the truck. Sleep came as he lay listening to the stream sing its soothing song.

At five he awoke. The gold, once he got it in the truck bed, was manhandled into the two large canvas shopping bags and he used the twine to secure the handles. He rested, ate the last of the rolls and drank some water before leaving at seven.

With nearly six hundred pounds of gold in the truck bed, he drove slowly and carefully back to Interstate 80 and then headed west. The ride to the Monastery took seven hours.

He arrived at the gates at three o'clock. The Brothers would be in the Chapel until three thirty so he had a little time to spare. The main gate was not closed, and he could drive the truck inside, turning into the small courtyard in front of the large double doors. These were shut as always during prayer. When prayer finished, the Administrator would open them again in welcome. Exiting the cab, he unloaded the canvas bags containing twenty-three bars of gold and placed them at the top of the steps. From his own bag he removed the envelope with the Wolenstein document in it. It was already sealed and addressed to, 'The Father Abbot'. He signed his name in the bottom right-hand corner. They would know who had left the bags and the Wolenstein papers would explain why.

Nothing stirred. After a final look round, he entered the truck and drove away. The bags would be safe until prayers finished, and the Administrator opened the doors in a few more minutes.

Turning west he started his long trip to San Diego. The six hundred mile trip took him eleven hours, and he arrived at three the next morning. Finding a small chain hotel on La Joya Village Drive he booked in, payed a cash deposit for two days and went straight to sleep. He felt very tired.

Chapter 5 – 'Redemption.'

Next morning he didn't wake until ten o'clock. It had been a long drive the previous day, and he needed fifteen minutes in alternating hot and cold water showers before he felt fully revived. He called room service for breakfast and shaved while he waited. Eating his ham, eggs and toast and drinking his coffee, he looked through the Yellow Pages and made notes. Dressing, and then fastening the heavy money belt round his waist under his loose shirt, he went outside and drove to the first address on his list.

The jewelers shop was on the Drive. It had a small parking lot in front. He left the truck there in full view. There was a door bell to press for entry and at the buzz he pushed and went in. Walking across the empty floor he stood in front of woman straightening watches in a display case.

"Good morning. I have gold to sell. Would you be interested?"

The woman looked up at him. "You mind waiting? I'll get Mr. Simmons the owner, for this."

He nodded and stood back. A minutes later a man came towards him.

"Hi there! I'm Fred Simmons. I own the store. Jeannie here said you have gold to sell?" A gray-haired man in his seventies, stood in front of him.

"Yes sir, I do."

"Fine. Let's go into my office over here, we'll take a look."

The office was a glass-fronted box at the rear or the store. They went in and Simmons closed the door. "Well sir, what do you have? Coins, jewelry or something?"

"No sir, I've got this." He rummaged under his shirt and removed one of the eight squares of gold he had cut, and put it on the counter. Simmons looked at him in surprise. "Wow! That looks like twenty-four carats." He picked it up and weighed it in his hand. "I'd say about three pounds

Avoirdupois. That would be almost fifty thousand dollars! Let me put it on the scale. We'll stick to layman's weight rather than Troy if that's fine with you?"

"That's good with me."

"Let me run a quick touchstone test first." Mr. Simmons took out an acid kit and did the test.

"Just what I thought. It is 24 Carat."

He put the metal on the scale. It registered 3.1217 Avoirdupois. He consulted his laptop.

"Well Sir, you have a value of $50,408.56 at today's gold price. If you want to sell it I can offer you a flat forty-eight thousand if you wish? I would have to send for the money, we don't have cash like that hanging around in the store!"

"That's Ok with me. Forty-eight thousand cash. Do I wait here or come back later?"

"Let's get the formalities done. I'll give you this form and you fill it out. We can make a copy and it will be your receipt. The time's eleven ten now. I can have the money here by noon. You can wait or come back. Up to you?"

"I'll come back this afternoon if that's no problem?"

"No sir, no problem. May I ask you a personal question?"

"Shoot."

"Do you have any more like that? I'd be interested in buying if you did."

"Matter of fact I do. Another twenty-two pounds."

"Twenty-two pounds? Wow. That's a lot of gold. Probably worth three hundred fifty thousand or so. You have that with you?"

"Yes, I've got it right here." He tapped his waist where the belt rested. Simmons looked at him for a moment and then seemed to make a decision.

"I think we had better close the blinds here." He stood and adjusted the blinds so the view out to the store was obscured.

James took the gold from the belt and put it on the desk. "May I?" asked Simmons, and James nodded. The other seven slabs were laid out and Simmons inspected each piece.

"Just like you said. There's about twenty-five pounds here. Now, I haven't heard that Fort Knox has been robbed or anything like that so I guess that these pieces were once a 400 ounce bar. Looking at the cuts I would say a hacksaw did the work. Indulge an old man if you would. Let me tell you a little story and you tell me how close I am, ok?"

"Go ahead."

"Well. Back in the 1830's and 40's, settlers from the east came to California. Not all of them went to mine for gold. Many were merchants looking to set up businesses to sell to the prospectors and miners. A much safer way to make money! Instead of digging they stood behind a counter and shortchanged the diggers when they bought in their dust and nuggets!" He smiled.

"This bar here isn't California gold. On two slices you can see part of an assay mark. I can tell you that the mark is from the Philadelphia mint. So Sir, I believe this bar came from Philadelphia to California. Somewhere along the way it went astray. Who knows how? Might have been a robbery, a flood or any sort of disaster that parted it from the owners. A long time afterwards someone found it and cut it up. They wanted to sell it so they thought it would be easier to get rid of in small pieces. Good thinking for a layman! So here you are."

He looked at James and nodded. "I won't ask how accurate that story is but I can tell it's not far off the truth. If you go along the Drive here in La Joya you'll find twenty jewelry shops this end and as many pawn shops at the other. Sell a few of these three pound hunks today and by tomorrow, every jeweler within five miles will know about it. Pretty sure the cop's will be interested as well! I don't think you want that to happen because for your own reasons you are taking steps to keep this quiet as possible, hence the small pieces. So what can we do?"

"You tell me." said James.

"Here's an offer. Take it or leave it. I'll buy everything. We can weigh it and you'll get a good price. You don't want it all in cash. It will limit what you can do and where you can go. I'll give you diamonds guaranteed to sell for at least $300 thousand. I have them here and they come with a certified gemologist receipt. The rest in cash, depending on the weight we calculate. No questions. No forms. I don't want to know who you are or where you're from. We do the deal and you walk out in an hour with what I promised. The deal stays here and nobody else knows a thing. I'm happy and you're happy. What say?"

An hour and a half later James put 100 thousand dollars into one of the canvas bags he fetched from the truck. The six diamonds, with the gemologist certificates, valued at a minimum of another 300 thousand, were wrapped in tissue paper, and put in a glassine envelope which went into his pocket. He shook hands with Mr. Simmons and walked out of the jewelry store. He never saw him again.

At a Bank on La Joya Village Drive they welcomed the new customer.

"A checking account deposit of five thousand dollars and a saving account with another thousand. No problem. A Bank debit card? Certainly! Just fill in the forms please. A safe deposit box? Yes Sir, follow our Deposit Box Manager downstairs and she will take care of everything for you. Have a good day!"

Into the box went most of the cash and the diamonds. He kept ten thousand back and in the quiet of the Bank vault, added that to fifteen thousand of the cash he had kept in the money belt. The Deposit Box Manager was happy to provide him with a heavy duty envelope. This he addressed to the Bank Manager at the institution he had robbed all those years ago. The address he had found that day in the Public Library. In a note he explained briefly what it was for. Naturally, he didn't sign it!

MICHAEL J. MERRY

When he finished he took his neckerchief and wiped everything he had touched, clean before carefully dropping it into the envelope which then went into his bag. The Manager offered to put the envelope in the Bank's outgoing mail but he refused. She did however, give him a dozen stamps from her desk drawer. He would mail the envelope along I-80 on the way to Coloma to pick up his car title in a day or so.

So now it was done. He drove back to the Hotel and took a swim in the pool. The Wolenstein's will had been executed, and he had soothed his own conscience. What he had kept, he reasoned, was not excessive when compared to what he had left at the Monastery. As for the Bank, he hadn't bought forgiveness, but he had paid back a debt, with interest. Now, all he had to was to make the most of his second chance.

'THE LADY.'

Chapter 1 – *'Falling in love.'*

I fell in love the first time I set eyes upon her. It was ten in the morning, December 21st, 1990. Of course, she was much older than me. She had just turned forty-six. Someone once said that between forty-one and fifty, a woman is like Great Britain, fading these days but with a glorious and all conquering past. That that made no difference to me! She was everything I had ever sought. Right down to the beautiful upturned nose. I've always been a sucker for upturned noses! For someone who had been around since 1944, she appeared to be in great shape. Naturally, like all attractive ladies, professionals had worked on her appearance. They had done a wonderful job.

She just sat there as I approached, moving slightly side to side as I came forward to pay homage. Her skin glowed as white as snow, not a wrinkle anywhere. She looked, if anything, mysterious.

I'd heard stories about her naturally enough. Stories from men who loved her passionately and from others who merely knew who she was. Their joint assessments all drew the same conclusion. This 'Lady' was the 'real' thing.

Up close you couldn't properly appreciate her. You had to stand back and with one scan of the eyes, absorb her completely. It was only then that her splendor could be fully realized, and at that moment you knew why Menelaus had launched 'a thousand ships' to release Helen from the grasp of Paris.

I'd searched before of course. For the past two years I'd traveled over a hundred thousand miles tracking down leads that took me to out of the way places, only to find that the lady I had come to see didn't fit the bill. Now, I had finally found my true love. How happy I was, very, very happy, and I knew that my journeys had not been wasted. With my camera I took a couple of pictures of her as she sat quietly waiting for her next lover to pamper and cosset her, and to spend ridiculous amounts of money to keep her beautiful. Then I hastened back to the small boatyard office to enquire how much the owner wanted for this incredible female, this magnificent Seaford S45, Flying Boat who I christened 'The Lady'.

Chapter 2 – *The 'Seaford.'*

The 'Seaford' Flying Boat was a development of Short Brothers. She was perhaps better known as the Short 'Sunderland'. Only eight were built. The RAF carried out military trials of these aircraft in April and May 1946, but decided not to adopt it. Seven of the eight were sent away to be converted to Solent Mk III's. The final one went to BOAC. It was her that I stood admiring in a small boatyard at Watson's Bay at the southern head of Sydney Harbor on that Friday in December. I had found out a great deal about her. For six months I'd been searching. There had been leads in South Africa, India, Brunei and Indonesia and I finally found her here in Australia.

A small Marina owner was now her proprietor. Four months before he had picked her up for five thousand dollars on a whim after a tip from a contact he had in Jakarta. He had her flown in. She was still airworthy. The four-man crew cost him four thousand US dollars and the almost four thousand mile trip used a lot of gas. There had been no offers on her when I contacted him Thursday. I flew down from Brisbane that afternoon and bright and early Friday morning, here I stood.

I had studied her history. BOAC, wanted to use her on a long distance route across the Pacific. They had her converted at the Short Brothers facility at Rochester in Kent and a great job they did on her.

She could carry 24 passengers and a crew of nine. Two pilots, a navigator, engineer, radio operator, a Chef and three attendants for the first-class only accommodations. There were three decks. The top deck included the cockpit, radio room and crew quarters and further back, the galley. Below, a second deck contained a passenger lounge and bar. Then came two bathrooms, both fitted with a shower, and at the rear, the sleeping berths. On the lower deck the war-time bomb bays had been removed and now held the main passenger cabin forward. Aft, were more fuel tanks, giving the aircraft a range of well over five thousand miles and plenty of room for water and storage. She was air-conditioned throughout.

'The Lady' had been operated by BOAC until 1954 and was then sold to the Sultan of Brunei who enjoyed traveling around his domains in great luxury. He could well afford to do so. Unfortunately the Sultan lost interest in her in the 1960's and for the next twenty-five years she was moored at Muara. The Navy took good care of her there. They kept her hull clean and maintained the engines. Once monthly she would be powered up and given a run around the bay. This event was always well attended by the locals. In 1985 she was finally sold to an entrepreneur in Jakarta who had visions of using her as a tourist attraction, flying around the islands and spending nights in various exotic ports.

He had the interior refurbished and modern plumbing installed. The mahogany paneling was bought back to its original polished state. A new galley went in with a microwave, stove, oven and refrigerator. In the cockpit, modernized and updated electronics were installed for navigation and communications, including a radio telephone. The big power-plant of four Bristol Hercules radial engines had been well maintained in Brunei. Still, our entrepreneur had them pulled apart and completely rebuilt using specially manufactured parts to replace any deemed worn or damaged. Overall, the upgrade gave the aircraft a cruising speed of two hundred and fifty miles per hour. Refurbishing took two years and half a million dollars and upon completion the owner decided to take his mistress for a short vacation aboard her.

His illicit honeymoon was all he had hoped for, and he arrived back three days later. After sending his mistress to her apartment in a taxi, he was driven home in his Rolls Royce.

Unfortunately for him his wife had him arrested as he entered the house. As a daughter of the wife of the Chief

Justice, she wielded a great deal of influence and was a rich woman in her own right. She was upset she had not been the second passenger on the trip and intended to make her husband very much aware of her displeasure. Indonesian law stipulates that adultery is to be punished with death by stoning, given there's enough evidence pointing to the action (i.e. with 4 trusted, impartial, and truthful witnesses in attendance). The crew of the 'Seaford', each whom had received a cash payment of five thousand U.S. dollars, were the witnesses.

After a week of letting him suffer she boarded her yacht and visited him at the prison island of Nusakambangan. After berating him for his unfaithfulness and promising to let the stoning death sentence be carried out, she finally let him off the hook. Calling in her attorney, who accompanied her on her trip, she had him present a document which essentially emasculated the husband. She became owner of his bank accounts, their house and his business. He, in effect, became her employee. He was also obliged to swear an Islamic oath that he would never cheat again.

Her last act was to have him sign a special authorization that would make her the person authorized to sell the Seaford. He docilely walked out of the prison with a dog lead around his neck, laughed at by the many fishermen who stood around near the pier where they embarked on her yacht.

The attorney sold the Seaford complete with crates of spares and tools, to a broker the next day and reported to the wife he had obtained ten thousand dollars for it. Happy it was gone and caring nothing for the sale price she readily agreed. The lawyer pocketed a twenty percent commission but didn't say anything about this windfall.

The 'Seaford' sat at the brokers until September 20th 1990 when the Marina at Watson's Bay in Australia purchased her for five thousand dollars. Two weeks later she arrived in Sydney.

The new owner just wanted to get rid of her for a fast profit. He didn't know me from Adam and at first told me he would 'sacrifice her for fifty-thousand'. When I told him who I worked for he asked me to wait a few minutes in his secretary's office. I heard him pick up the telephone and dial as I walked out. Ten minutes later he opened the door and invited me back in. His tone this time had changed.

"Mr. Bailey. You should have said who you were with when you gave me your name. International Productions! That would have saved me the cost of a long distance call! Never mind. That's water under the bridge. My names O'Connor. I own things here. Now, what about twenty?" He looked at me hopefully.

"Mr. O'Connor, I'll give you fourteen. That will include her staying docked here until I get a crew, fuel and having the authorities clear her for flight. Should take more than forty-eight hours. Deal?" He didn't really like it but put on a watery smile and we shook hands. To his surprise I paid him right away in U.S. dollars.

"A few other things Mr. O'Connor. She must be topped up with fuel early in the morning and I'll want the paperwork ready tomorrow at nine. I hope to be here then with a crew. The log books I'll take with me now please. As for crew I will need two multi-engine qualified pilots, a navigator plus an engineer. Who do I call?"

He wrote a number on the back of a card and told me that the company would probably find someone for me quickly. Thanking him, I pocketed a key which would allow me entry to the yard at any time, along with the aircraft keys and log books in a small duffle bag. Then I turned and left. My hotel wasn't far from the Marina so I took my time and walked the half mile. The sun was shining making it a warm day. It must have been almost eighty degrees.

Before going to my room I stopped by the restaurant. My stomach was growling. I hadn't eaten since early morning and felt quite hungry, plus the walk had left me with a dry mouth.

No one was visible but as I sat down, a white uniformed Chef complete with a toque perched absolutely straight on his head with no 'lean' either way, approached. He looked typically French, including the thin lips they always seem to have.

"Hello Guv! What can I do you for?" A cockney accent severely dented my ability to type by appearance.

"Good morning Chef. That sounds remarkably like an east end accent?" He laughed.

"You've got it mate! Poplar born and bred. Came out here after finishing school at Bloomsbury Square, you know, Le Cordon Bleu. Didn't want to stay in UK so I applied when I saw an announcement and I said to myself 'Willie, here's your chance!' and here I am! What about yerself?"

"My name's Jason Bailey. I'm work for a film business in the U.S. They have requirements for certain items needed for an upcoming production and that's what I've been looking for here at Watson's Bay. What I want is something special in the way of food. I've not had a really good meal in a week! What can you do for me?"

"I got some John Dory in this morning, fresh. Right out of the Harbor here from a local bloke. Fish and chips! Can't beat it! How about a nice cold Fosters while I get that going?"

"That'll be fine. Thanks."

The Chef walked back to the kitchen, and I sat back and enjoyed the view across the Harbor. An iced beer came, cold and refreshing. Then the fish and chips arrived and quickly vanished. I felt like having a nap but business was business and my boss, bless her heart, wanted results. Tired, I went up to my room and picked up the telephone.

The card had a local number on it. It took a few moments to convince the man I wasn't fooling around, but he said providing he was able to come up with crew he'd take them up to Watson's at nine in the morning. He would call me to confirm everything later.

Sitting down, I made a few calculations that the navigator would need. We would fly from Sydney to Majuro in the

Marshall Islands. It was a journey of about four thousand miles. Refuel and travel the twenty-five hundred miles to Hawaii. Refuel again and go to San Diego, California for delivery of the aircraft. I figured it would take us about four days with the overnight fueling stops.

We needed fuel, plus food and water onboard for the crew and myself as well as paper plates and plastic utensils. Five sleeping bags for the crew because the aircraft would be flying for extended periods of time and they had to rest.

By five o'clock I was certain that I had everything covered. I felt tired. Two weeks of following leads that had had me traveling half way around the world took its toll. I turned up the air conditioning and closed the blinds tightly. I called my office and dictated a note for my boss updating her on where we were with the mission. Finally I told reception I wanted to send a fax message. I went downstairs and the Desk Clerk helped me send three pictures of 'The Lady'. After telling him I wanted no further calls, I went to my room, undressed and got under the covers. In a few minutes I dropped off.

Chapter 3 – *'The journey.'*

I awoke at five in the morning and called reception. There were two messages. One came from the crew agency telling me he had what I wanted and would meet me at the Marina at nine. The second was from my boss acknowledging my call and the pictures and asking me to stay in touch. Nothing new.

I showered and dressed and went downstairs. The restaurant was open for breakfast at six o'clock. I saw no one around apart from the Desk Clerk so I walked in and over to the terrace. Willie came bustling out as he heard my footsteps on the wooden deck.

"'allo there! Up early eh? Ready for a nice Aussie breakfast?"

I was hungry I told him. He suggested 'the works'. The works came and I was amazed at the quantity of food. There were two fried eggs, a small Australian meat pie, and two rashers of bacon, two sausages, a fried tomato, baked beans and hot toast with butter. A mug of tea was set down by the side of the plate. I sat on the terrace and watched the sun, now well on its way up over the Harbor. There was light chop on the water and the early sunbeams hit the waves and the reflections blurred the view across to the National Park. I enjoyed the food and managed to eat most of it.

Back upstairs I got everything ready for my departure. Then I checked out and carrying the duffle, I walked down the road to the Marina. It was not yet eight, and no one seemed to be there. I opened the gate to the yard and left it ajar so that the agent and crew might enter later.

The 'Lady' was in the same position as I had left her the previous day. Her port wing overlapped the wharf by about twenty feet and the port float was almost touching the dock. I walked to the dock edge and out along the gangplank that led to a docking raft. The fuselage door was forward of two huge port side engines. Looking up, there were the cockpit windows and in front, that wonderful nose! At eye level with the door stretching along her side were six portholes

The fuselage entry port key was tagged, so I opened it and stepped through into a small foyer. On the left was the main cabin. Without the electric plant running it was quite dim, but enough light came through the portholes to see the seating. Luxurious arm-chairs were arranged in six rows of two, on each side of the aircraft. They had plenty of space between them. Lighting fixtures were over every seat. There was ample room to relax. The interior was polished mahogany and the carpet, red. The aisle separating the two rows was comfortably wide. On the right of the foyer a staircase led to the middle deck and beneath the staircase, a door which I was sure went to a fuel storage area. I climbed the stairs.

Emerging above the main passenger cabin I entered the lounge and bar. A dozen easy chairs, strategically placed throughout the long cabin looked very inviting. The bar and all the fixtures were mahogany and the glass shelves, devoid of any bottles or glasses, showed a little dust. I walked towards the rear and passed a staircase leading upwards. Then there were two bathrooms and after that came the sleeping berths. One up and one down in six rows of two. The bunks were made up but I could see built-in drawers beneath the lower bunks. I pulled one out and saw it contained bed clothes and pillows. Walking back to the staircase I went up to the flight deck. Everything looked new, the pilot chairs were shiny leather and the radio shack displayed several modern looking sets. Next came a small crew quarters with two bunks in it and to the rear, a modern looking galley with a refrigerator, microwave and electric stove and oven combination. She was magnificent!

Returning to the entrance door I went back to the dock to await the crew. They were not long in arriving. Shortly before nine I heard a vehicle drive into the parking area and a few moments later the door to the yard opened.

"Mr. Bailey? I'm Bill Evans. We spoke on the telephone. These gentlemen are Harry and Charlie Thompson, the pilots. Kevin O'Brian, radio operator and Vic Brown, the engineer. I've got their paperwork here." He indicated a briefcase held in his left hand.

I shook hands with each of them and suggested we go into the office and get started. As we were entering, a gas tanker arrived, and I showed the driver where the Seaford fuel tanks were located.

O'Connor let us use a small conference room, and we got going. The Thompsons came from New Zealand and had been around for years. Their logbooks showed that they were ferry pilots during WWII, flying Catalina amphibians over the Pacific so they were experienced with sea planes. They had last worked the month before with a DC3 charter company flying mining equipment to the interior of the country. I estimated they were in their late sixties. Kevin O'Brian, the radio operator/navigator was Australian and had been in the merchant marine on tankers and was in his thirties. His last job was with the Thompson's, operating the radio on the DC3 they flew. Vic Brown was English and a very experienced engineer who had started his career with Short in Rochester in the fifties. He was experienced with a variety of engines inside out and until recently, worked on contract with an airshow that toured the west coast of the country. An offer for a new tour with the show in New Zealand didn't appeal to him.

Within an hour we agreed on terms. Evans would drive them to their respective lodging and the men could pick up their belongings and catch a taxi back to the Marina. All the men had valid passports. Then I told them who I was and why we were taking The 'Lady' back to the states. They took it in their stride.

Vic Brown was given all logs and spares inventories carried aboard. He would check the engines over to make sure everything worked well. The Thompson's agreed they needed to go through the whole aircraft making sure nothing could come loose during the flight. Kevin O'Brian was tasked with powering up the radios and drawing us a course.

I would fax schedules to the Marshalls and Hawaii and get take-off permission from the Australian authorities. O'Connor agreed to have his secretary help with that. He also agreed to put me in touch with a small supermarket down the street and for the grocery delivery required.

At five o'clock that evening, after the food was on board and paid for, the Thompson's started the engines and a launch that O'Connor had called for, towed us out into the Harbor for take-off. Everything went smoothly, and I sat in the jump seat in the cockpit, watching Australian shoreline as it flashed by, and gradually receded as 'The Lady turned over Hunters Bay and headed north-east.

Once in the air I left the cockpit and made my way aft to the galley. I made a large pot of coffee and told the crew to help themselves. There were frozen meat pies to be heated in the microwave and I told everyone these would be ready about nine o'clock.

'The Lady' droned on course at fourteen thousand feet. The men ate their pies at nine and had more coffee. I stayed in the galley dozing on one of the sleeping bags we had purchased. O'Brian called me at nine thirty and we went together to the cockpit. The pilots sat in air-conditioned comfort, headphone covering their ears. The engine noise was loud up here. O'Brian pointed ahead.

"That's Noumea out there on the right. New Caledonia. Look further out and you can see that cloud build up against the moon. We have to turn slightly east now to avoid it. We had planned on the turn at about ten-thirty but we had better do it right away. Could be nothing but let's not take a chance. I've told Harry and Charlie about it and Vic says fuel isn't a problem. We'll be starting our turn in two minutes."

I went back to the galley. I felt the aircraft bank slightly as I laid the sleeping bag flat on the floor and tried to sleep.

O'Brian woke me an hour and a half later.

"Jason, there's a slight problem. We are north of Port Vila, that's Vanuatu. The two starboard engines are acting up. Let's go up to the cockpit and we can have a conference." We squeezed in, all five of us. The Thompsons took of their headsets.

O'Brian spoke. "I've told Jason what's going on with the starboards. I'll let Vic here tell you the options." At that moment there was a slight lurch to starboard and the note of the engines changed for perhaps five seconds, then returned to their calm roar.

"Well. There's the problem. You all felt that!" Said Vic Brown. "It's the oil pump for sure. If we lose oil pressure the engine can seize. The pump is dead-simple. It has two steel gears inside a close-tolerance aluminum housing and usually operates without problems. The housing can get scored if a chunk of metal passes through the pump even though the oil pickup tube has a suction screen to make sure that doesn't happen. If the pump housing is damaged, the pump normally has ample output to maintain adequate oil pressure in flight, and you won't know about any problems unless idling or taxiing. If there's a problem, the pump housing can be removed and replaced without tearing down the engine. One of our pumps is running at high temperature, the other not quite as high. I believe the high temp one has been damaged by metal slivers or something bigger."

"The second one may have shavings blocking the screen. The spares inventory I looked at said we had a spare pump. About half an hour ago I found it. We need to get back to Mele Bay near Port Vila on Vanuatu. It's an hour flight. Land there and I can change out the one pump and clean the other and have everything back together in two hours. Then off we go! From there its six hours flying time to the Marshalls." At that moment the engine note changed again, and the aircraft lurched starboard and gradually came back to normal.

"Harry's the Senior Pilot. So Harry, can we do it?" Vic looked questioningly at Harry. Harry nodded.

"Let's get on with it then." He started his turn eastward immediately. If all went well, in a few minutes they would be turning south and then west back towards Vanuatu. All didn't go well and as soon as Vic Brown got back to his cubicle he came out again and turned his thumbs down. "It's not going to be possible to get back to Mele Bay. We have to shut down the starboard outer at once." He nodded at Harry who selected the throttle and pulled it all way back. "Also, we need to cut down speed. The starboard inboard will overheat if we don't". Harry and Charlie throttled back on the other three engines and the noise lessened and their speed dropped.

"We must land in the next ten minutes. Kevin will have to pick a spot. Providing we can get down there will be no problem changing the pump. I've done it before and it's simple. We need an atoll and a smooth lagoon. There's plenty of them around here. We have to pick one and do a fly by to make sure it's OK."

Kevin had been listening from the radio room. He stuck his head out. "Tried the radio phone but nothing but static. Let me get up to the cockpit and see if we can find something suitable."

Two minutes later Kevin pointed out the small atoll they needed. It didn't appear on any maps but that wasn't unusual. There were so many of them in this area, nearly all uninhabited. Harry took 'The Lady' low. He leveled off at about two hundred feet and they flew around the small island. The moonlight showed it to be flat and surrounded by a reef. The inner lagoon looked calm.

"Can't do better than this. I'll take her in nice and slow. Looks smooth so should be OK" Harry lined up for the approach and they flew slowly down the lagoon before he put her down gently on the water. They ran two hundred yards and shutting off all but one engine, Harry bought them close to shore.

"I'll bring her to within about a hundred feet then someone has to get out and tie us up to one of those palm trees up on the beach." The trees were a mere fifty feet from the water. Kevin and Vick found a coil of rope and made one end fast to the float pylon. Then, Vick jumped into the shallow water and walked up the beach to the nearest tree and tied the rope to it. The two pilots and I went down to the open fuselage door. The early morning air felt warm and there was no breeze. Vic walked back to the aircraft.

"It's about four hours to sunrise. I can't start work until then. We need someone to sit here and watch the tide. Looks high now but as it goes out we need to slack off on the rope she stays in plenty of water. At six we can get something to eat and I'll start and have Kevin to help. Charlie and Harry can keep an eye on the tide. Jason, you not being an airman can cook if that's ok?" We all agreed, and leaving Jason to keep the first tide watch the others gathered up a sleeping bag each and stretched out on a bunk.

I let them sleep. At a quarter to six I had made coffee and fried up bacon to make sandwiches. By six fifteen sunshine was hitting the fuselage and Vic and Kevin were already up on top of the starboard outboard. As I wasn't tired, I told the Thompson's I felt like taking a walk. Everyone was wearing shorts for the heat and I took a baseball cap and sunglasses from my bag and found a machete in a sheath in the storage department. I grabbed a bottle of water from the refrigerator before leaving and wading to the beach, turned east and started walking.

It was hot. The plastic bottle of water had lost some of its coldness already. Looking back I could see that Vic had part of the outer engine cowling off. I hoped that his confidence in his abilities weren't over- optimistic.

The sand felt firm, and I made good progress down the beach. The palm trees waved in a single line about five feet apart all the way along. Inland I could see shrubs and bushes covering the many low rock formations. Something caught my eye. The symmetrical row of palms was suddenly broken up. For a space of perhaps a hundred feet, the tall palms became stumps. I walked closer. Something had sliced into the trees and I noticed the shrubs behind the break were lower than those either side where the trees grew tall. I walked into the gap.

To my left there was what appeared to be a large rock covered by vines and grass. It didn't seem quite right. The 'rock' had straight lines. Very unusual and hardly ever occurring naturally. Drawing close I stretched out to pull at the vines. They came away fairly easily and beneath I could see metal. Using the machete, I cut more and uncovered not a rock but what was definitely the front of a radial aircraft engine, the prop bent but still attached. It dawned on me that this could be a plane lost in the Pacific during WWII. Hundreds were shot down, crashed or simply vanished, never to be found. This was surely one of them.

The other side of the broken trees turned up another engine, rusted and bent. Walking inland along the line of shortened grass and shrubs I found the wingless fuselage of a plane overgrown with more grass and vines. Its undercarriage was gone, and it sat a few feet above the ground. The windscreen was starred and cracked and looking in I could make out two skeletons in the pilots seats.

That was enough. I took a few pictures and a close up of the faded number on the fuselage, NR16020. Then for some reason I stopped for moment and said a short prayer. This is where they had died and where they would stay forever.

It wasn't far back to 'The Lady'. Vic waved. "Nearly finished! It's what I thought, bits of metal screwed up the outer and the screen was blocked with shavings in the inner. Half an hour or less and we can get out of here." I called back my congratulations and immediately the Thompsons asked me to get the rope inboard and be ready for take-off.

After stowing the rope I went to the galley. There were some frozen pizzas in the refrigerator and I started these cooking in the microwave. It was too hot for coffee and a jug of iced lemonade seemed appropriate. Half an hour later we were on our way, everyone happy eating and sipping the cold lemonade. One thing I did do was have Harry write down the exact GPS coordinates of the atoll we had visited. He was happy to oblige.

When we were a couple of hours out from San Diego I used the radiophone and arranged the studio accounting people to meet us and have return tickets and wages ready for the crew. I asked them to include a bonus and told them about the repairs. They readily agreed, and we made the payoff dockside and said goodbye to each other.

Later I went to the studio to make my report and the props people took over 'The Lady'. The following year I sat enthralled as she dominated the screen in the studio's new production. They sold her after that for almost a million dollars to a company specializing in auctioning movie props. She was beautiful and famous. Many people would want her. That's the way it goes with women I guess, they look for what's best for them. But, even after all this time I can take comfort in the fact that for a few days, she belonged to me.

Before all that happened there was another event that eventually bought me lot of unwanted publicity. The day after I got back I wrote to the National Transportation Safety Board giving the details of my find including the GPS coordinates. I included a photographs of the remains and the faded number on the fuselage, NR 16020. I didn't hear anything for two months and then one day I received a call at the studio.

"Mr. Bailey?" the voice asked.

"That's me."

"Mr. Bailey. My name's Evers, Sydney Evers. I'm a senior investigator at the NTSB. A couple of months back we received a letter from you with some photographs and a GPS coordinate. We have only just got round to investigating the event you described. I apologize for the delay. You gave us the position of an atoll you visited on a flight back from Australia. I am correct?"

"You are correct."

"Mr. Bailey. In the letter you provided the aircraft identification number you found on the fuselage. You also sent a photograph of the number and said you saw two engines. Is that right?"

I wondered what this concerned, but I politely told him he was right.

"Mr. Bailey you are not connected to any aviation concern nor are you a pilot or crew correct?"

"Correct."

"I imagine that you are not an aviation buff either?"

"No. I'm not."

"Ah! Then that explains it. Anyone with aviation connections would have recognized that I.D. number. You see, Mr. Bailey, NR16020 was the aircraft identification number of Amelia Earhart and Fred Noonan's twin engine Electra. You have helped us solve a mystery that has baffled everyone for over fifty years. Mr. Bailey, Mr. Bailey? Are you there?"

'GHOSTBUSTERS.'

Chapter 1 – *'E.A.C.H.'*

I look for 'Ghosts'. No, not those things dressed in a long white sheets you see on Halloween. I mean 'Ghosts', you know, what people connected with the intelligence services call folks who work hard at being inconspicuous.

A person you walk by on the street and you hardly notice. The guy sitting next to you at a concert that sits and listens. Doesn't sing along or anything. At the bar in a crowded pub he moves to one side so you can order your drink. You wouldn't know them from Adam, but I would.

You see that's my job. Knowing. Being able to pick out a Ghost in a crowd. Looking for the person who does everything properly. Never jumps the queue. Put's the divider down after his groceries in the supermarket. Waits for the pedestrian light before crossing the street. Plus a thousand other things. These are the people that have to be observed carefully. Why you might ask? Well, they want to stay out of any kind of trouble. So they do everything right. That makes them different from most of us.

When I did my training they told me that about three percent of the population happened to be that careful. That means that three out of ten folks who behave that way, either have a reason for doing so or behave that way naturally. Believe me, for most of us it's not a natural trait. Everyone makes a wrong move occasionally. According to statistics that means every couple of hours. So, do you think that if you keep an eye on someone for two hours and they don't put a foot wrong then they have a reason of some sort? Not really. It's complicated you see.

I'm a 'Ghostbuster'. No, I don't have a vacuum cleaner device strapped on my back to suck up these wisps of trouble. My clothes are simple and I have a normal haircut. But I carry a 'plastic' firearm. Yes, a 'plastic' firearm.

Perhaps I should explain a little further. The 9/11/2001 incident gave the U.S. a kick in the pants and made us just a little more ruthless when dealing with our enemies. After all, they don't take us into consideration when performing their acts. Our intelligence agencies applauded the decision to become more proactive when dealing with terrorists. Perhaps at last the gloves might be removed?

Unfortunately, they remained on. While military administrators rushed to make sure Muslim menus were in place for the Guantanamo prisoners, Jihad John cut the heads of his captives. Something more drastic had to be done to fight back.

So, the Embedded Agent Control (Homeland), (EACH) was created. We work exclusively for the Director of National Intelligence, the DNI. It's a top secret organization and outside of the DNI, few know about us. Individual Agents are given extraordinary decision-making powers. There are sixty Agents. One for each State, Territory, Commonwealth and Protectorate. We can, under certain circumstances, act as Judge, Jury and executioner. That decision came from the President of the United States. It's not recorded anywhere in writing.

Agents are selected from every walk of life. It's not necessary to have attended a University or College or to have served in the armed forces. You don't have to have any other special attributes. You will not even be approached until you have been checked out through restricted intelligence channels. Age? Well you will be under thirty-five, that's the only prerequisite. What else do they look for? Even I can't tell you that. I don't know. The recruiting process is very subtle and you won't know it's taking place until they say they want you. Then, if you say 'yes' the process starts.

You are told how to ease out of your present lifestyle and vanish from the face of the earth. You are given a new name and background. My name these days is Tim Stacey. Then you are subjected to two years of initiation. Nine months of this will be spent with the Special Forces Training Unit. You will be provided with a temporary I.D. for the duration. After that comes visits to Latin America, Europe and Asia. A month in each location with a specialized trainer. Then it's back to the U.S. for the final year. Everything is explained to you, there are no secrets. If you survive those final twelve months then you will be activated and assigned a territory.

The Special Forces training isn't secret. Many people have undergone the 'Q Course'. You go to Ft. Mackall in North Carolina for the orientation course. That's a little over three weeks. Then it's on to Bragg for orientation for seven weeks. After that Phase II is given over to Language and Culture. Another six months. Long and hard but when you finish your confidence level is high and your second language has improved.

What is secret is the final year. All I can say is that you learn what makes people different. Patterns of behavior are recognized. What to do in certain circumstances although you always understand that the final decisions may well have to be taken by you. You will be provided with DNI identification. It will have an electronic chip embedded in it, that when scanned, along with a live fingerprint, proves your identity at once. Access to air and sea port secure areas and military establishments will be instantly approved. Every security organization will be advised to provide cooperation.

You will go on a two-week weapons course with your 'plastic' firearm, the one mentioned earlier. These really are top secret. In an emergency they can be carried through TAS checkpoints and will not set off an alarm. Made entirely of fiberglass by Bates Industries of Houston, Texas, they were developed in 2011 at the request of the DNI. There are less than two hundred in circulation. The ammunition is classified. If you call Bates and ask about the weapon, they will deny any knowledge of it but will ask you for your name and telephone number. You will get a return call, but not from Bates.

Contact methods are learned and a special cellular telephones and tablet PC's issued. A completely new identification will be established for you and it will be secure so that any investigation into your past will be subtly diverted and the enquiring party investigated. On the side of the tablet is a small tag. Beneath is a red button. Push it and the PC is wiped clean at once. The cellular phone has something similar.

After assignment to a certain area you will receive your briefings on a daily basis. They will arrive every day at five in the morning and must be acknowledged within fifteen minutes, otherwise they are automatically deleted and it takes a special call to re-establish communication. You don't want that to occur. You will be assigned a personal contact. Available night and day. I called my guy Michael Clancy.

The e-mail briefings will update 'Ghost' activities in your area. Names, addresses and a special identification number will be provided for any Ghost. His or her movements are always included when known. You will know who they call and whether the communication reveals anything relevant to security. These will not be the 'normal' suspicious persons. They will be the deep cover people that have established themselves here and live normal lives until they are 'triggered' to perform or assist with, an act of terror. We probably know about sixty percent of EA's. The rest are out there but unless they make a false move or we get specific Intel, there they will stay. Much to our chagrin.

There will be an apartment or house for you. A vehicle will be registered in your name. Insurance will be taken care of. You yourself will establish bank accounts and credit cards. The mechanism is in place so that the process will run smoothly. You will be just another citizen. But, one day you might receive a Blue alert.

Chapter 2 – 'Alerts.'

EACH Agents may receive a Blue alert any time. Blue's come via cellphone so, every time that phone rings, your heart skips a beat. We have three levels of contact. Red is elevated but not imminent. White is elevated imminent and Blue an all-out emergency. We were told while training to have two hand bags ready at all times. One at home, one in your vehicle. Mine are inexpensive small carry-on duffels. Inside is a clean polo shirt and socks, a two changes of underwear, an extra pair of pants, a light jacket and a baseball cap. A toiletries bag, sun glasses and a few breakfast bars and that's it. Easy to carry and always ready.

Your vehicle must be gassed up every two days. In the trunk you carry a full five gallon fuel can and a large plastic container of water. There's also a sophisticated first aid kit. They told me you could do most things with it, open heart surgery excluded.

I had been with the Force for two years before I got my first White. It was November 4th a Wednesday. At four o'clock that morning the phone rang. Already awake, I picked it up right away, pen and paper ready. A metallic voice, probably recorded, edited and then played:

'White. Immediate. ID 41Xray299FL. Subject has meeting News Café noon today 4th. KYEO and report.'

The call terminated, and I went to the tablet to see what subject 41X299FL had been up to lately. A White call was not a complete surprise. I was aware 41 lived on the outskirts of the City proper. An apartment on the third floor of an anonymous condominium. I had details of his vehicle as well as his insurance company and the name of his physician. Our 41 arrived in the US from Guatemala. Originally from Syria, he became a Guatemalan citizen. Then he got a Green Card through a US Government Lottery and now worked as a waiter in a small Miami restaurant. There had been several jobs, all waiting tables. We had information on him because he had visited Syria for six weeks a year previously. There was no incriminating evidence against him. He was a regular EA, a Ghost. His Syrian name was Ayueb Homsi, and his Guatemalan one, Abdiel Sanchez. I checked on him every three weeks.

The News Café? That's on 8th Street and Ocean Drive, South Beach. I thought it touristy but if the other person happened to be staying close, not a bad choice.

Arriving early, I found a parking lot with space available. You had to be careful. The traffic wardens were unforgiving. I slipped a waiter a twenty, and he agreed to hold a table besides mine until I took my hat off. He would then 'find' the table in the always crowded location. While I sat on the terrace, my new friend put a red 'reserved' sign on the small table next to mine. I ordered coffee and a burger. My target turned up a little before twelve. When I removed my straw hat, the waiter made his move and pointed out the table. I was just a tourist in my Bermuda's, T shirt, flip flops and sun glasses. His friend, turned up a few minutes later. A tall man, he wasn't a Latin but had olive skin. He addressed the other in Arabic.

"How are you my friend?"

"I'm well. And you?"

The greetings over, they sat. The big man seemed friendly. There were lots of 'habibi' and 'Ahlan sadiqi' thrown around while they ordered tabbouleh and babaganush and then got down to business. I took two pictures of each of them with the camera hidden in my sunglasses. These would be uploaded and sent to the DNI later.

I noted nothing strange in their conversation. References to 'our mutual friends', nothing more. I watched them out of the corner of my eye. The friend was the amateur and 41, the pro. It was he who used his hands to signify the volume of the conversation should be lowered and tapped the side of his head as if to say 'think' if the friend went off track. It was he who covered his hand when writing something on a paper napkin. They ate and as they stood up to leave I listened the tail end of 41's goodbyes. He was saying '...up at your room at five then', and they walked out. That might mean this evening or tomorrow morning. I followed the friend. He was staying at a very expensive Ocean Drive Hotel known for the bevy of thousand dollar a night girls that frequented its bar. I went back to my apartment and sent a report with the photographs. A fast reply said that instructions would be received within the hour.

The reply came, a White code. Another KYEO message meaning keep your eyes open. Gevarghese Olikara, was the name of the 'friend' a rich, well educated, Syrian playboy who made a nuisance of himself by sucking up to Hazzm and running errands for them. He had arrived in Atlanta a week ago and appeared in Florida the previous evening. Probably he had driven to Miami. They had a file on him but nothing to red flag his visit. Olikara was a messenger. He had given a message to 41 or made arrangements to deliver something.

I changed clothes and arrived outside the Hotel at four forty-five. The target, 41 arrived on foot at four fifty five, went in to the Lobby, and headed for the elevators. He entered alone, and the light showed he stopped at the sixth floor. I sat in the Lobby to wait. Fifteen minutes later he came out of one of the elevators with two fishing rods in his left hand and what looked like a cloth rod carrying bag in his right. The bag had no curve, it stayed completely straight and his right shoulder dipped, it must heavier than the two rods. I followed him to a nearby car park where he put the rods and bag into the trunk of a vehicle and drove off. The evening before I had looked at 41's record, it didn't mention anything about him being a fisherman.

In the Lobby I waited, and thirty minutes later Olikara came down in the elevator with a suitcase, calling the concierge to get him a cab to the Airport.

Back at my apartment I sent a message asking for more details on 41 and a check to be sure Olikara had caught a flight out of MIA that evening. Then I went to bed and looked at TV for an hour before going to sleep.

I had a reply on the tablet when I awoke. Olikara had taken a late flight to Guatemala the evening before. What I found more interesting was that 41, Abdiel Sanchez, or Ayueb Homsi had definitely received sniper training at an Ahrar al-Sham camp in northern Syria. Did I have any more information?

I replied mentioning the fishing rods and the suspicious black bag. Five minutes later the White message said to keep a close eye on 41. The President would be in Miami on a campaign stop on Friday November 6th. Details forthcoming.

Chapter 3 – *'Ayueb Homsi, EA 41.'*

Oh. Tim Stacy! *Ahmaq Kabir*! You are indeed a great fool! Agent of the United States Embedded Agent Control. Put to watch me, Ayueb Homsi. I have seen you several times over the past year. You dress in different clothes but I always notice you. That walk. It is special and I recognize it. Also, you always wear the same sunglasses. Perhaps you see me shopping or walking to the cinema but you never stay long. Your visits are on a Wednesday or Friday when you know I got to the little store near the apartment and buy a Lottery ticket. One day I will win the prize. I dream numbers and I look out for groups of numbers when I am working and I play these. One day, Yes! One day! So Stacey I see you looking from your car. I know you Tim Stacey! You do not know that I know you though.

Stacey, you are very innocent! Like so many Americans, you are so secure that you know more than others when in reality, you actually know so much less! The other day you sat at the next table to Gevy and myself. The stupid tourist outfit almost made Gevy laugh out loud and I had to restrain him. I must admit you looked very foolish. However, you heard enough, and that's the important thing. Today you will follow me when I got to the fishing camp. Don't get lost! I will drive slowly!

Did you find out that Gevy left Wednesday evening? Of course you did. Your people tapped into the departures and found his name. I bet that once you found that, you were happy. I bet you checked no further. If you had you would have found out that Gevy returned Thursday morning!

Do you realize, great fool, that I was first honored by the Syrian Muslim Brotherhood and now by Hazzm. Then I came here to watch and wait. Now it is time to act. For the past four years I have watched, waited and listened. First with the Brotherhood and now Hazzm and the Levant Front. In the next few days the whole world will know us and bend to our wishes.

Yes, Stacey. Like your fairy tale of Hansel and Gretel and the white pebbles, I will strew a trail for you to follow. You Stacey, will follow the trail to wherever I wish to make it go. But I will scatter your path with red herrings! How we will laugh as you run along it!

Chapter 4 – 'A day fishing.'

At six in the morning I parked down the road from his apartment, waiting. He drove out at six thirty and went north and then west, picking up US-27. There was little traffic, and I stayed well back to avoid being spotted. Finally, in the distance, I watched him turn off right. As I drew close, I saw the fishing camp. One of those that rents a small Jon boat with a 5cc motor and fishing rods with bait to tourists for a few hours. I parked on the roadside by a canal and waited for twenty minutes until I noticed a small boat leaving the Marina. It looked like 41. I went to the trunk of the car and found my binoculars. Abdiel Sanchez was out for a day's fishing, or was he?

The canal was long and straight. I didn't move for half an hour and he could be seen. Those boats were slow. Then he turned right. I waited and then started the car and drove along the highway until I saw where he had made the turn. There was another straight canal, and he was a quarter of a mile down already. I couldn't get close, so I parked the car to one side of the canal entrance, opened the windows and sat to wait.

Ten minutes later came the first shot. I got out of the car and looked down the canal through the binoculars. Nothing. Then, another shot that came from where I had last seen the boat. I waited and over the next quarter hour there were an additional twenty or so reports. There was nothing out there to shoot at so he was probably target shooting or sighting a weapon of some sort. Everything was coming together. I waited, and shortly the boat returned along the canal and went back to the Marina.

I felt sure about 41's intentions. However I wanted to see where he would go when he finished his fishing adventure. I waited two hundred yards down from the Marina in a small layby until he exited half an hour later and turned back on

US-27 to Miami. I stayed well behind. It was not a busy highway on a Thursday afternoon so the tail was simple. He turned off at I-75 and followed that to I-595 and then I-95 North. It looked like he intended to go to Ft. Lauderdale. He didn't keep me waiting long because he made his way to East Las Olas Boulevard and down to a Marina. There he made several circles around the Marina and the surrounding streets. Then, when he started back, I dropped in behind him again, keeping well behind while he took I-95 back to Miami.

He headed to Coconut Grove and left his car with the valet at the Sonnesta Hotel on McFarlane. I parked down the street and waited. He was out in thirty minutes and went back down-town and seemed very interested in the AA Arena. It was almost two o'clock when he got back to his apartment. He left his car in the parking lot and went inside.

I returned home and checked my messages. An abbreviated schedule for the President's visit. He would be at a fund raising lunch near Las Olas at noon and another at three in the afternoon at a residence near McFarlane Road, Coconut Grove. He was due to make a speech at the AA Arena at seven and would go from there to the Airport and back to Washington. I called in a White with my details. They asked me to hold and then Michael Clancy, my direct contact, came on the line.

"Stacey. Clancy. Any concrete ideas about the black bag?"

"No. It might be a gun but I didn't see it."

"We need to find out. Can you do a look-see on the car?"

"Yes. I have the VIN and can do it after dark. It's a Corolla."

"Give me the VIN. I'll arrange a key" I repeated the VIN and was told to expect a message within the hour. I had to check the black bag and call back soonest. Fifty minutes later a message arrived saying a key taped to the top of the vehicles front right-hand wheel. It got dark at six so I headed to the apartment. The car was in the lot. An elderly lady parked and removed a plastic bag from the back seat and walked into the back door. The key was there, and it took only a few seconds to get into the trunk. Unzipping the black bag I turned on my small flashlight and inspected a Remington 700 with a Leupold 10x40 scope. A box of 7.62mm ammunition sat by the gun. This was a sniper rifle. You could buy them at most gun shows for about fifteen hundred dollars. Perfect for an assassination.

I was out of the trunk and had it closed in less than half a minute. The key went into my pocket. Back in my car I contacted Clancy and gave him the information. He said he would call back. On the way to my place I realized they previous day I had left my straw hat at the News Café. It was a nice hat, so I took a swing by to ask if they had put it on one side in case I returned. There was no parking anywhere around so I decided to try early in the morning, they were open twenty-four hours.

Chapter 5 – *'Running around in circles.'*

I didn't sleep very well and was up at four. No messages but at four twenty Clancy called. He had news. They had investigated my information and the Secret Service had been advised. Our friend 41, Sanchez had rented a room at the Sonnesta a week previously. It was on the eighth floor with a view that overlooked McFarlane Road in the Grove. There was a fund raiser for the President to be held in a private residence there. The Service would wait for him when he arrived today and take him into custody as soon as he walked into his room with the black bag. Good job. KYEO!

That called for a celebration. I went to the News Café to ask about my hat.

There was parking at five in the morning. The previous night's crowd had left and the early birds were arriving. I purchased a newspaper and walked the two blocks to the restaurant.

There were plenty of tables available and I at down. Two minutes later I heard a voice.

"Good morning boss. I think this is yours."

It was the waiter from Wednesday. He was standing in front of me smiling and holding my hat.

"Wow! Thanks! I was going to ask about the hat. Left it Wednesday."

"Yep. I get you. For that kind of tip we offer special service." He laughed and handed me the hat.

"Coffee? Eggs Benedict?"

I ordered the eggs and coffee and then opened the paper. It was full of the President's visit later today. It told me what I was already aware of. Visits to Lauderdale, Coconut Grove and the AA Arena. I called Clancy. He answered on the second ring.

"Can you find out if Olikara really checked out of his Hotel Wednesday night?"

"Will call right back." He hung up. I waited ten minutes until his call came in. He spoke without preamble.

"He left. Said he would be back in a day or so. We'll tell you when we have something new."

I drove home. It was six thirty, and I needed a nap for a couple of hours. At nine the phone rang.

"Stacey. Nothing from Sanchez. A dead end. His cell phone is tapped, but he only made one call last night and that was for a pizza delivery. We could pick him up on a pretense but that might cause a diplomatic problem. Let's be vigilant and wait."

I decided to visit 41 and drove over to check the apartment. Five minutes later I was in the parking lot. The Corolla was still there, but what about the owner?

Parking down the street I waited. Nothing. At eleven forty-five I called Clancy and told him what had happened. He told me to check the trunk of the Corolla and call back. Five minutes later, after waiting for the garbage truck to exit the parking lot, I opened the trunk of 41's vehicle. The bag was still there. I called Clancy. 'Houston, we have a problem!'

Chapter 6 – 'Vanished.'

Oh. Tim Stacy! Great fool that you are! I watched you last evening as you opened the Corolla. When you left I packed the few things I would need. This morning at nine I walked to the little store. It is Friday so I have to buy my Lottery ticket. I have special numbers for this week! Always keep the same schedule, it lulls people to sleep. Then I hailed a taxi. I did not go near to the Corolla, it would not be needed again. I asked the taxi to go to the Airport. The driver dropped me at the AA departures terminal. I got out of the cab, walked in and went to a bathroom.

It took a few minutes to dress in the white scrubs and put my other clothes away. I now sported a thick mustache and large sunglasses. I went downstairs to the arrival's area and picked up another cab. This time I asked for the Mutiny Hotel in the Grove. I called Gevy to tell him I was on my way. Wasn't I bothered about the cell phone being tapped? Of course not. I have four cell phones. I gave two to Gevy Wednesday. It is so easy to buy a phone, get a number and use it. Who would guess it was me or Gevy calling? No one.

So now I am at the Mutiny. Gevy and I are in the suite preparing for this afternoon and going over everything to make sure we can leave without problems. Ah Stacey! What is it that you are doing right now eh? Are you sitting outside my apartment waiting for me to pick up my car and drive to the Sonnesta? Or are you biting your fingernails because you have found I have left and you have no idea where I am?

You of course found out Gevy went to Guatemala. But this was to put you off the scent because he came back on Thursday morning. He rented an SUV and drove to Hialeah and purchased fifty packs of fireworks. Piccolo Pete's, six to a pack, with a noise level of about 117db's. These went into the trunk. Then he drove to the medical supply company and picked up his wheelchair that had been ordered a few days earlier. At the Mayfair Shops in the Grove he found a remote parking spot. Five minutes with the trunk open allowed him to finish his arrangements. One cell phone he left there. It had plenty of battery available to keep it on for seventy-two hours.

He used the bathroom in the lot to fix his appearance and a few minutes later an elderly gentleman in a wheelchair hailed a taxi outside of the Shops.

Now what Stacey? You went to Gevy's Hotel again this morning I am sure. What did you find? You found he had checked out Wednesday evening, right?

You are a fool Stacey and easy to deceive. Now we are both gone and you don't have any idea where. Gevy's reservation at the Mutiny was made weeks ago in name nobody knows and paid for with a credit card belonging to someone that does not exist. The reservation is for an elderly invalid. He uses a wheelchair.

This is how he arrived at the Hotel. In a taxi with his wheelchair. An old man with white hair and spectacles. The porter pushed him up the ramp so he could register. They told him his suitcases had arrived and were waiting for him. There would be a private nurse coming tomorrow he said to the clerk. Please make sure he is shown up when he gets here. They pushed him in the chair to the elevator and on to his eleventh-floor suite. There he stayed, enjoying the luxury. That evening, he ordered from Atchana's East West Kitchen, the Hotel's Thai restaurant

We will do what has to be done a little later today and then we will vanish and then reappear in a few weeks as heroes in our own land.

Here in the Hotel everything is ready. I had made the arrangements yesterday and two suitcases were waiting when Gevy arrived. We have many friends that help out with small missions such as this. In one suitcase there is an RPG29 Vampir Grenade launcher. It has a 2.7x1P38 optical sight mounted on the tube. There is one round of TBG-29V thermobaric anti-personnel ammunition. Gevy has trained on the weapon and has told me only one round will be needed. It has a range of about 500 meters and eight fins keep it steady in flight.

Dressed as a male nurse I arrived at ten in the morning. I was shown up to the suite. We had to get the staff used to us so I pushed Gevy in the wheelchair all over the Hotel. Through the garden, around the Lobby and then we circled the pool. There were some sympathetic glances. Gevy said afterwards it was hard not to laugh. Back in the suite we ordered lunch, from the room service menu. Gevy appeared to be in a good mood.

"With my reward I'll no longer rely on my father for money. I'll have all I need for the rest of my life! What about you Ayu?"

"I will go back to my country. Buy a house, have many women and become fat! But first I'll look and find out if have won the Lottery. I buy twice every week. One day I'll get the right numbers and win. See this, here is my ticket for Saturday. These are very good numbers!" I pushed the ticket across the table to him.

The telephone rang. It was room service. I answered it as Gevy was still sitting in the wheelchair. Did we want both green and black olives? Yes, I said, bring both. As I stood up I looked out of the side window. The house for the fund raiser could be seen through the ferns and trees in its garden. There was a construction site to the side of the Hotel. It already had ten skeleton floors erected. A tower crane lifted steel beams from a flatbed to the right of the Hotel and swung them to the site on the left. Steelworkers unhooked them, placed them and started riveting. It was fascinating to watch. The crane, a single unmoving tower, had a horizontal arm that allowed it to maneuver its load.

But you Stacey, you don't care about this? By now you are worried. 'What is going on?' you ask. Is Abdiel Sanchez in his apartment waiting for the right moment to drive to the

Sonnesta? Or has he changed plans. Find out because now the time is slipping away. Almost one o'clock on Friday. You must move Stacey!

There was a knock on the door and we found our lunch had arrived.

Chapter 7 – 'Search.'

"Damn right we've got a problem. The President's next appearance is at three. It's quiet in Lauderdale. No problems. Sanchez doesn't answer his cell phone. We tried calling using a Miami cut-out number, but he doesn't pick up. We are having the Miami Fire Department pull a fire drill on the apartment at twelve thirty. ID yourself when the fire truck pulls in. They will give you a uniform so you can be there when his apartment is checked. It will be any minute now."

And it was. They asked no questions as I pulled on the long coat and a fire helmet they gave me and followed the Inspector and two firemen up the stairs to the third floor. They hit the fire button and off went the bell and horns. Three of the four apartments opened their doors open within ten seconds. The fourth stayed shut. The Inspector asked the Property Manager to use a master key to open it. There was no one inside. I called Clancy.

"All local cab companies are searching their records. They are looking for pick-ups in that area early today. Back to you in ten." He hung up. Thanking the firemen I went downstairs. I checked the Corolla again. The bag and the Remington were still there. Perhaps he had got cold feet?

When had he left? Then I remembered. Every Friday morning he bought a Lottery ticket in the small store by the side of the apartment. I walked in and found it empty. There was an elderly man, probably the owner, standing behind the counter.

"Good morning. Did Mr. Sanchez come in yet?"

"Oh, yes sir. Mr. Sanchez always comes in Friday for Lottery! He said this week he felt sure he would win as he picked some special numbers! But they all say that!" The man laughed.

I thanked him and walked outside. Clancy's call a few minutes later made cold feet a possibility. He'd been dropped off at the AA departures terminal at nine-twenty and went inside. They were checking all airline to find out where he had gone to. Stay on the line. I waited for a little and Clancy returned. "Nothing. He hasn't left. He has no reservations. We are doing another cab check. Anyone who took a cab from the Airport between nine twenty and ten o'clock." He asked me to hold on. It was two o'clock.

A short time later his voice came over the line. "No one matching Sanchez's description has been picked up."

"Try the arrivals downstairs. Anyone, no families, single man going to the Grove. Get a description."

More time passed. "Got a hit. Male dressed in scrubs. Mustache and glasses. Went to the Mutiny in the Grove. There are no other hits for single males going there. Secret Service will meet you at the Desk. Look for the Agent's lapel indicator. It's a blue circle with 6 inside it." It was two thirty.

Miami traffic on Friday's is brutal. Add to the confusion of the President coming down I-95 on his way to the fund raiser and you can imagine the tie-ups. It took me thirty minutes to get to the Mayfair Shops in the Grove. From there it was a hundred yards to the Mutiny. As I left the car I heard the sirens wailing. I parked in a no parking zone, it seemed faster to walk what with all the traffic.

I recognized the Service man as I walked into the marble floored Lobby. He nodded but stayed at the side of reception.

I approached the Assistant Manager at the side of the Desk and waved the Agent over.

Chapter 8 – 'Ready!'

Ah Gevy! Here he comes! Lots of sirens, and as we looked west from the suite we could see the convoy through the trees as it arrived at the front of the house. We had the windows opened and Gevy put a chair on a table to allow him to rest his elbow when he aimed the RPG 29. He had a perfect view of the garden of the residence. There were all kinds of law enforcement vehicles present.

We stood back and watched and then, a few minutes later saw movement and what seemed to be Secret Service Agents, appeared on the patio of the house. They spread out. We waited to see what happened next. The sirens stopped and all that could be heard was the groaning of the construction crane lifting the steel beams. Then a flash of color and women appeared in the garden.

"Is he there Gevy?" I asked.

He lifted the RPG and peered through the optical sight.

"I cannot be sure. Get the phone ready!"

I took his extra cell phone from the table. By its side rested a number that corresponded to the phone in the back of the SUV parked at the Shops. When I dialed the number the detonator attached to the cell phone would receive an electric charge and set off the Piccolo Pete's. That would add confusion to whatever happened next as the police responded to the explosion.

"It is him! It is him! Dial fast Ayu. Fast!"

I dialed the number.

Down in the Lobby, Stacey spoke to the Agent "Tell him who you are." The Agent flashed an ID and the Assistant Manger's face paled.

"A man in scrubs…" That was all Stacey could get out. Then a tremendous explosion took place. That, although Stacey didn't realize it, was the 300 Piccolo's exploding in the SUV that Gevy parked at the Shops.

Everyone flinched, and some dropped to the floor. Sirens whined.

Up in the suite Gevy sighted and fired. The thermobaric round rushed from the tube. There was an explosion, small compared with the previous one. They had no time to check results or talk right now.

In the Lobby the Agent talked on his communications microphone clipped to his collar. He nodded and pulled me aside "My name is Stevens. It's an explosion at the Mayfair Shops about a hundred yards down the street. Also, something else exploded as it hit a steel girder hanging from that big crane that swings in front of the Hotel. They are moving the President as I speak."

The man in scrubs must be found. I grabbed the Assistant Manager.

Chapter 9 – 'Escape.'

Gevy dropped the RPG and in five seconds was in the wheelchair. I unlocked the door and pushed him into the corridor. The elevator opened, and we got in. We descended slowly, stopping at three of the floors to pick up passengers. Then we arrived at the Lobby. There was a lot of confusion.

I pushed Gevy through the pool door of the Hotel, past the sun lounges and through a small gap in the hedge. We had to wait for traffic on South Bayshore but we got across and then through the boat parking to McFarlane. Once there I got the wheelchair onto the small path that leads to the Marina. Along the pier we went, passing docked charter boats until we reached the 'Atargatis', the boat that would take us east towards Bimini. There we were to be picked up with the help of GPS, by a Libya owned freighter hired by Hamzz. It was in international waters and no one should stop us. The charter Captain, who had been paid well not to ask questions, was waiting and very quickly we were on our way.

Then came the bad news over the radio. There had been something fired or thrown from a high floor in the Mutiny Hotel towards a house on McFarlane where the President was attending a fundraiser. Whatever it was, struck a steel construction beam being swung by a crane moving girders across the side of the Hotel. There had been an explosion but there were no reported injuries.

Police were investigating at the Mayfair Shops which at first, diverted attention. A vehicle in the parking garage had exploded. Again no injuries and various law enforcement agencies were investigating. Police were on the lookout for a man dressed in hospital scrubs that may have been at the Mutiny Hotel earlier. The President canceled his AA Arena appearance and had gone to MIA to return to Washington.

So Stacey. You think you have won? We will see, we will see! I am away and you are still in Miami. Who is the clever one Stacey? You or me?

We increased speed heading north-west. The ride would take about three hours at 25 knots. Bay waters were calm, and the boat made good speed. There were plenty of other craft around this Friday afternoon but at four thirty most of them were headed towards Miami. It would be dark in less than two hours and they wanted to be back at their Marinas by then. The Bay is a tricky place and the ever-shifting sandbars made Captains nervous.

We crossed Key Biscayne, under the bridge and headed due east towards Alice Town, Bimini. No one spoke on board. The Captain had been retained because he had a reputation for keeping his mouth shut. The boat sped on its course. I had the GPS coordinates memorized and would give them to the Captain in a few minutes. It was light at five o'clock but the horizon was slowly darkening. The boat ran on. We had to slow down soon. The conditions made it impossible to run at full speed although we had radar. Besides, the closer we got to Bimini, the more vessels were around. I went to the bridge and spoke to the Captain.

"The GPS coordinates are 25.625-79.35833. We will be met there."

He made a note, nodded, but didn't reply.

Another two hours I estimated. The freighter had to be there. Then the long ride back across the Atlantic and through the Mediterranean to Latakia. We failed in our task, but the scare we put into the heart of the American authorities would keep them on edge for months.

Chapter 10 – *'A boat ride.'*

Back at the Hotel Stacy asked again, "The man in scrubs? I need every bit of information. Now!" The Assistant Manager recovered his composure. "Please wait. I will find out." Walking to the reception he spoke to the Desk Clerk. I looked at him as he questioned the man. He nodded and made notes in a small book. The Clerk made several entries into the PC and spoke to the Assistant Manager as he did so. Then he returned to where we were standing.

"The man said he was a male nurse and had to take care of a guest in an 11th floor suite, Mr. A'meen Hisham. A reservation came in several weeks back, prepaid. He arrived Thursday in a wheelchair and seemed old and frail. The nurse arrived earlier today, and they gave him permission to go up to the suite after the clerk called ahead. He saw them not long ago. The nurse pushed the man around the pool. Earlier he said he was doing the same thing. It didn't look suspicious."

"Let's check the suite."

We rode up to the eleventh-floor and the Assistant Manager unlocked the door. The RPG lay under a table in front of an open side window. I looked out and saw the hive of activity across McFarlane.

The remains of lunch were strewed across the table. A pot of coffee and black and green olives. On the floor was a Florida Lottery ticket. I picked it up and put it in my shirt pocket.

We left the suite and went downstairs.

"Thanks." I said to the Assistant Manager. "Close off that room. A Secret Service team will be here shortly. Show them up. You speak to no one before you speak to them. We'll go check the back."

Stevens, after speaking into his collar microphone, went out with me to the pool at the rear. There were several groups of people chatting near the bar.

Stevens flashed his Service ID. "Did anyone see a man in a wheelchair go through here a few minutes ago?"

"Sure. There was a male nurse pushing him. They went through the hedge over there." He pointed to a gap in the hedge. We ran over and through the space. A path led past some sheds, a small fence and then more sheds and down a slight slope to South Bayshore Drive.

We crossed the divided road and came upon a fenced boat parking lot. The double doors were open, and we ran through. A Marina Bull boat mover came noisily towards us and we waved to stop it. Out came the Agent's ID again.

"We're looking for a man in a wheelchair and a male nurse. Have you seen anything like that through here?"

The driver looked over at us, a large boat balanced on the front forks of the lift. He turned off the engine.

"Sorry. Can't hear a thing with that running. What did you want?"

Stevens repeated the question.

"Well, 'bout fifteen minutes ago I pulled this Malibu out of the water along the pier on the other side of McFarlane. Owner parks it here at the back Marina lot. Cheaper you understand. Anyway, I saw this guy in scrubs on the deck of a 40 foot Viking. Nice boat. 'Aint seen it before 'round here but it took off fast heading out to sea. Didn't pay no attention to it after that. I was too busy with this baby!" He pointed to the Malibu.

"Thanks. We'll go that way."

They crossed McFarlane and went into the Marina yard. On the far side stood a pier. There were half a dozen boats tied up by the bows. Their quarry had long gone. Stacey looked at the Agent. "Perhaps the Coast Guard can help us out. They have fast Cutters at their South Beach location."

"OK. You call there. I'll phone my Supervisor and let him know where we stand."

They made their calls and Stacey received immediate confirmation that the CG Cutter Paul Clark would move out right away. Was it possible to get a chopper ride to South Point Park? The Cutter could pick them up there, much faster than them trying to get to South Beach in the Friday traffic. A call to the Miami Police Department resulted in confirmation that a chopper would be at the Marina in fifteen minutes. I called Clancy and updated him. He said to go with the Cutter after the Viking. Stevens said he'd travel with me. Thirty minutes later we were on board the Cutter and headed east. The Commander, whose name was DeFoe, listened to our story. When we finished he nodded.

"They will head for the Bahamas or perhaps, Bimini. That seems certain. There are hundreds of vessels around this weekend, it's the biggest fishing tournament of the year. We have no idea which craft is the target. I'll show you the mess on the radar. We can go to the bridge in a minute and look. If we don't know where your guys are heading we might chase twenty or thirty of these boats and be wrong every time." He shook his head.

"If we find her, and it's a big 'if', you have to tell me what to do. My boss said you guys are in charge. We've got a MK38 25mm which is plenty of firepower. There's also four M2 Browning's if needed. This Cutter can run at twenty-five knots and I'm sure what we are chasing won't be going anywhere near that speed in the dark. Let's take a look."

They went up to the bridge and DeFoe pointed out the radar. They were far enough away from the coast now and the screen showed dozens of blips.

"It could be any of them. Take your pick." He turned back to where we stood waiting.

"You can use our communications if you wish but try you own first, they should work fine here, we're not that far out. I'll take you out on deck. It's a nice night and you can sit and admire the view for an hour." He led them outside, and they sat on a locker. Both took out their cell phones.

I called Clancy. "Ok we are at sea on the Cutter. We are an hour to where we might intercept. What do you want done?"

"Well, I guess the Captain told you about firepower. There should be no worries with that. First you have to find the right boat. I hear there's a fishing tournament this weekend. That's the problem. What's the Viking going to do? They might go around Bimini to Nassau or Freeport. There's hundreds of islands around that area. While it's dark they could vanish. The Service agrees we want these people alive and back here soonest. That means taking them in with no problems. The Agent with you, Stevens, will be told the same thing. The Captain has been advised. Oh! By the way. The President is asking for hourly updates on this! Stay in touch."

Stevens confirmed his instructions were the same as mine. He looked over and asked, "Any ideas?"

I slipped my cellphone into my shirt pocket. It rustled against something. I pulled out the Lottery ticket.

"Mr. Stevens, I have an idea where we can find them. The answer to our boat location is right there in this Lottery ticket." I found Defoe and explained.

An hour later we could see the Viking. The Cutter illuminated her with its spotlight and fired a burst from one of the M2 Browning's over her charthouse. The tracers seemed to emphasize the seriousness of the situation. We came alongside and a boarding party soon had all three handcuffed and shackled. As this took place, we noticed a large freighter a quarter mile downwind from the Viking. It slowly moved off south.

I asked Defoe to lock up Olikara and the boat skipper but he told me the skipper wanted to talk and that Stevens intended to interview him. As for the Viking, they already had a crew on board and it would follow us back to Miami once the Cutter weighed anchor.

I called Clancy. He seemed pleased. I was to expect a call back. Then I went to the 1st Lieutenant's cabin. Two armed seamen guarded the prisoner.

"Good evening Mr. Homsi, or should I say Sanchez?"

"My name is Homsi. I know you Stacey. For two years I have known you. You are not very subtle. Nothing will be said now. You have to advise me of my rights even although your act of piracy taking vessel is illegal."

"Mr. Homsi. Your Captain invited us aboard. There's nothing illegal about it."

"It does not matter. I want legal representation as soon as we reach land. I will not speak until then."

"No problem Mr. Homsi. That's your choice."

"I have one question. How did you find out which boat was ours? We saw you on our radar. You made no deviations."

"Well Mr. Homsi. If you hadn't played the Lottery this week then we might never have caught you. But you did play, and you left the ticket at the Mutiny under the spilled lunch table. Your numbers were 25 62 57 93 58 33. If we put those into GPS formula such as 25.625 -79.35833 it would place us exactly where we are anchored right now! I'll check the winning numbers tomorrow!"

'COHEN's empanadas.'

Chapter 1 – *'Gossip.'*

It was the morning of the biggest social event of the year. The two reception lobbies at Secure Vault were full of clients who had come to take belongings out of their deposit boxes. There were two lobbies because there were two major political parties in the country and in the past, the principal players had not mixed socially. That had changed somewhat these days.

The Democrats were out of power at the moment and the Reformists ruled the roost. However, that did not prevent *Doña* Jacinta Flores de Rivera holding court as she awaited the summons that would see her guided down to the Vault proper to open her large box. At any other place besides Secure Vault, Jacinta would have insisted she be given priority access. However, the opportunity to lord it over the dozen or so other ladies present, some young and a few just a tiny bit older, was too much of a temptation.

She helped herself to another of the small *empanadas* the Cohen brother's, owners of Secure Vault, always offered to their clients as they sat in the lobbies. Jacob Cohen, one of the owners, swore that fifty percent of his clients merely came to check their boxes so they could partake of his wife's delicious meat pies and his famous Cuban coffee. Jacinta extended her *demitasse* to a passing waiter, and he immediately filled it. Leaning back in the comfortable armchair, one of a dozen arranged in a large semi-circle, she continued her one-sided conversation with as many of her companions who would listen.

"Yes! I heard that Juanita Gomez our accountant at the Management office where our Gulfstream is parked told someone that the President had important business in the Interior last Thursday. So important that he took his 'Personal Assistant', *Señorita* Pricilla Alvarez, with him. Huh! Personal Assistant indeed! Her six-inch heels and short skirt were quite inappropriate for a business trip. Juanita said that the President stood at the foot of the steps and ogled her backside as she went up. Now, is that the kind of behavior we expect from the leader of our Government?" She looked around for support. It was provided by *Señora* Wilma Cortez de Cortez, whose husband had been the Minister of the Interior in the past Government. "*Querida* Jacinta. You are right of course. My Diego, as a Minister in the last Government, often used the aircraft for Interior trips. I can tell you, he would never ever take such a woman on one of those flights!" She tossed her long black curls. No one said anything. Most present understood that her Diego was gay and had no time for beautiful women such as Pricilla Alvarez. However, her companions merely nodded in agreement.

A guard entered from the small reception area and spoke discretely to Jacinta. She got out of her armchair and turned to face the other ladies.

"I have to get my things now girls. I trust we may continue our conversation this evening." She walked with the guard towards the Vault. As she reached it she glanced at a notice posted on the door. It stated that Secure Vault would be closed from noon Saturday until ten on Monday and there was no access to boxes whatsoever during that time.

Customers were asked to make sure they returned valuables before the deadline.

In the other Lobby, the First Lady of the Republic, *Doña* Margarita de Los Angeles Smith, whispered to her companion, the wife of the Finance Minister, *Doña* Flora Gonzalez de Constantino.

"Ramon, my Driver told me that Juanita Gomez, the Rivera's accountant said that the President traveled with the Alvarez woman last Thursday and he ogled her short skirt. Their Gulfstream is in the same hanger as the Presidential aircraft, so she sees a lot. That *hijo de puta!* If we didn't have to attend the Red Cross Ball tonight I would go home right now and have it out with him."

"Ah Marga. Men are all the same. They love young *culo*. Enrique tells me he pays no attention to all the pretty little things at the Ministry. He also told me last night at dinner that he had heard about this story. He said it was *pura mierda!*"

The women laughed.

"All the same, that Juanita Gomez has a big mouth. She will have to go."

"How will you accomplish that my dear Marga? She doesn't work for you."

"Flora. People always want something from the President. I will ask him what Jacinta's husband is lobbying for and see if we can arrange a compromise."

"Marga, you are a born conspirator! I wish you luck! Be careful when you ask your husband and remember tonight is the Red Cross Ball. No one wants weepy eyes or grimaces to spoil it."

There were two big community events during the year. The Red Cross Ball on the second Thursday of December and the Arts Gala Dance, which helped fund three orphanages, in mid-January. Tickets for these events cost $1,000 per person and obtaining them was a major social success. Custom dictated a truce between all attendees on those evenings.

Politics were not discussed and everyone tended to be polite to everyone else. That however would change the next day when everything returned to normal.

The December Ball coincided with the start of school vacations. The January event, celebrated the overthrow of the Dictator some fifty years previously. Traditionally everyone took a long weekend and went to their beach houses.

They were the busiest days of the year for Secure Vault. After the Ball the Company would open at ten o'clock on the Saturday but remain open only until noon. After that, Secure Vault would close until the following Monday morning.

Chapter 2 – *'Marga and Ricardo.'*

Doña Margarita de Los Angeles Smith arrived back at the Presidential Residence about two in the afternoon. A servant opened the door of the Mercedes and offered his hand to help her out. Before she climbed out the made sure she left her gloves on the seat. A guard closed the door, and the Driver started the car. He waited, unnecessarily adjusting the rear mirror of the vehicle.

She walked into the house, past the servant. Then, with an exasperated sigh she turned back, as she seemed to realize something.

She called to the Driver, "Moreno. My gloves. I left them on the back seat of the car. Get them and bring them to my room after you park." She crossed to the circular staircase and walked upstairs.

Once in her room she put her jewelry case on a table and undressed. At forty-eight she was still a striking women and frequent visits to the spa and massages every morning, kept her body tight. She went into the large bathroom and gargled. As she returned to the bedroom there was a knock, and Ramon Moreno, the Driver, entered. No surprise showed on his face as he stood waiting.

Margarita said nothing, merely beckoned. He walked over to the bed and waited as she unzipped him.

It was finished in two minutes and with no fuss, he left the room. Margarita gargled again and then took a leisurely shower.

The First Lady of the Republic, *Doña* Margarita de Los Angeles Smith, required sex frequently. She hand-picked all staff members and providing they had the necessary skills she would enquire, very indirectly of course, as to their willingness to help her fulfill certain other requirements. These were very discrete encounters, never lasting beyond a few minutes but they kept *Doña* Margarita's complexion fresh and young and she felt that was very important. After all, her husband got what he wanted whenever he wanted it. Why shouldn't she?

She toweled off and lay on her bed to think. The last thing in the world she wanted was a scandal involving her husband's philandering. So, she had to make an example of the storyteller, Juanita Gomez. Unfortunately, Pricilla Alvarez was beyond her reach as she had no direct evidence of infidelity. Plus, as a Government employee, messing with her might start the scandal she wished to avoid. So, she needed something that would push Jacinta Flores to fire Juanita.

Perhaps it might not be too difficult. After all, they had been at school together thirty years ago and politics apart, were not enemies. What she had to do was get her husband, Ricardo, to give up a small favor to bring Jacinta round to her way of thinking. She looked at her watch on the bedside table. It was after three. A nap and she might expect Ricardo home. She would be waiting.

She felt his hand stroking her backside and awoke, turning to face him.

"Ricardo, you are early!"

"Early and finished for the day. Did you get your jewels?"

"Yes. They're on the table. The emeralds will be perfect with the new dress." Then remembering what she required, she spoke again.

"I bumped into Flora. We had coffee and those delightful *empanadas* that Cohen always has. Guess what I heard."

"I don't have to guess. I had lunch with Alvaro Constantino. He said tongues were wagging about my Assistant wearing a short skirt for Thursday's business trip. That's bullshit!"

Marga laughed. "That's what Flora said."

"So, forget it. You can't be President and not have people taking crap about you. We both know that."

"Dear Ricardo, I understand. I won't say another word. But..." her voice trailed off.

"But what?"

"Well, we can't have that kind of talk going round. That woman, Gomez, She has to go. People have to learn they can't gossip and lie about us and get away free!"

"Marga, she works for Carlos and Jacinta's Management Company. We can't mess with their staff."

"Suppose they fire her?" she said innocently.

"And why would they do that?" Then his eyes opening wider, he answered his own question. "An exchange?"

"Exactly!"

He looked down at her on the bed. "Not only do you have a very nice ass, you're very clever!"

He walked to the window and closed the sun blinds. The room became dark and for the next half an hour there were no words exchanged, just squeaks and grunts.

Over a quiet dinner at the Residence before the Ball, the plot was hatched. Carlos Rivera, President of the largest construction company in the Republic, had bid for and won the recent competition for repairing the Airport Highway. It had been a fair process but politics as usual, held up the official award. Rivera Construction had equipment standing idle, and idle equipment means money. Ricardo could sign the contract and clear the way. The following Monday the Gazette would publish the award. In return Juanita had to lose her job. They left for the Ball at nine o'clock, Marga happy she had the ammunition she needed to get her own way and Ricardo anxious to have a word with Pricilla Alvarez about being more careful or everything might be spoiled!

Chapter 3 – *'A favor requested.'*

At nine fifteen the President and First Lady arrived at the Red Cross Ball. Their limousine was preceded by four motorcycle outriders with lights flashing, then came the Presidential Mercedes and another SUV with six bodyguards following that. They were ushered into the Parliamentary Union, the Nations' premier Private Club. Their entry into the ballroom coincided with enthusiastic applause from the mainly Reformist guests who had the first opportunity to buy this year's tickets. There was a slightly more restrained response from the Democrat's.

The couple were greeted by the Head of Protocol who had the enviable, or perhaps unenviable, task of allowing access to the Chief Executive and his wife at their special table. The Head had already taken substantial payments from several aspiring petitioners, all of whom had been cleared by the President himself before giving him the OK.

First came the Ministers and their wives and then several selected lesser citizens who had lined the pocket of the Head of Protocol. When the last one had left the President motioned to the Head.

"Daniel. I want the Rivera's over here in five minutes. Discretely please."

The Head nodded and sidled away. The President turned to his wife. "They will be over in a minute. I'll speak with Carlos and you make sure Jacinta is on board."

"Thy will be done!" She replied in a mocking tone.

The Rivera's came through the cordoned-off area, led by the Head.

"*Señor* and *Señora* Rivera, Sir." He walked quietly away.

The President and his wife stood.

"Carlos, Jacinta. Welcome! Please sit here", he indicated chairs next to their own. "It's rarely we get the chance for a chat." The Rivera's sat, and the President turned to speak with Carlos as Marga addressed Jacinta.

"Jacinta. The children are well I hope, and your esteemed mother?"

"Thank you Marga. The emeralds look fabulous! All's well. The kids getting ready for college next year. My mother does not get about so much these days because of her leg trouble. She was not happy being left home this evening I can tell you!" The both laughed easily. After all, they had known each other for years and attended school together.

"Jacinta. I spoke with Ricardo this evening over dinner. Unfortunately the matter of the Airport Highway came up. We drove there last week to meet the kids when they returned from their college hunting trip and we found it full of potholes and bumps. A terrible showing for the tourists arriving. Now, between you and me the contract is, as usual, being held up by some of our more misguided functionaries. You know what I mean?"

"Yes Marga. I understand what you're saying."

"Well, I said to Ricardo this was intolerable and something had to be done immediately. That's what I said. Immediately!"

"I understand Marga," replied Jacinta, knowing full well that the next sentence would outline the terms under which Carlos's project would get going and they would not lose any more money while the equipment couldn't be used.

"I require a small favor Jacinta. If of course you believe you can accommodate me." Jacinta glanced at Carlos, he was in deep conversation with the President. Might it be a personal financial arrangement that the President wanted going through his wife instead of directly? No. That was against all etiquette. She was aware that the Minister of Public Works had already been compensated. It had to be something else. But what?

"Of course Marga. Whatever I can do for you!"

"Thank you Jacinta. It's that Juanita Gomez. The one that's works for your Management Company. I'm sure you know that she is spreading rumors about Ricardo?"

Jacinta weighed her words. She now had a good idea what it was Marga wanted. She wasn't against it. After all, employees should keep their mouths shut when it came to talking about their employers. However, as Marga had more or less committed to getting the contract signed she rapidly calculated what else she might be able to negotiate.

"Marga. You are right. She is a spiteful little bitch. I realized that as soon as that terrible rumor came up I would have to let her go." She smiled at Marga as if to say 'you didn't have to ask, I was going to do it tomorrow!'

"Jacinta. Thank you. It's all settled then. By Monday that woman will be gone and Carlos will have the President's signature on his contract. By the way, the diamonds look wonderful."

She realized she had been outmaneuvered but right now it was important that she resolve this little problem. There would be another request from the Rivera's, but it wouldn't be coming right now.

"The wheels are already turning Marga. I do hope that in the future I can turn to you for help if we run into any other problems?"

There it was, the hook. "Anything at all Jacinta. Anything at all!"

Jacinta Rivera returned with her husband to their table. A smile of satisfaction on her face.

Chapter 4 – *'A favor granted.'*

On the Friday morning following the Ball *Doña* Jacinta Flores de Rivera made a telephone call to the Civil Airport where their Gulfstream was parked. The Management Company that handled their aircraft, answered. Jacinta gave Marcos Applebaum, the Supervisor, instructions to terminate Juanita Gomez forthwith and to provide her with the benefits due by law. He should add two thousand dollars to the final amount to be paid. Juanita would have no reason for complaint. She also told him that discretely, Juanita should be given excellent references and mentioned that she would not be upset if Applebaum assisted her with getting new employment. This wouldn't be difficult. The Applebaum's were a large family of business people, stalwarts in the Jewish community.

Now, believing that Marga Smith had in no way pushed her to do anything, she called for her car and Driver and returned her diamonds to Secure Vault. While there she managed to devour three delicious *empanadas*.

Also, on that Friday morning, President, Ricardo Smith, took a ride on the Presidential Citation Sovereign to the northern border. Aboard was the Commander of the National Defense Force and his Deputy. They were to make an inspection of the Block Force in place to prevent smugglers, terrorists and other assorted unwanted characters from crossing over the jungle borders into the Republic. The President's Personal Assistant, Pricilla Alvarez, accompanied them.

During the hour flight and there the President had plenty of privacy to speak with Pricilla regarding appropriate dress. She pouted for a little but after spending fifteen minutes alone with him in his private quarters, she returned to the front cabin with a smile on her face.

During the return flight the President radioed his office and had his Chief of Staff prepare the Airport Highway contract for immediate signature. At four in the afternoon he called Carlos Rivera to let him know he had done his part. Carlos told him that Jacinta had completed her side of the bargain so all was well. They exchanged mutual respects and closed their respective telephones.

Juanita Gomez got a call from Marcos Applebaum at two o'clock on Friday afternoon. He said to come in immediately. By three o'clock Juanita was on her way back home. In her purse she had a check for severance for her two years' service and an envelope with two thousand dollars enclosed, in 'special regard' for her assistance. The Rivera's were cutting down on expenses Applebaum explained. Juanita however, had no doubts why she was being fired.

Once home she called Ramon Moreno. He had just arrived at his farm after working a morning shift.

"It's me. Get your ass over here right away. We need to talk!" She closed the telephone, confident he would arrive shortly.

Sure enough, in twenty minutes the access intercom sounded and she buzzed him in.

"I got fired today. If I thought it had anything to do with what I told you about the President and Pricilla Alvarez I'd kill you!" she looked daggers at him.

"Darling. How could you accuse me of such a thing? I would never hurt you. You know that." He was the consummate actor.

Mollified somewhat by his show of surprise, she calmed down.

"Well anyway. I think somehow the President's wife heard something and asked Jacinta to fire me. The bitch!"

"Now dear. Calm down. It's just a job. I'm sure that there's plenty of other opportunities out there!"

"Hypocrites all of them! Everyone talks about everyone else and I get in trouble for a tiny indiscretion. It's not fair.

I bet they got together yesterday when they went to pick up their jewels and had a good time stabbing me in the back. *Putas*, all of them."

"Take it easy. What's done is done. What exactly did they say to you?"

"Well, old Applebaum, the Supervisor, told me the official reason for getting rid of me was that the Rivera's were cutting down on staff. Unofficially I know it had to do with what I said about Pricilla. I got everything I was due plus a bonus of two thousand dollars. He also hinted he might get me another position with *'mishpocheh'*. The Jewish families here are very close. I have to wait a few days and he'll send me to an interview."

"That's great! You came out smelling like a rose!"

"That's what you say. All those old bitches sitting round in Secure Vault eating the Cohen's *empanadas* and talking about me! I hate them!"

"Is that what they do in there? I always have to stay with the car. They call as soon as a client is ready and you have to be down the ramp and at the pickup pretty quickly or the security measures start up and then you have to go around and wait until you get cleared again."

"I went in with Jacinta once depositing and picking up. It's very well decorated but being in the basement there's no windows or anything. You can have coffee or Champagne with those great *empanadas*."

"Christ! Imagine the wealth that the Cohen's have in there. It must be tens of millions! Marga's emeralds alone are insured for half a million. I know because she told Flora Constantino that in the car the other day."

"It would serve them right if someone stole the lot. Then the fights with the insurance company's would start and we could all sit back and enjoy ourselves. Now, come over here. I intend to do to you what Jacinta Rivera just did to me."

For the next hour all that was heard was heavy rain against the large picture windows of Juanita's apartment.

Chapter 5 – *'A new job for Juanita.'*

It was not until the following Friday that Ramon and Juanita met again. They ate dinner and returned to his farm to pass an idle evening.

Juanita lay back on her pillows. Marcos Applebaum phoned during the week and she had an interview with Levi Cohen of Secure Vault on the Monday. Levi was a cousin of Marcos and as Jacinta had astutely noted, family always obliged family.

As they lay there Juanita started to think out loud.

"I keep thinking about those jewels. Hundreds of millions. That's a lot of money. What say we steal some of it?" Ramon laughed.

"Sure. I'll just walk in and tell the Cohen's to hand over some *empanadas* and a few jewels. That should work!" He laughed again.

"Shut up! Think. Can it be done? If so, how?"

"It's impossible. Secure Vault has a half dozen guards on duty most of the time. They're all armed with Heckler and Koch MP7's with forty round magazines. The 30mm ammunition can go through body armor! I learned about these when the President sent me to that Driver Defense School in Miami last year."

"Ok smart guy. Apart from the guards what do they have?"

"Well. They're located in a basement with no windows. Then inside I guess they have about a thousand deposit boxes. They must be tough to break into!"

"So. We're talking of stealing millions but we don't know shit about the place we're intend to rob! Unless we get a great deal of information, it's a waste of time to keep contemplating."

"Jesus Juanita. Are you serious about this?"

"Why not? If I get the job Monday I can find out a lot. Let's get all the info together and then see what might be possible. Agreed?"

"Agreed. My bosses are going to the country place tomorrow afternoon. Marga always gets stuff out of the Vault before they leave. I'll keep my eyes open. Let's see what kind of information I can get."

"Fine with me. Let's meet here next week. That give us both a few days to investigate. I'll call you to tell you which day so we don't cross each other up, I'll stick to what's inside you stick to the outside."

That agreed upon, Ramon left, but before he walked out of the door Juanita could have sworn he had a strange look in his eyes.

It's incredible what one can find out these days with a little personal investigation and the help of the Internet. So many of the previous inaccessible answers to questions are available to all, with some research.

Ramon went home and sat at his computer. He had agreed to stick to the 'outside' elements. Typing in 'Secure Vault' he hit 'enter'. There were many entries, but none pertaining to the Cohen's business. He tried again putting in the country name and then the words 'Secure Vault.' There it was. 'Cohen's Secure Vault'.

The description took the enquirer to the Secure Vault web page which told Ramon it was the 'Premier' safety deposit company in the Republic. It had its own security force, eliminating any possible corruption from outside sources. They were armed with Heckler and Koch MP7's. The site didn't mention what kind of ammunition they used.

The prices of the boxes were listed along with sizes. Deposit and redemption hours were included. You couldn't walk into Cohen's, you had to telephone for an appointment. Then if your credentials were approved, either Jacob or Levi Cohen would set up a meeting. It went through the steps to be taken. Finally, it boasted that it had never had a robbery attempt in its twelve years of existence. Very impressive!

He was thinking; it doesn't say much about the location, just the fact that there were multiple guards on duty at all times. Why? Ramon pondered the reason. It hit him at once. This wasn't a bank Vault. It was a regular office building with a basement that relied on human beings and not steel and concrete to protect it. It had to be vulnerable. The armed guards gave the impression of safety. Now, who did he know that might be able to help? Then an idea entered his head. Someone he had spoken to, not so long ago. Someone who had struck Ramon as being an adventurous type and not having any problems whether what he was doing was strictly legal.

He looked up his contact list and found the man who he was looking for. They had been together on the Drivers Defense course the year before. Samuel Harris was his name. He called up Skype on his PC and dialed a 44 prefix number for the UK.

Sam Harris was a Cambridge graduate who had studied History and had decided that he wanted to see action and not Museums. He had applied for and was accepted to do the forty-four week Sandhurst course. He went from there straight into 1 Para, the First Battalion of the Parachute Regiment. This is where most of the SFSG (Special Forces Support Group) troops are drawn from. Later when seeking employment he always omitted with whom and where he had served but when asked for references, those he supplied were more than adequate. Right now he had no job. He was last employed as a 'protector' for a private currency dealer. This was terminated when an investigation of his finances by the Inland Revenue turned up irregularities. He was presently awaiting trial. Sam was fine for a few months but he needed to find something soon. When his telephone rang he was about to go to bed, aware that his bank account would need replenishing within ninety days.

"Sam? It's Ramon Moreno. We were together in Miami on that Driver Defense course last year."

"I remember you well Ramon. We had a few nights out if I recall!" He laughed to himself. Yes! They had been out and enjoyed themselves. They didn't overdo it because the course was difficult, and you needed your wits about you. Moreno was a good driver and Sam remembered he worked for the President of his country. This might be interesting.

"Right Sam. We did. Look, I don't know if you are the person I need to speak to but I recall you saying you studied art, and that you had been an Army officer. Let me read you the following memo I put together and you tell me if my hunch is right."

"Sure, I could do with an interesting story right now. Shoot."

Ramon picked up on his curiosity. He had no memo to read but he could ad-lib well with the assistance of the on-line brochure.

"Here we go then. 'Secure Vault' is a safe depositary company owned by the well know businessmen Jacob and Levi Cohen. They manage one thousand boxes of all sizes. Secure Vault is located in the basement of the National Security Insurance Company, a ten-floor building in the City's banking area. It has its own protection force with armed guards on premises twenty-four hours a day. They have never had a security problem. It's estimated (and Ramon made this up) that Secure Vault has under its care over one hundred million dollars of wealth at any time. Clients alone have access to the boxes. There is no 'dual access'. This ensures absolute safety and confidentiality as the client is the only one who can gain access to his or hers receptacle.' That's a précis of why I called." He stopped speaking, waiting for a response.

"Interesting Ramon but where do I come in?"

"Sam. Secure Vault isn't as secure as their brochure would like you to believe. There may be a chance to breach what there is with minimum risk and reap the rewards. I have a partner who has inside information and we think there is an opportunity for a substantial unauthorized withdrawal. Are you interested in coming over for a visit so we can talk further?"

"Providing you pay my first class airfare, my food and put me up at a four-star hotel I could come for a few days. No promises mind you."

"Sam. Buy yourself a discounted ticket on the Internet. You can stay at my farm. I'll pay meals and a taxi back to the Airport if you decide not to participate. You'll need a visa from the Consulate in London. They open Saturday's. It will take a day. E-mail me as soon as you get things fixed."

"Ah what the hell! I wasn't busy right now anyway. I'll see you Wednesday hopefully. Lookout for the e-mail."

And with that, Sam hung up.

The next morning he called the Consulate, and they told him he needed to present his fingerprints certified by an authorized agency and a form, signed by a medical facility, listing his blood type. These two items, along with two passport photographs would entitle him to a ninety-day visa. It could be issued immediately.

He got dressed and caught a bus to the City. It took most of the morning to get the papers he required and at the blood bank they made the inevitable request as to whether his would like to donate his rare O-negative blood. However, once these were in hand he went to the Consulate and filled in the form for a visa. At three thirty he stopped by a discount travel agency and reserved a flight to the Republic for early Monday. The return date he left open. When he got home he emailed Ramon the details.

Chapter 6 – *'Information.'*

Ramon reported for work Saturday, sure the President's wife would call him to drive her to Secure Vault. She might meet friends there and stay for a while for coffee and the Cohen *empanadas*. At that time he could take a look inside the National Security Insurance Company building.

At ten o'clock Ramon eased the Mercedes down the tight winding access road to the basement entrance of Secure Vault while Marga called to announce her arrival. Ramon opened the car door, and she went in with Jacob Cohen who greeted her.

He drove up the ramp, parked on the first floor and adjusting his *guayabera* so it concealed his firearm, he walked through the side door into the Lobby. It was deserted, vacations had started.

The receptionist at the Desk looked up and smiled at him. The Presidential staff all wore dark blue *guayabera's* with the gold and red Presidential seal on the left-hand pocket. She assumed he must be at the building on business. Probably, like everyone else of importance, returning or picking up jewelry before the noon deadline. She beckoned him over.

"Hi! I guess you work for the President?" Ramon looked carefully at her. She missed being pretty due to her thin lips and eyeglasses but he could see a nice top half over the high counter.

"That's right. The uniform is a dead giveaway. The Presidential Service." He smiled at her and held her gaze until she demurely looked away.

"I bet it's exciting close to all the famous people?"

Ramon saw an opportunity looming and cast his line.

"Well. It depends. You realize I can't say anything about my work. We are all sworn to secrecy in this job."

"Oh! Of course not!" She blushed. "You must have something important to do. How can I help?" She had taken the bait.

He leaned closer over the counter and said in a low voice. "I'm just observing the security here. The First Lady is at Secure Vault so I need to check things out." He winked at her and she blushed again.

"Well everything is protected here. You know there's no access to Secure Vault from the main building."

"None? Not even via the elevator?"

"No. When Secure Vault purchased the basement they fixed it so the elevators don't go below this first floor. To get in downstairs you go to the basement entrance or through the door you came through to the parking lot. You know they have all those guards on duty." She removed her glasses. Blinking a few times she continued.

"This Desk is open until nine each evening except Saturday and Sunday. There's someone here seven in the morning to nine at night weekdays. That's because the National Insurance Company has people to take details of accidents that happen late. We work two shifts. One person works seven to two and the other two to nine. Weekends, there's just the morning person until noon Saturday when we close up. Anyone who doesn't turn up or who comes late three times is fired. They're very strict."

"Wow. That's pretty tight! What happens when maintenance has to be done in the building? Cleaning, painting, elevator problems."

"The cleaners come in weekday evenings at seven and must be out by nine o'clock. They sign in and sign out. Any painting is done early mornings on weekends. They make arrangements in advance. The Company doesn't want the smell around while there are clients in the building. As for the elevators they are checked every month. The Sanyo people usually tell us a few days before they come in. It's always on a weekend because we don't want one of the elevators out of commission during working hours. I don't work weekends but I understand they cordon off the elevator they want to work on and hang notices on each floor. When they finish they take them down, close everything up and leave. Very occasionally, if there's a big problem, they come Saturday, leave at noon and then return Monday to finish."

"I understand. Very efficient. I am sure my boss will be happy everything's under control. What's your name? She always likes to know about people that help us out."

"Oh thank you! My name is Dolores Matos."

"Dolores. Thanks. I'm Ramon Moreno."

He turned and walked towards the side door, waving as he passed through. She gazed after him, thinking thoughts that every twenty year old girl has occasionally. She put her glasses back on.

Ramon no sooner opened the Mercedes door when his phone rang. It was one of the security guards from the Vault to tell him that the First Lady would be at the entrance momentarily. He drove down to pick her up.

The President was leaving on a trip Saturday afternoon. Ramon would be free until the following Thursday. He drove the President to the heliport and then took the car back to the Presidential Residence. After picking up a few personal items he drove home to the farm outside the City where he had lived since his parents passed away. Then, he decided to take a nap.

When he awoke he checked his e-mails. Sam Harris would be arriving at three on Monday afternoon. He called Juanita and left a message for her to come over six o'clock Monday.

Most of Sunday he spent searching the Internet for information that would be needed. At five o'clock he realized he hadn't eaten lunch and not wanting to go out, he took a beer from the refrigerator and made himself a sandwich, staying working until eight. He watched the television for an hour before going to sleep.

Chapter 7 – *'Planning.'*

Ramon awoke early that Monday morning. He ate a bowl of cereal and then checked on Sam's flight. It was scheduled for a two-thirty arrival, slightly earlier than anticipated. Then he typed and printed, all the information he had gleaned to date. He made three copies. When he finished he fixed the pull-out couch bed and then went to the nearest supermarket to stock up on groceries and beer. He also bought two extension cords for their computers.

He ate lunch and called Juanita. She said she got the job at Secure Vault after her interview with Levi Cohen and started work Tuesday. She could be at his place by six. It was a forty-five minute drive to the Airport, but the farm was on the way so traffic would be light. He left at one thirty to give himself plenty of time.

Most people were already at the beaches and others at relatives country homes in the interior. He parked and walked into the arrival's area. The flight was announced and ten minutes later Sam walked out carrying a shoulder duffle. They shook hands and exchanged the usual amenities on their way to the car. Driving to the farm they talked.

Forty-five minutes later Ramon had told Sam about the two big yearly social events and how they affected Secure Vault. He added what he thought could be the most important thing of all.

"The main elevators only go from the first to the tenth floor. The shafts go all the way down to the basement but not the elevators. When Secure Vault bought the space they did something, I don't know what, to prevent them from descending any further than floor one. I think that may be our entry point. Why do I say this? Because the elevator used to go down to the basement so the exit doors are still there!"

"Sounds like it. They wouldn't have to do much to stop the elevator at the first floor. Make the adjustments in the main control box. That's usually located for convenience right on the ground floor. All it would take was for the technician to punch in the access code for the basement and then disable it with another code. However, we need to be sure."

They arrived at the farm shortly after three and spent the next half an hour getting Sam settled on and showing him where everything was. Juanita arrived at six.

After the introductions they sat around the central coffee table and took out their respective computers and plugged them in. Ramon had an excellent high-speed wireless Internet connection and everyone logged on.

Ramon started the ball rolling by repeating what Dolores Matos had told him.

"I've told Sam what this is all about and he agrees with me it sounds feasible to get into Secure Vault if the planning is right. That's why we are here. To discuss everything. I've got all my notes and we will go over them in a minute. I agreed with Juanita that my job would be anything outside and she would try to get the information about anything inside. Of course, things will overlap. That's not a problem and will allow us to compare our notes. So, here's what I've got."

Ramon handed them copies of his notes and read through them, explaining everything he had learned from Dolores Matos. When he finished, Juanita took out her own annotations.

"Well, you are looking at the new Office Manager for Secure Vault! The Cohen's are cousins of Marcos Applebaum, my ex-boss. I went there this morning and Levi and Jacob Cohen interviewed me and said to start tomorrow. They spent three hours telling me about the Company!"

She wouldn't be dealing with clients but was responsible for the guards and their schedules, the accounting and sending out bills. She had to order all supplies. Jacob told her he personally took his wife's famous *empanadas* each morning to the office to be gently heated in the microwave and offered to the clients. He told her the employees were forbidden to partake of the small, delicious pies!

Ramon couldn't believe his ears! He hugged Juanita and stroked her cheek.

"Incredible! Absolutely incredible. What a break! Tell us all about it."

Juanita, basking in Ramon's praise, started her story.

"Secure Vault is owned by the Cohen brothers, Jacob and Levi. Jacob is the glad-hander, greets the guests and plays nice as well as handling the financial side. Sarah, his wife is in charge of the *empanadas*." She smiled.

"Levi is operations, the staff, and everything on that side of the business. I'll work for him. My hours are Monday to Friday eight to five." She smiled.

"The business is well run. Been around twelve years. No losses or attempted robberies. They purchased the basement from National Security Insurance. Got a good price because no one wanted to be underground without windows. For the Cohen's it was ideal. They have no political affiliations and even provide segregated waiting rooms for the Democrats and Reformists. That's a left-over from years back when the parties were feuding. Things are different these days." She looked at her notes.

"Now for the details. They gave me a six page memo with all the details. The actual Vault itself is located at the middle rear of the property. There is a reception area inside the front door, about twenty feet across and eighteen feet deep."

"Levi took me all round the premises. There is one door guard, and another who patrols all around the offices. After the reception area you can turn right or left and enter one of the lobbies. These have comfortable arm-chairs and sofas to sit on while you wait to be called to your box. A guard sits behind a Desk in each Lobby. At the front of the Vault, to the left of the front door, is office space for the administration. I'll work there. To the right are the Cohen's offices and a kitchen." She keyed her computer and started reading again.

"The whole Vault is lined with quarter-inch stainless steel. Between the actual Vault entrance and the divider between the lobbies, there is a small space. There are two guards located here. One for the entrance door from the reception and Lobby, and one for the actual Vault door. The Vault door is six feet wide and eight feet high and is made of stainless steel. It's opened with a card. One guard always has a card. Levi Cohen has another."

"The boxes run across the rear of the Vault. On the right are four cubicles where clients can take their drawers and examine them on a table. As far as I could estimate, the elevator shafts are behind where these cubicles sit. There are light doors on each of the cubicles for privacy. Electric receptacles and cable Internet are available in each cubicle. The Vault is protected by an Ansul Halon fire suppression system. The temperature is maintained at seventy degrees."

"There are nine hundred and forty boxes. Nine hundred and ten are in use, meaning rented out right now. Prices range from two hundred dollars a month for the largest box down to fifty dollars a month for the smallest one. The boxes are an obscure brand, made in Brazil." She removed a print showing a rack of boxes from her folder and they passed it around.

"Trust the Cohen's to buy something like that, probably got a discount. Note one thing, there are two card slots on the box. I'll explain my thoughts about that later. Levi didn't explain the reason. The lock has four anchor points similar to most modern boxes. All the locks are wired back to a central computer in the Vault. The cards are all-pre-programmed with the box number printed on them and loaded with the entry data."

"The guard lets you into the Vault ante-chamber. Before you enter the Vault proper you put your own card into the reader and your thumb on a pad that reads the print. A central computer checks both and if they match the Vault proper will open. You're probably asking 'what if you lose your card and someone else picks it up?' Nothing can happen.

The combination of card and print have to match or there's no entry into the Vault proper. Lost cards can be replaced and a new one programmed. There is a machine for that. They use it because the customer will retain the same box but the new card will have a different code." She smiled and looked at her computer again.

"I won't bother you with the P and L of Secure Vault but I can tell you, it's healthy. Weekdays there are seven armed guards, one of these who relieves each of the others for any breaks, bathroom, lunch, or anything else. There's two catering and cleaning staff and four office employees plus the Cohen brothers, one of whom is always on duty."

"It's simple. The client phones ahead for a withdrawal or deposit and gives the time of arrival. This is entered on a computer to which the front door guard has access. When the client gets out of their vehicle they produce an entry card, programmed with their data, and put this into a receptor. If everything checks out the guard releases the door lock, and they are buzzed in."

"The administrator finds out what is required and puts the details into the computer while the client goes to one of the two lobbies and sits down. Jacob Cohen or an assistant, depending who the client is, brings *empanadas* and coffee or Champagne is offered. When things are ready the Lobby guard advises the guest they can enter. He will approach and escort the client to the antechamber door in front of the Vault proper. The guard inserts his card and the door will open. Client enters, door closes. Client then inserts card in scanner and puts thumb on scan pad. Guard puts in his card and if everything checks out, the actual Vault door opens. Guard stays with the clients while they use their put their card key in the top slot to unlock their box. The security computer for opening the boxes themselves is kept right there in the Vault. It's not connected to any of the other systems." She checked her notes again.

"There is only one card per client and they boast there is no 'master card' kept by the owners. I don't think that's right. All those boxes have two slots for cards. Why, if the client is the only one with access?" She shook her head.

"I think, and this is a guess, that the Cohens have copies of all the box key cards. Of course, I can't swear to this, it's a hunch." She shrugged and continued. "We have to find out somehow,"

"The customer, or the guard, if the client wants, carries the box to a cubicle, and takes out or puts in items. Then the customer exits the cubicle, and the guard helps replace the box. The client is escorted from the Vault and may leave after having the administrator at the front door call for their vehicle. When it arrives the door guards open up, and that's that." She looked around.

"Just a couple more items. The Vault is closed on National Holidays. On the two special weekends during the year, when the charity events take place, the Company opens on the Saturday following the Thursday from ten to twelve. It's staffed then but I don't think I have to work. At noon everyone except five guards, leave. The two front door guards and the two in the space leading to the main Vault, stay. One extra guard roams around and does the reliefs. There is an alarm system that can be activated by a guard from the front door, the two administration offices or the security space leading to the Vault proper. It will sound in the Lobby of the building and trigger the police emergency number." She paused.

"To reiterate. There is one card key per client. If you lose it that's a problem. You must report it and then your security checks have to be re-done. No one can get into the Vault proper without their new card and a thumb scan. That makes for excellent security. No one can deposit or retrieve anything from the box until everything is changed in the Company computer. Clients will be charged a thousand dollars for a lost card. That's to cover all the inconvenience." She looked up and nodded her head.

"However, people like the idea no one can get in their box. Only the cardholder. No one else has a system like that in the Republic. Finally, the Cohens, and everyone else for that matter, believe that live guards with automatic weapons are the best solution for guarding valuables. It's just the fact that each box has two slots for cards. That has me intrigued. By the way, I will have a card to get me into the front door, nowhere else." She sat back on her chair.

"That's about everything I know as of now. After tomorrow I'll learn more." She looked over at Sam.

"Well Sam. That's our side of it. How about you talk about yourself and tell us what you can do to help pull this off."

Sam nodded. "Juanita, that's a huge amount of valuable information and it came at the right time. Now, how about a beer first? I've been on an aircraft for the past ten hours, I'm thirsty and I need to use the bathroom!" Everyone smiled. Ramon and Juanita went to the kitchen. There were beers in the fridge and Juanita put some snacks out. Once they were seated, Sam started talking.

"My name's Sam Harris. I attended University at Cambridge. I studied History and Arts and got MPhil in the History of Art and Architecture. As an officer in the British Army I served twelve years, mostly in Iraq and Afghanistan. First with 1st Battalion, Parachute Regiment. That's usually known as 1 Para. Then with the SAS, that's our Special Air Service Force for four years. When I got out I went to work for the Royal Army of Oman. The country is ruled by the Sultan, Qaboos bin Said al Said. There were quite a few of us training and leading their forces. I know the area and I know people. When I left there I went to work back in the U.K. as protection for a currency dealer. These people can make or break small countries by trading their currencies up or down. They are not liked and in constant danger. I was hired to protect one such man. The job paid well but my boss thought he was smarter than the U.K. revenue people and came a cropper."

"That was over a month ago. I'm not working right now. What I bring to the table is that I've done things that normal people never even dream about. I've been in situations where life or death decisions have to be made and I mean it was my life that was in the balance. Was I good at it? Well, I'm sitting here so there's your answer. I'm not bothered by taking chances. Not stupid chances but chances where the success rate is over fifty percent."

"I know weapons and I have a lot of contacts in my gray world. Some of them will provide the information lacking in your reports, which by the way, I thought were very good. Christ knows how and where you got the information but it's excellent." He sipped his beer.

"Now. You may have ideas, good ideas I might add, regarding entry into the Vault. We don't information on exactly how to get inside Secure Vault. We will need an elevator expert to tell us more about that. You don't have the information about how to get into the boxes. They may be discount boxes but the Cohens obviously know a thing or two. You saw from the picture that there are no external hinges to hammer off so it means either drilling, laser cutting or the sledge and pick method which I'll explain later. Of course, if Juanita is right and the Cohen's have copies of the cards, where do they keep them? Obvious answer is in a box in the Vault! Somehow Juanita needs to get to the bottom of that mystery. If she can find out, a hell of a lot of work can be saved." He pulled out a small notebook.

"You don't know what's in any one box. That means we need time to open a lot of boxes and cherry pick the best contents. Securities and stocks are no good. We want cash, valuable re-sellable jewelry and art or antiques. There may be pre-Columbian artifacts, burial grounds have been discovered here. We have to be careful about how much we can take out.

That will be decided once a plan is developed. We should be able to accomplish that during my visit. Then we need to get the merchandise out of the country and into the hands of someone who can buy if from us. The going rate we can expect for good jewelry is about forty percent of the value. The sixty percent or so we give up will get us the security we will need. That means our names won't be bantered around and everything will be kept under wraps." He drained his beer.

"Finally we have to get into the Vault itself. The quarter-inch steel lining must be breached or perhaps the door. We can't make a lot of noise. If the elevator doors in the basement exist that's our key. Let's talk about things."

It was six o'clock by the time the three had each given their presentations and they started to talk together. At eight Ramon phoned out for a pizza delivery and at nine they took a break after eating.

At midnight they decided they needed to sleep. It was agreed they would meet for lunch at noon the next day at Ramon's.

He promised that by the time they arrived he would have their preliminary ideas printed up to look at.

Juanita left and the two men went to bed tired but satisfied with the progress made.

They had agreed that the Arts Ball would be the ideal time to carry out their plan. That was scheduled to take place on, January 16th, a Thursday.

Chapter 8 – *'Oman.'*

At midday on Tuesday the 22nd of December they met for lunch at Ramon's farm. He had been up since eight, preparing the initial plan and then printing up the copies. He also made a list of what they would need and who would do what for the next twenty-four days.

The requirement list was separate from the plan. It outlined tasks for each of them. Sam must return to Europe and then go to Asia to meet with his middle-east contacts. He would find out everything about the elevator and what was needed so it could possibly be used in in the heist. Ramon's job was to focus on the laser cutting equipment, high-speed drills, bits and the pick and sledge necessities. Juanita was responsible for the timetables and the entry. She had to investigate the second slot in the boxes and if the Cohen's possibly kept copies of cards. If they did where did they keep them?

At the luncheon they agreed on a third split of the profits after deducting expenses incurred. That afternoon Sam arranged a flight home for late Tuesday evening. Ramon dropped Sam off at eight o'clock for his ten-hour flight. They shook hands and wished each other luck.

On the aircraft, Sam started to put out feelers through e-mails to the people that he thought might provide him with information. He sent messages and took care what he said. He was satisfied that he gave nothing away. By the time he landed at Heathrow, there were replies to some of these, agreeing to speak with him upon his return to London. He took the Heathrow express to Paddington and then a taxi to his flat near Bayswater Road. It was six o'clock and traffic was accumulating.

There was a small fast-food shop on the corner of his street and he picked up a sandwich before going into his building. He didn't unpack but took the list of people to call and sat down at the telephone.

It was ten on Wednesday morning in Oman and his first call went to a contact there. One by one he dialed his numbers. Few calls lasted for more than five minutes. Others were not so successful and after an exchange of greetings, terminated even more quickly. By noon he had spoken with the people who replied to his e-mails. He finally went to the kitchen, made tea and then ate his sandwich.

Then he walked two blocks to the mail box he rented. He found only one flyer in it. His Company, 'Sam-Art' used the box as an office address. He paid all his bills this company. It was convenient

He now had a plan and where might get help. Using the Internet he made reservations to fly to Oman. He arranged a flight via Qatar that evening. Then there was a short hop from there to Muscat. It would leave at eight fifteen and arrive at just after four in the morning Thursday after a stopover in Qatar.

Arriving in Oman he checked into the Samara Hotel in Al-Khuwair, about fifteen minutes from the Airport. Turning the air conditioning up high he slept until ten in the morning. At the coffee shop in the Lobby he ordered coffee and toast and then made his first call. It was to an old Cambridge and Army friend who, like Harris, had opted for the military instead of the world of Art. He was attached to the recently formed Oman Border Security Brigade,

Dan Watkins, happened to be an intelligence officer with an eye for business deals. He was expecting the call, and they arranged to meet for lunch at the Hotel at noon.

It was a good meeting for Sam. Dan gave him contact names for two persons who might be interested in any valuable jewelry available, no questions asked. He also told Sam an art dealer would call him. Watkins was an inquisitive man but when Sam told him that his enquiries had nothing to do with intelligence in the middle-east, he politely kept quiet, telling Sam to give him an hour to contact the people he mentioned and then to make his calls. He made it clear he had an interest in any deal and would help out. After lunch Sam returned to his room and later, spoke with two people. His first meeting was downstairs in the Hotel at eight o'clock. His man, wearing a smart business suit, came directly to his table.

"Good evening Mr. Harris. My name is Amari. Major Watkins called me. That is why I am here. Tell me, when did you arrive?" They drank Turkish coffee and talked generalities for twenty minutes. Then Amari got down to business.

"Mr. Harris. I understand there is jewelry for sale. May I ask, stones or set pieces?"

"Set pieces. Emeralds and diamonds."

"This is not a problem. However, the pieces have to be dissembled to avoid any recognition. These days many pieces are recorded by the insurance company's and there is an excellent shared database to look up stolen items. Not of course that I am saying you are handling stolen goods!" He smiled at Sam.

"If you break them up does that deflate their value by much?"

"It certainly does. Half the value is in the setting. However, good stones can be sold anywhere."

"What might I expect per carat?"

Amari laughed.

"If this were an ideal, less complicated world I could give you a quick course entitled 'gem pricing for beginners', but alas the world of stones is not so simple. The price is as complicated as their color. There is no fixed list for gems. If there was, everyone would want one. Ah! If I only understood everything about pricing stones I would be a rich man. Nobody knows it all, believe me. It's a world of color and shapes. Hues, tones and a hundred other things. There are many factors that determine the price per carat of stones. Here is a very simple example; a one carat stone could cost five hundred dollars. However a stone of two carats does not automatically cost a thousand dollars. That's because a two carat is rarer and therefore costs a good deal more. The most important colored gems are rubies emeralds and sapphires. Diamonds are something else!" Amari looked at him and raised his eyebrows.

"Stones rarer than others, command a higher price per carat. Rubies are far more rare than saphires. A Burma ruby is priced higher than a Thai ruby because it is rarer than the Thai!" He drank the dregs of his coffee.

"So, what it comes down to really is the exclusivity of the stone and finally what a dealer will purchase it for after calculating his re-sale price and adding profit. I have to see and examine a stone before I put a price on it. That means you have to show me the stones, I price them and an exchange, stones for currency takes place. It does not take long to examine a stone. If you had a hundred fair sized stones we could be finished in an hour. The smaller stones we lump together and a lot price given. I'm sure you don't want to wait around while each one was individually examined?" They ordered more coffee.

"Anyway. I know this is boring but let's get to what you want. An estimate perhaps? I saw a Columbian emerald of thirty-four carats sell for under nine hundred thousand retail. That about twenty-five thousand a carat. On the other hand, a one carat emerald might sell for four thousand a carat. There are many one carat stones but few of thirty-four carats. See what I mean? Exclusivity! We have to look at them and I would give you a price. It will be far less than a jeweler might pay but selling to me buys silence. That's important, no?"

"Very important. The goods will be available before the end of January. I'll call you to advise my itinerary. Can you arrange the necessary security?"

"That will not be a problem. I suggest first you bring pictures and perhaps, a sample. Someone will be at the Airport. When you step off the aircraft you will be taken through Customs and Immigration as a valued visitor. If you have any doubts call Watkins. He will tell you what you want to know." They shook hands and Amari left. Sam's next appointment was at ten o'clock so he went to his room to freshen up.

At ten he returned to the coffee shop again. A man in Arab robes approached his table. "Mr. Harris. Mr. Watkins said you would be here. I am called Ghali." His English was not as polished as that of Amari.

Sam rose to shake hands, and they ordered coffee. Again the niceties were exchanged for fifteen minutes and then Ghali started business proper. He adjusted his long white cotton robe and straightened his headdress.

"Mr. Harris you have jewelry to sell?" He looked expectantly at Sam as if the items would be produced then and there at the table.

"I'm sure Mr. Watkins told you Mr. Ghali, I might have jewelry for sale. Right now that jewelry is not with me here in Oman."

"When will you have it then?" He seemed in an awful hurry.

"Perhaps in a month, maybe a little longer. I'm not sure. However, if you are interested I will call you when I return?"

"So. You do not have it now? You are sure?"

"I'm sure."

"Well then Mr. Harris. I will bid you a good evening. Without the jewelry present I can do nothing. I hope you will contact me when and if you come back. Here is a card." He passed a small rectangle of cardboard across the table. There were Arabic letters on it.

"Thank you. When I have the items I will call I appreciate you coming here today, my apologies for the disappointment. Please forgive me." They shook hands and Ghali left.

Harris went up to his room. He felt exhausted. Despite the coffee, he couldn't sleep so he walked to the Al Zawawi Mosque, illuminated and shining like gold in the moonlight.

The calmness of the location relaxed him and after half an hour he walked back to the Hotel. As he walked, he realized that tomorrow was Christmas day.

The telephone rang at ten in the morning, waking him from a deep, jet lag sleep. It was Watkins.

"Good morning Sam. Dan here. Look, it's Christmas Day, not that they celebrate in Oman! I'll pick you up in an hour, take you to my elevator man and we can come back to my place for lunch. I have six bottles of Bodegas Hermanos Sastre 'Pesus' from Ribera del Duero. They were given to me for a small favor I did. Knowing your tastes, you will be in heaven!"

"That's great Dan. I'll be outside in an hour." He hung up and got ready.

In the shower he wondered about the 'small favor' Dan had done to be rewarded with six bottles of the Spanish wine. From experience he was sure it retailed at close to three hundred dollars a bottle!

An hour later Dan dropped him off at a café and pointed out his contact. "That's Aamir. He's expecting you. I'll be back here in thirty minutes."

Aamir turned out to be a friendly person. He stood, and they shook hands and then, in the usual Arabic way, they slipped into a conversation which entailed Sam telling him of his service on the Yemen border and the problems there. Aamir told him he had served with the Jebel Regiment in the interior of the country. After the accepted niceties Sam opened the conversation proper.

"Tell me about elevators Aamir. Sanyo SEE CPO1 forerunners. I'll take notes and you talk."

"Ok Sam. Stainless steel frame with PVC floor. Acrylic top panels. Door steel. PVC floor. Usually built for a thousand KG capacity but can go to two thousand if necessary. I can give you shaft sizes and control room dimensions." He smiled.

"No. Not necessary thanks. Is the shaft enclosed and where do they put the computer controls on these?"

"The shaft isn't enclosed. It will have steel girders and these will support the actual elevator runners. You could see the concrete walls of the building if you were unlucky enough to be between floors when the doors opened! The computer control box they usually put in an accessible place. By the side of the elevators on the first floor. It will be built into the wall. There may be another auxiliary box in the basement."

"OK. Now a hypothetical question. If I had such an elevator in my building and it went from a basement to ten floors. What if I wanted to stop the elevator at the first floor and eliminate access to the basement permanently?"

"Simple. You go to the computer box and program it. It can be done with a few key strokes. If you wanted it to be really permanent you would seal the basement doors. That's easy to do. Weld a steel bar across from girder to girder not touching the door, to avoid damage. If you want access later, remove the bar."

"Can anyone program the computer?"

"Well. What you will find is that the companies that sell elevators always have highly trained technicians to maintain them. However, providing the elevator doesn't have a problem, a layman may do this with simple instructions."

"Could you do this, you know, a diagram with the instructions all written out?"

"Come here tomorrow, same time. You will have your diagram. No charge. A favor from one soldier to another!"

Dan pulled up to the curb and the two men shook hands. Sam climbed into the SUV.

"Get what you wanted?"

"Yes. Thanks Dan. Ghali didn't pan out but Amari certainly is a great contact."

"Well, you can't win them all! Now let's get food and try that wine. I'm waiting to hear from my antiques and art man. I hope he'll call today. When do you go back?"

"If I can finish tomorrow then Sunday at the latest. I have to see Aamir again. Then your art guy, and that's it."

He hoped he might finish up and get home as quickly as possible. There was a lot to do. After an excellent lunch and a bottle of wine inside of him, Sam returned to the Hotel. It took an hour to update his notes and then he went to bed.

The next morning he walked to the café and found Aamir waiting. A large manila envelope rested on the table in front of him. After exchanging the usual greetings, Aamir handed him the envelope.

"Sam. Everything you need to know about the elevator is in here. I made out a list of instructions that any technician would carry out doing maintenance. It shows you how to stop the elevator between floors for work to be done but more important it explains how to get the elevator from the first floor down to the previously blocked basement by imputing the right codes." He tapped the envelope.

"As a bonus there's a master key in there that will fit your SEE CPO1 control box and the elevator itself. You shouldn't have any problems."

"How do I thank you Aamir? This is terrific!"

"Perhaps one day you may able to assist me my friend. Until then, go in peace."

They said their goodbyes and Sam returned to the Hotel. He had a message at the Front Desk. Watkins note said that he should meet 'Caleb' at noon in the coffee shop. Caleb would know him.

It was a fruitful meeting. Caleb, an experienced dealer, understood both sides of the business. The above board and the below board. Sam was interested in the second of these skills. After their introductions he explained to Caleb that there might be art for sale. It wasn't art that might be offered at auction. Caleb nodded.

"I understand Mr. Harris. You know that the Art Loss Register has over four hundred thousand stolen works on file. To sell a known work on the black market expect to get less than ten percent of its true price if you are lucky. That's why the stolen Cezanne masterpiece 'Boy in a Red Waistcoat' got returned in two thousand twelve. Much too hot to handle!"

"So you are telling me that art isn't a good deal, the kind I'm talking about?"

"Artifacts are better. Bring me something from the tomb of Qin Shi Huang for instance. Something that has never been seen. That's what you need to do. Best of all, some of the Inca artifacts or pre-Columbian gold items. Those I can sell for an excellent price. Private collectors love them. So forget paintings Mr. Harris!"

The talked for a further ten minutes and Harris was impressed with Caleb's honesty. He didn't offer anything he couldn't deliver. They parted company after exchanging telephone numbers.

Back in his room, he made a reservation for the afternoon flight to London. He called Watkins to thank him and tell him he'd call when he had more news. He then mailed Ramon saying he would return on the 12th and to pick him up after he arrived.

Chapter 9 – *'Moving forward.'*

Juanita started at Secure Vault on the Tuesday. A quick learner, she picked up fast as Levi spent the next three days going over her duties.

All Juanita had to do now was to find out the mystery of the two card slots on the boxes and whether the Cohen's did actually have duplicate cards. If so, where did they keep them? As it turned out the answer to that question appeared a few days later.

Levi asked her if she would work over Christmas and she put in a full shift on the 24th and 25th. He also told her that the annual Company dinner would be on January 16th.

The memo that Levi had given her outlined the operations of the Vault. She studied this when she arrived home from work each day. In the office she also learned a lot more. The list of clients and their addresses for billing were password protected and stored in the computer system. Juanita, as Office Manager in charge of the billing, received the code. Levi said there were nine hundred and ten boxes in use.

She stayed, like a very conscientious employee, after the office staff lad left at noon Christmas Day. Then she entered her code and accessed the billing list. Box number, size, price charged and a blank space for any notes. All were listed. She saw nothing unusual there. Pricing constant, boxes in numerical order.

She went through page by page, there were fifty entries per page. On page nineteen the last entry appeared on line nine. Something didn't add up. If nine hundred and ten boxes were in use the last line should be line ten, not line nine. One box in the system wasn't listed! It took ten minutes to find it. On page fourteen the numbers went from seven hundred one to seven hundred thirteen. Then continued with seven fifteen.

Number seven fourteen, one of the large sizes, wasn't included in the numerical order. Could that be the Cohen's box?

Although she believed she now had important information she still didn't know for sure why there were two slots on each box. Perhaps one for the client's card and one for the Cohen's? It might indicate the Cohens, in spite of their denial, had their own way of entry.

She had seen the Vault once. Only clients, the Cohen's and guards were allowed in there. She would have to hope her hunch turned out to be correct.

Ramon had been busy gather information and checking logistics. If Sam returned on 11th of January that gave them until the sixteenth, Saturday, before they would breach the Vault. They would have plenty of time. It closed at noon and wouldn't open until Monday at ten in the morning. He was assuming they would use the elevator shaft for entry. Front Desk staff and perhaps others were always at the National Security Insurance building until noon Saturday. The Desk had to be convinced that the Sanyo elevator people would be working there on the weekend.

He would need uniforms and a van with the Sanyo logo on it. Once inside, he had to find out how to get from the elevator shaft, into the Vault by cutting or breaking through a wall and the steel liner of the Vault. Next, how to get into the boxes? If Juanita's belief turned out to be right and the Cohen's had copies of the cards hidden in a box, it was simple. But if not?

How would they escape when they finished? What would be done with the proceeds of the robbery? There were a million things to be arranged and Ramon, after a very quiet Christmas, spent most of his days seeking answers on the Internet and most of his night worrying!

Oxy-fuel cutting is the oldest and simplest of the methods and it will go through quarter-inch steel easily. Concrete is simple, you use a hand-help pneumatic saw and diamond blades. A high-speed drill with diamond tipped bits was required to open the boxes if needed. Someone had to show him how to cut and drill but that wouldn't be a problem.

If Juanita's theory didn't pan out they might have to crack the boxes with a hammer and pick. Sam had told him about this. He had to get two pickaxes and a metal grinder to sharpen the points on the picks. Tongs and sledge-hammers were no problems to buy.

They needed a trolley to move items back and forth plus bags to store the proceeds. Hessian sacks would be best. Food and water might be required as they might spend quite some time in the Vault. He thought that a few blankets would help if it was cold down there.

On Monday the 28th Ramon left early in the morning on a shopping trip. He drove the two hundred miles to the frontier and after showing his passport, crossed into the next Republic.

Like all frontier towns it seemed bustling and busy. He checked into a Hotel and went downstairs to enquire where the stores he had looked up the day before were located. The owner helped him and using a small tourist map he marked the places.

When Ramon returned to his Hotel that evening the trunk of his truck contained the oxy cutting torch and a tank he would need. In addition, he had obtained a hand-held pneumatic saw and half a dozen diamond blades and a heavy duty high-speed drill with diamond tipped bits. Twenty feet of yellow security fencing with 'Danger' signs to attach to it, a sledge hammer, two stainless steel spikes, each five foot long, plus industrial tongs were all safely in the truck. The equipment was covered by throwing two dozen hessian sacks over it. To learn about cutting with the torch, he had spent the afternoon helping the owner of the place where he had purchased the torch, slice through several dozen old concrete pilings. They were needed for fill on a building site after being reduced in size. The owner laughed when Sam asked how much the lessons cost and said they were free as he had helped out a lot!

Tired, he slept early. The next morning, before returning, he found a graphics store and picked up an assortment of plastic letters, and a small mechanical logo machine with the cards it used. They would need ID's. Then he made a visit to a shop which supplied uniforms and got what he wanted there. There was a picture of a Sanyo technician servicing an elevator in an Internet announcement and had taken a note of the color of the uniform. He now had a very good match. Crossing the border ten minutes later, he started back.

He arrived at the farm before twelve. That afternoon he purchased a metal grinder and finally arriving back home he parked the car in the large garage and closed the door.

Once inside, he called Juanita to tell her what he had accomplished so far and what they planned for after the New Year's holidays. They agreed to meet on the second of January after she had seen her family for the festivities.

On Saturday the 2nd Juanita came over and they went to the garage where he showed her what he had bought. That afternoon she helped him grind the spikes to a sharp point. He took out the three uniforms, one small and two large. These could be altered as needed after he and Sam tried them on. She also told him about the Company dinner on the 16th at six o'clock. She would have to attend.

Transportation would be required for all the equipment Ramon had purchased, plus the items he still had to buy. Where would they get a vehicle to use? There were so many things to do. They went out for dinner to talk it over.

In London, Sam spent the next ten days visiting several Museums and shops. At the Victoria and Albert and the British Museum he spent time studying gems. In Hatton Garden, the precious stone center, he picked up more information. Finally, at a theatrical supply shop, he purchased wigs, plain lens eye glasses, stick on beards and mustaches. An idea formed in his head about how they might use them.

He arranged flights to New York and on to Tucson, Arizona where he would stay a few days and travel on to the Republic on the 11th. He found an inexpensive Hotel there, the Solimar, and made a reservation.

On January 8th he took a flight to New York and traveled down to Tucson. He wanted to see the Tucson Museum of Art, famous for its pre-Columbian pieces. After registering at a small Hotel in the downtown Presidio district, he walked to the Museum on North Main.

It housed an amazing collection, and he got a good idea of what were the most valuable items should they come across any in the deposit boxes he intended to rob. After e-mailing Ramon with his flight and Hotel details he flew to Miami, changed planes and got to the Republic in the afternoon of the eleventh of January. The flight arrived an hour late and Ramon waited around until he cleared Customs and then took him to the Solimar Hotel to register. He wanted to be sure he had a permanent address. That completed, they went to the farm. A call to Juanita confirmed she would be there at six o'clock.

While they waited for Juanita, Ramon showed Sam the items they had purchased. Sam felt particularly pleased with the sharpened steel spikes, convinced that these would do the job if the access cards were not found.

The ID's were finished. There were photos of Ramon and Juanita on two of them and they had trolled the Internet and found an old picture of Sam in the Army which they used for his card.

Juanita arrived, and they ate sandwiches and drank beer before getting down to business.

Point by point they covered all aspects of the robbery. They agreed the disguises were a master touch! Alibis were discussed, and they came up with a plan for those. One thing they decided was to get in and out as quickly as possible. They set a deadline of ten Saturday night. Being greedy wasn't smart. They would take what they could in the hours available. Then it might be a good idea to be seen in public after cleaning out the van at the farm. The City had a busy nightlife and arriving at a Hotel bar or club at midnight would be normal. When they had finished talking it was close to eleven o'clock. They arranged to meet again the next evening for an update.

In the morning Ramon drove Sam to a commercial vehicle rental company. There he signed up for a week's hire of a Ford Econo-Line, giving his Hotel as his address. They took the van to Ramon's farm and in the garage, started work on the decals.

That evening they met again and updated Juanita. The van had been thoroughly washed and left to dry out before the decals were attached the following day. Juanita would call the National Security Insurance Front Desk late Friday telling them the elevators would be serviced Saturday. It should be a fast job and they expected to be out when the building closed at noon. Their disguises were ready. The wigs, plain lens glasses, beards and mustaches laid out on the table. The stomach padding would come last of all.

There seemed to be nothing pending, except what they would do when the heist was complete!

Meanwhile, Sam could sleep at the Hotel and Ramon would call him about being picked up each morning. On the Wednesday they put the decals on the van. They looked very convincing. The uniforms were ready and Juanita had bought three baseball caps. The decals for these they made by mounting them in plastic holders. These were attached to the caps and jackets using small letters. Everyone would wear gloves throughout the entire operation.

Juanita explained about the Company dinner. She had to be there. It would also make a good alibi. Fortunately the restaurant was close to the National Insurance Company building. She could walk there in a few minutes.

Ramon and Juanita had their jobs to attend to and Sam stayed at the farm thinking about what to do after Saturday.

He also spent a long time studying the elevator diagrams given to him by Aamir.

When Ramon returned that evening he told him they had better have somewhere to get rid of the equipment when they finished. Ramon took him to the garage and found two shovels. At the side of the yard they dug a four foot pit beneath a pig-pen used when his parents had owned the farm. The dirt was piled by the side. Old, dirty straw could be laid on top when they finished.

Then, in the garage he showed Sam a hide under one of the large paving stones that made up the floor. The hide was invisible unless you were aware of it. The slab looked no different to all the others. There was however, a small hole that seemed to be an imperfection in the concrete at one end. Most of the stones had similar holes in them. Ramon went to a tool bench and from a shelf, pulled down a four foot length of wire with a tiny loop on one end. He walked to the stone and slipped it into the hole and turned it. Pulling on the wire, he met resistance and using his strength, lifted it from its resting place. Beneath lay a cement-lined box, big enough to hold a tall man.

"During the days of the Civil War some fifty years ago, this was a hide hole for patriots on the run. My father became involved in the resistance movement and often hid people here. If you look at one end you'll see a grill. It allows air in from between the gaps in the other stones. They don't meet perfectly and air circulates. This is ideal for hiding the proceeds."

Sam immediately agreed, and they returned to the main house. They both examined the plan over and over again and could find no problems with it. It only remained to get out with what they would be taking and return to the farm. If all went well no alarm would be given until the Cohen's arrived on Monday morning. Sam must stay at the Hotel until Wednesday and then return the van. At that point he would decide how and when to leave the country. Ramon dropped him off and took the van back to the farm. Sam stayed a few minutes in the Lobby talking to the Desk Clerk before taking his key and going up to bed.

Chapter 10 – *'The robbery.'*

Ramon and Juanita left the farm at nine thirty Saturday, and picked Sam up a few blocks from his Hotel. In the van he pulled on his overalls and fixed his facial hair. There was little traffic, and they got to the parking lot just after ten. Before exiting they checked each other's disguises. Sam had a blonde wig tied into a pony tail and protruding through the gap in the cap. He sported a fu-man-chu, mustache and thick-rimmed glasses. Ramon wore a dark wig, long and curly almost to his shoulders and a bushy black mustache. Juanita's hair fitted tightly under her cap. A full beard covered most of her face and she had on tinted glasses.

Ramon and Sam had padded out their trim waistlines with towels. The parking lot was filled with the cars of people returning their gems before the noon deadline. No one paid them any attention.

The side door was open and Sam and Ramon, dressed in their elevator repairman uniforms and sporting their wigs protruding from under their caps, their mustaches and beards, padded stomach's, and plastic gloves, walked through.

A bored Desk Clerk, more interested in his coffee, donuts and cell phone than in elevator service, waved them away as if to say 'go right ahead'. Sam went back to the van where Juanita waited. They loaded a toolbox, the 'Danger' signs and the yellow safety fence onto the trolley and pushed into the Lobby. The attendant stayed eating and talking on his phone. Ten feet from the Desk, only the top of his head was visible.

The safety fence were placed and 'Danger' signs hung. Juanita took the 'Elevator under Repair' signs and went floor by floor hanging them on the elevator key pads. Sam used Aamir's master key to open the computer box. His diagram appeared simple. First it highlighted in colored marker, which buttons to press to start the elevator in slow mode so they could stop it between floors. In a few minutes the doors were opened and Juanita reappeared. Sam started work. He hit the entries and with the doors open, the elevator rose slowly. Another keystroke and it stopped about five feet above the level of the first floor. Looking over the edge he saw nothing impeding its descent to the basement! He keyed the codes in to allow the elevator to descend. It sunk down until half the cab was below floor level. Keying again the elevator rose. Stopping it he looked into the gaping hole.

Concrete walls and the steel support columns were visible. Exactly what they wanted! At the Front Desk, the receptionist couldn't be seen. Walking forward, he caught a glimpse of the man's reflection in the smooth, tiled wall surface behind the counter. He sat with his phone to his ear. Perfect!

Two minutes later Ramon entered the elevator and went down to the basement. He pushed the 'open' button and saw a concrete wall. That's what he wanted to know. He banged on the door and Sam bought him up and listed to his report.

"Open the doors and there's the wall. Looks like the Cohens did everything on the cheap. Behind it should be the steel."

"Fine. The clerk isn't interested in us. Call out to him we are leaving everything here until Monday. Tell him the job needs more equipment or something and we will be back Monday. We will leave and then you get in the elevator and wait for my call. I'll go with Juanita. It's now eleven fifteen. At twelve fifteen we'll come back. He's only seen two of us so if you stay here, he'll be none the wiser." He looked towards the Desk.

"Check your watch. The elevator is programmed for maintenance. It will stay on the first floor and there should be no problem. The other one is working normally and can be used. When I call, open this one up and then go to the side door. It's a simple lever lock."

Ramon called out to the receptionist and saw an arm wave in acknowledgement. Then he nodded to Sam and entered the elevator. The door closed behind him.

Sam drove Juanita to her Bank's drive-in ATM. She withdrew fifty dollars and put the receipt in her handbag. They went to the drive-by window of a fast-food place. Sam took off his cap, wig and glasses and drove to the window. He ordered two coffees with milk and sugar to go. He paid with a credit card and saved the receipt. That was two alibis established. They drove back to the building and parked the van. His watch said twelve o'clock.

At twelve fifteen Ramon's phone rang. He punched the 'open' button and the elevator door slid to one side. The Desk Clerk had already left. He pushed the trolley across to the side entrance and opened it. Juanita went in while Sam and Ramon loaded the rest of their equipment. In the back of the van hung a garment bag. It contained a change of clothes and shoes for Juanita's dinner appointment, a mirror and her makeup kit.

Ramon pulled off his cap and mustache and wig, it was his turn to leave for a few minutes. He went to the van and drove out of the parking lot, along the seafront and then, five minutes later, turned into a branch of his Bank. In the drive-through lane he deposited his payroll check and took a receipt from the machine. When he got back to the building and parked, Sam and Juanita were waiting. All made sure they had their plastic gloves on.

They locked the side door and loaded the elevator. Sam keyed in the codes that allowed it to descend to the basement. When they opened the doors the concrete wall appeared inches away. Ramon started up the hand-help pneumatic saw with the diamond blades and cut across the top and then down the sides. The concrete crumbled into the elevator well. Behind it the steel wall could be seen. Next he used the oxy cutting torch to get through the wall. It sliced through like a hot knife through butter! He pushed hard and the thin steel buckled inwards.

The collapsed wall had collapsed on the table in one of the small booths. Sam climbed through, followed by Ramon who turned to help Juanita. As he did so, he brushed the jagged edge and winced as it cut through his overalls and sliced his arm. It was superficial, but a lot of blood ran down the wall and on to the floor. They stopped the bleeding with a handkerchief and bound it tightly with tape.

The deposit boxes were at the rear. They started by using the heavy duty high-speed drill with the diamond tipped bit on box seven fourteen. It took about three minutes to drill directly into and through the card slots, disabling the locks. Juanita pulled out the box and put it on a booth table. Lifting the metal cover, they counted twenty albums. Slipping open the first one they noticed it was similar to a business card holder, each containing a card in a plastic pouch. On every rectangle appeared a sticker with a number. There were fifty cards in each album. They had found the Cohen's weak spot!

"Ok. This looks like what we needed. It will save time and eliminate the noise. Juanita said the Vault was soundproof, but you never know, especially after seeing some of the other claims the Cohens made. We won't use the pick or the saw. Great! Now, we'll never open everything. There are far too many. Let's start with the bigger boxes first. This has to be all business, we can't stop to gape. Juanita can use the key cards, Ramon pulls open the boxes and I will go through them to see if we can find and separate the more valuable items."

"Ok here we go. The box numbers run across. Smaller ones are zero, zero, one, all the way to seven hundred, the bigger ones at the bottom will have numbers above seven hundred. Let's see how we do!"

She looked through and found an album starting with seven zero. Pulling out the first key card she found the box. Putting it into the bottom slot they heard a soft 'click'. "Well, the key cards are all pre-programmed like the originals. That's great!"

Ramon pulled out the large box. Surprised at the weight, Sam had to help him carry it to a table. He pulled back the lid. A row of gold coins glinted in the light of the neon overhead.

"Krugerrands. Half ounce. About five hundred bucks a piece. Too heavy for us. What's underneath?

Below the coins were packages of hundred dollar bills. Sam estimated thirty packs with a hundred bills to a pack, three hundred thousand dollars. They removed the money and returned and locked the box with the coins in it.

"Next box." She extracted another card and slotted it in. Again the soft clicking sound and Ramon removed the box. He lifted the metal lid and there below, cushioned in tissue paper, lay a crude pre-Columbian tiara of gold and emeralds, magnificent in its simplicity.

"That's a keeper. Probably worth more than a hundred thousand to a collector. Put that aside Ramon." He delved underneath finding half a dozen pieces of crude gold and bejeweled pre-Columbian broaches. "All good for sale. Keep a running total of the cash. Don't worry about the rest." Juanita made a note on a pad. All the boxes were put back and locked.

They started again. Many boxes had nothing but legal documents, deeds and shares. However, a great deal contained cash. By three o'clock Juanita said they had over three million dollars in various sized bills. There was also jewelry, loose stones and set pieces. Among these were Marga's emeralds and Jacinta's diamonds, both identified by papers in the respective boxes.

At five o'clock they had filed three of the hessian sacks with cash and another with artifacts and jewelry. Sam called a halt to the work.

"Look. We've opened over a hundred boxes and according to Juanita's notes, there's about ten million in cash, twenty in jewelry and I'm guessing another fifteen in artifacts. I believe we have enough. We can leave just before six and drop off Juanita at her dinner. Ramon and myself will go to the farm and get everything ready." They nodded in agreement.

"We drive into town and each goes his own way. Make sure you are seen and you use a credit card to pay for anything you eat or drink. I'll get a cab to my Hotel later. Same for Juanita. If she's asked why she didn't drive she can always say it's because she intended to have a few drinks. Ramon can go back to the farm. We replaced all the boxes. It will take days to find out which boxes were opened and what people will admit got stolen. Do you agree?" The both responded affirmatively.

"Tomorrow be seen! Go out, spend money and establish your alibi. Monday they will find out about the robbery. Either because the building will call the elevator people or because Cohen will come in and see what has happened. Ramon and Juanita have to report for work that day. Ramon shouldn't have a problem but Juanita is sure to be questioned. She went to her Bank in the morning and the party in the evening and was seen Sunday. Let's hope that leaves her in the clear." He paused.

"We know however the police won't stop there. I'll stay at the Hotel and take a tour or something. When things calm down in a few days, I'll return the van and leave. Our takings will stay at the farm. No one touches them. I'll be back within a month. By then I'll have set up meetings for selling the artifacts and jewels. I also hope to have a solution for the cash." He thought for a moment.

"Let's continue here for a bit and then get moving. We'll leave the elevator on the first floor. Everything normal. Pick up the safety signs and out we go. Providing we do that and it's working, the early Front Desk person shouldn't know a thing. Now, any questions?"

They both shook their heads and carried on working until after five thirty. They found almost two million more in cash, jewelry and several additional artifacts.

Everything was loaded into the elevator and taken to the first floor. From there the trolley took it to the van, and they loaded up. Juanita climbed in and peeled off her disguise. It took her twenty minutes to put on makeup and dress but at six fifty-five she was ready. They took a last look around the Lobby. The elevator stayed stopped on the first floor looking completely normal. They cleaned up using wet cloths. Nothing seemed out of place. The side door locked automatically as they exited. There were no cars in the parking lot. They stripped the decals from the van quickly before leaving. It now looked like a thousand other vehicles in the City. Juanita got dropped off on a corner just yards from the street. She would have a five-minute walk to get to her dinner. Sam and Ramon drove to the farm.

It took almost two hours to empty the van and wash it completely inside and out. By then it had started to rain. All equipment, uniforms and disguises were buried and the fresh earth covered with the old straw. Rain should flatten it out in no time and it would become unnoticeable. The hessian sacks went into the hide hold and they closed it up. Finally they removed their plastic gloves.

After showering and dressing, Sam drove to his Hotel. It was eight thirty. The Desk Clerk gave him the name of a good restaurant and twenty minutes later he sat at a table with a large steak and half a bottle of excellent Spanish wine. Later he went to the Casino at one of the bigger hotels and gambled for an hour. He arrived back at his Hotel, asked for his key and was asleep by midnight.

Ramon drove into the City twenty minutes after Sam left. On the way he stopped at a gas station and filled his tank. At a café on the seafront road he ate dinner alone, leaving a big tip when he signed the credit card slip. Afterwards he went to a late movie and kept falling asleep as it played. Finally at eleven thirty he drove home.

Juanita arrived at the restaurant with some of the other staff. The Cohen's were there along with their wives. It was a festive occasion with lots of wine and laughter. She left at nine o'clock. Levi and his wife dropped her off at her apartment. It had been a long day. Sunday Sam went on a tourist bus for an eight hour ride to all the beauty spots. It was interesting, and he enjoyed both the company and the lunch. Juanita went to the beach with friends and then had dinner. Ramon took his car to be thoroughly detailed, sitting drinking beer while they cleaned it and then going for lunch.

Chapter 11 – *'Aftermath.'*

Juanita went to Secure Vault on the Monday morning. Police cars were in abundance. She sat in her car for a minute and forced herself to relax. Approaching the front door a policeman stopped her, and she had to produce identification. Seeing her name he opened the door and beckoned a uniformed officer over. He had another man in plain clothes with him.

"Juanita Gomez? I'm Captain Gonzalez. This is Detective Dumas. I must advise you that Secure Vault has suffered a break in. We think jewelry and cash were stolen. We are contacting the owners of all boxes as we don't know which ones were opened. Now, can you tell me where you were this weekend?"

"Well, I worked here Friday. Saturday morning I woke late, passed by my Bank and spent the afternoon home. I attended the Company dinner in the evening. Mr. Cohen and his wife drove me back to my apartment. Yesterday I was at the beach with friends then we had dinner together. That's about it."

"Thank you, Ms. Gomez. I suppose if you went to your Bank you took out or deposited money?"

"Right. The General Bank. The main branch. I withdrew fifty dollars. I've got the receipt here somewhere." She opened her handbag.

Dumas held up his hand. "That won't be necessary. Please tell me where you had dinner on Sunday?"

"Oh! The Luxor Café. It's just off the seafront."

"I know it. Thank you. We will want to talk to you later."

"OK. I'll be here."

She turned to the administration area where Levi Cohen stood wringing his hands.

"Terrible. A disaster! Who would do such a thing? Years of work ruined! Ah Juanita. You will have to help. I need to know about which clients were affected. We only found out about the robbery half an hour ago when I arrived. Get me a list of clients and boxes. We'll make a start. Everyone has to be contacted. I have no idea which boxes, if indeed any, have been opened. They all look fine except one right now. This is dreadful!" He walked away shaking his head.

Juanita spent the rest of the day checking the information. Clients said that one hundred and twenty boxes seemed to have been robbed so far. Most people were didn't mention cash losses, only jewelry. At six in the afternoon there were still about twenty clients waiting to check their belongings. A further ten had yet to be contacted. Juanita didn't get home until eight o'clock.

Ramon had a quiet morning until ten thirty. Then the problems started. Marga received a call from the President who told her about the robbery. Ramon drove her immediately to Secure Vault where Jacob Cohen personally met her. She was the first client to check a box and her face confirmed Levi's worst fears. Her emeralds had been taken but not several other pieces which were less valuable. She was sure a hundred thousand in cash had vanished but she didn't mention that to Jacob. As the news spread, more and more clients arrived.

At the crime scene the police found bloodstains. The Chief of the robbery detail, Captain Horacio Gonzalez sent for a rush analysis. Within an hour they received the results. 'O' negative. A break perhaps? 'O' negative happened to be the category of only five percent of the population worldwide. However, he realized the Republic had no data base to trace people by blood type. The new Driving Licenses which would start being issued later in the year would have the information but right now there was nothing he could use. For a moment he was stuck. Then he remembered all foreigners were obliged to be fingerprinted and submit their blood type for a visa. It was an outside chance, but he called Customs and asked them to run blood types of visitors for the past month. They put him on hold. He waited nervously. Thirty seconds later they told him only one visitor in the past thirty days had 'O' negative. His name was Samuel Harris who listed his address as the Solimar Hotel.

Sam had been on a chartered boat for a day's fishing. When he got back to the Hotel that evening he found a Detective waiting for him. He walked up to the Front Desk and asked for his key. The Detective walked over.

"Mr. Harris. I'm Detective Alfonso Reyes. I'm sorry to bother you. There has been a robbery. At the scene we found fresh blood stains and believe one of the thieves sustained an injury. I have to ask two things. First, where were you on Saturday? And secondly have you been injured in the past few days, a cut maybe?"

"I slept here Saturday. I had breakfast at a fast-food joint and walked around the City. Came back in the evening and then went out for dinner. I asked the Desk Clerk to recommend a restaurant. I didn't get assaulted or anything. No injuries. Why do you ask me in particular might I ask?"

"Because, Mr. Harris you are registered on your visa as having O negative blood, the type we identified at the robbery site. As you probably know it's a rare type, hence our enquiries."

Sam realized the blood came from Ramon so what was happening? He had better play this one carefully.

"Detective. I'm willing to go with you to any doctor you wish and have him check me out for a wound if that will help?"

"Mr. Harris. There's a Doctor right here. Can we go to your room please and he will examine you there?" He pointed to a man holding a small black bag.

These guys were smart though Sam. Everything set up and ready!

"Sure thing. Let me get the key."

They took the elevator to his room, and the Doctor asked him to remove his clothes. After two minutes the doctor shook his head.

"Mr. Harris, you have some nice old scars but no wounds!" He turned to the Detective. "Nothing at all here." Reyes apologized profusely and he and the Doctor left.

That, more or less was the extent of Sam and Juanita's interaction with the police. No one questioned Ramon, Sam returned the van without complications.

They met three days later at the farm and related their stories. Sam expressed surprise to find that Ramon actually did have O negative blood, a million to one coincidence.

Using his phone, Sam took pictures of the gems and artifacts and emailed them to his Company address in London. He then erased everything on the phone, just in case and flew home the next day. His carry-on duffle was searched at the Airport but of course, they found nothing. Sam had counted that they would only search his bag. In the change pouch of his wallet he had placed two diamonds along with some local coins. He casually dropped the wallet in the plastic tray with his watch. The Security Guard pushed it across the top of the scanner and glanced at the items briefly. There was no alarm.

Two days later he showed Amari photographs of the jewelry and the two stones. Amari said they were very good and once he saw the rest he would make a firm offer. Meanwhile, it looked like the haul would be worth at least fifteen million. Amari purchased the two diamond on the spot for thirty thousand dollars. Sam opened an account in Oman later that morning. He needed money for expenses. At the same time he arranged with his new Bank to rent a large security box.

That afternoon Caleb drooled over the photographs of the artifacts. There were a total of forty-one. Watkins attended the meeting.

"These are incredible. They can never go on the open market but I know of a minor Prince that will snap them up for his own collection. They could go for over ten million. Most excellent Mr. Harris. When can you get them here?"

"I'll need help Caleb. I also have a large amount of American dollars I need to wash."

"That won't be any trouble. In Lebanon I've got an excellent contact at the Casino de Liban. It can be arranged that you win there, declare your winnings, pay a commission and all will be well. We can discuss that when the goods arrive. Tomorrow I will tell you how to get them here. Contact me in the afternoon. I'll have full details."

Watkins told Sam there should not be a problem. He would guarantee everything. In his position, Sam believed this was entirely possible. The amount of cash he had promised Watkins purchased reliability. However, he kept the key to the deposit box.

He flew back to the Republic in early February, checking into the Hilton this time. Ramon picked him up two blocks away at six o'clock. They went to the farm and Juanita arrived a few minutes later. Hugs and handshakes were exchanged. Sitting down, the updates started.

Sam told them what he had been doing and who he had seen. He gave them the good news about the value of the items. Then he described how the proceeds would be carried from the Republic within a week by a cruise ship passenger traveling to Muscat. He told them they needed to buy three large, strong suitcases and explained exactly how the contents should be packed. The suitcases would go to the Hilton and be picked up there by the passenger. No Customs problems were expected. Caleb and Watkins could ensure that.

The artifacts would be fenced by Caleb, the gems by Amari. After paying their commissions and settling up with Watkins, the proceeds would go into the security box. Everything had to remain the same. No travel, no spending, no talking. It had to be at least a year before they could travel to Oman and share out the funds. Each of them should make their own arrangements after that. They both agreed.

Juanita told Sam that Secure Vault was in liquidation. She would be out of a job in two weeks. The Cohen's had had multiple disasters to contend with and could not continue in business.

Ramon took up the tale. The police had found nothing. There were no fingerprints and the only lead seemed to be the blood stains. That was checked but turned out to be a dead end. The Desk Clerk saw two Sanyo elevator men Saturday morning. He said they both had facial hair, and he'd watched them carefully. They had left just after eleven. He swore nobody else came in while he was on duty. Sanyo said no employees worked at the building that day. There was talk of suing the Cohen's for misrepresentation about the safety of the Vault. That was ongoing, but the best story of all was still to come.

A week after the robbery, the Police interviewed Jacob and Sarah Cohens' personal staff. They went to the house and spoke to everyone who worked there. Naturally, someone had leaked word to the Press and the reporters and TV cameras waited outside. One small fact was revealed during the visit, it didn't help the investigation but it turned into the biggest scandal in the Republic for years.

It made headlines in all the newspapers and on the television. Cartoons appeared and comedians joked about it. Apparently the secret behind Sarah Cohen's tasty *empanadas* was because they were stuffed with seasoned iguana meat! The Cohen's had a dozen in cages in their garden, ready to be butchered! The humiliation and ridicule the Cohens ensured after that, pushed them over the edge. They filed for bankruptcy. Two months later they left the Republic to live in Israel. They never returned.

'TWO PRIESTS.'

Chapter 1 – *'A friendship.'*

Steven Blogs was a superb footballer. In fact, the best young football player in the local school and many people said, in the whole district.

Steven loved football but his passion unfortunately lead to some neglect of his regular school classes. Mr. Baldock, the Headmaster had frequently spoken to Steven about it and Steven always promised to do better. Baldock, like everyone else at the school and in the village, liked Steven. He was a very polite boy and would always raise his cap in greeting when passing a neighbor on his way to classes or offer to assist the elderly across the High Street. As an Altar Boy, he served at St. Mary's on Sunday's and was an enthusiastic member of the local scout troop.

Sunday was his favorite day because most of the men and boys would meet at the recreation ground, pick sides and play their hearts out for two hours until the one o'clock meal time.

Steven could usually be found at the rec ground after school. He ran home first to do his various chores, and with a shout of 'I'm off to the rec to play footie' he left the house, boots in hand to make his way down to the park. Steven enjoyed his uncomplicated life. In this rural community most of the men were employed around the area working on the farms. He, like them, became a dedicated supporter of the Rovers, the local side that played in the fourth division of the Football League. What could be better? Listen to the radio broadcast of the Rover's game on a Saturday and then on Sunday, go to Mass and out to the rec to play footie!

At ten, he became friends with Patrick Malone. They had known each other since early in Primary School and often said 'hello' at Mass, but they had never had been close. Paddy, a tall thin boy with no aptitude for playing sports, stood out as the brightest student in the school and seemed to be perpetually have his head in a book. Perhaps because of this the other boys sometimes made fun of him. It was this occasional harassment that bought Steven and Patrick together.

As school finished one rainy day, a group of pupils began tease Paddy about being a bookworm. It wasn't really serious but some pushing and shoving drew Steven's attention. Because of the rain he hadn't rushed off home and on to the rec today, so he came to Paddy's rescue.

"Get away from him! Leave him alone. He's not hurting anyone. Let him study if he wishes! Go on, shove off!" He stared at them and because they respected Steven as the best center half in the district, they walked away.

He nodded at Paddy and turned to leave and go home, but Paddy caught up with him.

"Thank you Steven. Thank you for seeing them off. I'm not a good fighter so thanks for the help."

"It's fine. Don't worry. They won't bother you again."

He turned and called over his shoulder, "I've got to get my cassock washed so I'm going by the Church. Walk along with me, I know you live that way."

They walked, and they talked. Steven told Patrick about being an Altar Boy and Patrick told Steven that although he didn't play soccer he supported the Rovers. At St. Mary's Catholic Church, Steven introduced Patrick to Father

Dunstan, the Parish Priest. There were not a lot of Catholics in the district so the Parish was small and poor. Father Dunstan, like many before him, was serving the final years of his Priesthood there. A cheerful soul, he soon had Patrick asking questions. Before leaving, he agreed to come on Sunday to learn what was required to be an Altar server. That day saw the start of a long and enduring friendship between the boys. They saved their pocket money diligently and every six weeks would have enough to go to the Rovers ground and pay the boy's entry fee to watch them play.

Only five years after World War II, the country remained deeply in debt. Money was scarce and the only way to get to a Grammar school involved passing a scholarship. Patrick had no problems getting in but poor Steve struggled. However, with Paddy's tutoring he passed the entrance examination and was also accepted at St. Peters Catholic Grammar School in the nearby town.

As an eleven year old Steven won a place in the school soccer team made up of boys of fifteen and sixteen. Paddy would come to the Saturday games to cheer him on. He seemed destined to have a great career as a footballer and he never missed a training session during those years.

At sixteen boys could either leave school or continue with advanced studies until eighteen and go to University. Steven thought long and hard. Conscription for two years still existed in the United Kingdom and he was sure he would have to serve sooner or later. He felt sure University was out of the question. Paddy would make it and get an exemption from military service, but not him. If he got it over with, then before he reached twenty he could come back and hopefully try out for a professional club.

He left school and worked at a local store for the next year. Then at seventeen he went to the nearest recruiting office.

Chapter 2 – *'Growing up.'*

Joining the Army at seventeen and a half, he was posted to the Suffolk Regiment. After twelve weeks he came home on leave and after a brief reunion with Paddy Malone, went to Cyprus. He spent eighteen months there fighting EOKA, the Greek Cypriot independence movement. Steven survived several ambushes during his service there and, in nineteen fifty eight, shortly before the cease fire was signed, he returned to England with Sergeant's stripes on his sleeve and a chunk of his right calf missing, the result of a land mine explosion while on patrol. His dream of being a professional footballer would remain a dream. He was almost twenty years old.

Paddy was studying Philosophy at University but they got together a few weeks later when the mid-term holidays came around.

Sitting in the sunshine in Steven's back garden they sipped their Guinness while Steven told Paddy all about his service. It seemed like a confession and Paddy was a good listener. Steven had never spoken to anyone of his experiences in the hot, dusty and dangerous villages outside Nicosia but he bared his soul to Paddy that day about the wounding's and killings.

They didn't speak of it again but both realized that afternoon had changed them both. Paddy went back to the University the next day and Steven started work with his father at a nearby farm. He remained employed there for a year until he met Paddy again.

At a Rovers game they bumped in to each other and their reunion was a happy one. They went to the bar and Paddy gave him the news that he would be entering a Seminary to study for the Priesthood the following week. Steven found it hard to believe until Paddy told him he had decided after the two had met in Steven's garden when he returned from

Cyprus. Steven then understood why Paddy made his decision.

On his way home he stopped by St. Mary's. Father Dunstan had just finished with the evening service and he joined him in the sacristy. They talked for two hours. The Father told him he was leaving the ministry later in the year to go to a home for retired Priests. He had just turned seventy-five years old. Steven told him what he wanted to do, and the Father gave him the information and references he required.

He spent that evening writing letters and a few weeks later received replies from his ex-commanding officer in the Suffolk Regiment and from the Bishop in Brentwood.

With these in hand he made an appointment to visit one of the many 'Red Brick' universities springing up throughout the United Kingdom. The meeting resulted in his acceptance to study History.

He called Paddy, and they met that weekend. Steven explained that he felt a calling from the Church and had decided to study and then attend a Seminary. Paddy smiled. Inside he'd always known.

Chapter 3 – 'Paddy.'

Paddy explained to Steven that to advance in the Church, you needed a specialty. With his finance degree, he would graduate from the Seminary in a month. He was going to the Vatican Bank in Rome to study there. Steven was impressed but Paddy, after a couple of Guinness, seemed the same old friend as ever. They parted that evening and were not to see each other for quite some time.

Paddy stayed in Rome for seven years, his financial and organizational skills winning accolades from his superiors. The word around the Vatican hinted that the Purple would not be long in coming. They were right. He became Monsignor Malone after leaving the Vatican Bank. The next step found him attending Pontifical University where he obtained a Doctor of Theology degree. I he thought he would be returning to the Bank but the Catholic Church works in strange ways.

He was told he would not be going back into finance. Perhaps to keep him humble, a common occurrence in the Church, he was being sent to San Pedro in Paraguay. Before going off to his new assignment he visited England, and of course met with Steven.

He stayed for three years in South America, serving as a Parish Priest in a region dominated by cattle ranches. The people were known for their friendliness and they extended a warm welcome to Padre Patricio as he was known. He liked it there and learned Spanish from his Parishioners. The climate was warm and wet but in winter the temperature would drop down to fifty degrees and the nights could be cold. During his two years there he learned humility. The rich cattlemen didn't have much time for the Monsignor from the Vatican but the people did. They invited him into their homes and saw his fervent belief in the Church. He learned how to be a Parish Priest in San Pedro.

At age thirty-seven, to his surprise, he was recalled to become Secretary to Cardinal Octavio Salazar at the Secretariat of the Economy. Salazar, a favorite of his Holiness, the Pope, served as his special advisor. Paddy, as the Cardinal's Secretary was now exposed to the inner circles of the Vatican. With his organizational skills Paddy became the administrative leader of the Secretariat, and Salazar, advancing in years, left more and more of the day to day running of the organization to him. His efforts did not go unnoticed.

At forty-two the Holy Father approved Paddy's selection as Bishop and a few months later he went to New York to serve under His Eminence Henry, Cardinal O'Malley, the Archbishop. There he presided over a suburban Diocese for eight years and was then sent to the Diocese of Brentwood in the United Kingdom as Bishop. He spent six years there before returning to Rome. During that time he met Steven twice. Once at the lunch they enjoyed upon his arrival and then on a Saturday visit to see the Rovers play. Paddy was a very busy Bishop.

Back in Rome Paddy became a minor Church celebrity. His various important appointments indicated his standing, and like a star, he was expected to shine brightly. This he did.

The Holy Father, now in his eighties, named Paddy as Acting Head of the Secretariat of the Economy. At fifty-three he was very young to hold the post. He justified the Pontiff's faith in him and the Churches finances, astutely invested, reached new heights, allowing money to be allocated to evangelical missions all over the world.

After the Holy Father passed away four years later Paddy, as custom required, resigned from his post. The new Pope, an admirer of Paddy's skills, appointed him Cardinal and sent him as Archbishop to Westminster, as Prelate of the Catholic Church in the United Kingdom. He returned to London almost immediately. He was fifty-seven years old.

Chapter 4 – 'Steven.'

University learning was difficult for Steven's brain but very easy in every other way. He was only a little older than most students but his experience went far and beyond theirs. Starting soccer again he found he hadn't lost his touch. Naturally he couldn't shoot as hard as he used to, due to the injury, but once in shape he made the University team in his 'freshy' year.

He learned how to study properly and by the end of his second year he got excellent grades. One weekend a month he spent at home and during his vacations, helped at Saint Mary's near where he lived. Father Donovan was another elderly Priest spending his final couple of years before retirement at the small, inconspicuous post. Donovan had been a Chaplain in the Parachute Regiment and had dropped at Arnhem in WWII. Steven got on well with him and they spent quite a few evenings at the Rectory attached to the Church. He enjoyed a Guinness as did Steven. The Father explained many things about the Priesthood to his younger helper and had infinite patience when answering questions.

Paddy came with him once but didn't seem to have the same rapport with the older Priest. He said afterwards that the Church was modernizing and dinosaurs like Father Donovan, were needed in Parish positions, but that to advance in the Church one needed the three 'S's'. A specialty, a sponsor and 'suerte', the Spanish word for good luck.

After four years Steven had his degree and was accepted into a Seminary. There he spent a further five years studying and the year after that was assigned to a Parish Church on the outskirts of Liverpool. For the next six years he toiled there as an Assistant Pastor. He still played soccer every chance he got, and his efforts made him a popular figure amongst the younger members of the Parish.

One of the bright spots of his stay there was Paddy's vacation visit while he served in Paraguay. He spent the night at the Parish Rectory where the Priest, Father Feldon, was astounded to learn of the close friendship that existed between the Monsignor and the Assistant Pastor.

They had dinner together and Paddy regaled them with stories of the Vatican. He kept it light, but it was obvious that he was familiar with most of the players in the Church hierarchy.

The very next day, Father Feldon, taking no chances that any information regarding his Parish would be bandied about, had asked that Steven be transferred elsewhere.

Fortunately, word of Feldon's request reached the Monsignor's ears as he visited the Cardinal Archbishop's office in Westminster before leaving England. When he heard what had been requested he was able, through his UK contacts, to have Steven sent to his home, east of London, as Assistant Pastor at St. Mary's in the Diocese of Brentwood.

For Steven it seemed wonderful to be back again. At thirty-five he led an untroubled life in his principal role as mentor to the children and young men of the town. He was a quiet man and attracted little interest from his superiors. What they did know was that he had a gift with youngsters and under his tutelage, Confirmations increased every year. He was secure in his post and becoming respected and admired by his Parishioners for his simple way of life and his dedication to the younger people.

He felt at last that he had found his calling and was very content. Some of the men had worked the surrounding farms for more than fifty years and their children and their children's children attended St. Mary's. They were bell ringers, choir members and ushers as well as other helpers. One, old Henry Mosley, was the gravedigger who boasted that at seventy-four he could dig a six footer in one morning. It was William that had made him the wedge for the ever-drooping window in his bedroom and William who had carved new balusters for the Altar rail.

Several Parish Priest's came and went over the next fifteen years. They were usually men who were completing their time in the Priesthood. Some were like saints and others merely mortals whose vocations and energy slowly faded with the days. All got on well with Steven as he toiled every Sunday afternoon getting his young charges prepared for their first Communions, and later their Confirmations.

In winter time he could usually get to see the Rovers play home games. He had been named their Chaplain a few years earlier when one of the Directors, a Parishioner, learned of his interest in the Club. Those Saturday afternoons were greatly looked forward to, giving the blessing in the dressing room and then watching the match.

Teaching the Parish children was his special gift. There was always one child in the Confirmations group who would attempt to confound him with an obtuse question regarding the Church. Most enquiries he had heard already over the years but as usual, he answered them in a jocular manner which usually had the remainder of the class laughing and the questioner humbled but not ridiculed. Today it was a young man called Thomas Smith who had decided to be the instigator. Towards the end of the lesson he raised his hand.

"Yes, Thomas?"

"Father. Why is it in the front of the Church they have those large, enclosed boxes where the big-nobs sit but in the back the people only have regular bench pews?"

Steven didn't bother about Thomas Smith's occasional attempts to wind him up. He came from a well-off family and besides that, was an enthusiastic soccer player and a Rovers supporter. That with Steven, was worth a lot. But today he decided to him some fun himself. The pews had been paid for by one of the richest farmers in the district almost a hundred years previously and, as was custom in those days, the farmer built a large, enclosed pew at the front of the Altar for his family.

"Ah Thomas. You always have hard questions. This time though I know the answer!"

The class squirmed and muffled their first sounds of laughter. Father Steven was famous for his answers to these kinds of questions. He continued.

"Now Thomas. Have you ever been on an aircraft?"

"Of course I have Father. We went to Spain on one last year."

"Good. That's good Thomas!" He looked around and rubbing his hands, surveying the class. They leaned forward in anticipation.

"Well Thomas. Spain eh? How nice! Now, describe the aircraft. Tell me about it."

Thomas, seeing a chance to boast a little, started out.

"Well Father. These planes are big. We went on one from Stansted. It took over two hours to get to Madrid. They had a lady that served cold sodas and peanuts to us. I really liked it!"

"Wow! That sounds like it cost a lot of money Thomas?"

"It did but my Dad has a few bob!"

"Tell me Thomas. Where did you sit on the plane? In the front or the back?"

"In the back of course Father. Up front is First Class. They have big wide seats there and you need a lot of money to sit…"

His voice trailed off as the laughter started.

"Thomas. You've answered your own question! Now how about a game of footie?" Even young Thomas smiled.

As usual, when lessons finished, he'd call for volunteers for football and he and the boys would go to the field beside the Church for a pickup game. Steve played in his old army boots which he had been wearing during winters for the past 30 years. It was a rural environment and when visiting Parishioners he often had to take muddy paths.

The sight of Steve holding up his cassock, his white legs ending in old army boots, always elicited good-natured laughter from the boys as they played. And play they did! Usually for an hour before it got dark, and the players scuttled off for their dinners. Steve would then return to the Rectory and take a bath before having a sandwich for dinner and afterwards, doing his weekly house cleaning. In such a poor Parish they couldn't afford a housekeeper.

The Parish Priest had retired two weeks earlier in mid-November and Steven was alone. He rather liked the independence. Then, one afternoon close to the end of the month, he received a telephone call. Paddy was on the line. He had been appointed Bishop for the Diocese of Brentwood and had just arrived. Could Steven come to visit him?

It was six miles to the Bishop's Residence at Cathedral House in Brentwood and Steven rode there on his bicycle. He had a noon lunch appointment. The Tuesday morning was cold, and he bundled up, a thick scarf hiding his clerical collar. He arrived after an hour's hard peddling and cycled up the driveway, dismounting at the steps of the house. A young Monsignor came through the front door and asked what he wanted.

"Young man. I wish to see the Bishop please." He answered.

"You do eh? Well you have to make an appointment for that fellow. He doesn't just see anyone you understand?"

"I'm sure he doesn't Monsignor. I hope he will oblige me though. My name is Blogs, Steven Blogs."

"I'll take a look. Stay here Blogs while I check the appointment book."

"Oh. By the way Monsignor, I'm Father Blogs in case you can't find it." He loosened his scarf so his collar showed. The Monsignor looked annoyed.

"Father, you might have told me that earlier in the conversation. I recall now that His Excellency mentioned he wanted to see you. Heaven knows what you've done."

Obviously he knew nothing of the friendship between the Bishop and this lowly Priest thought Steven. I'll have a little fun before going in.

"Monsignor. I don't think I've done anything bad. Could it be that he wants to meet me?"

"I think not. He's far too busy to bother with every Pastor who drops by here. Now, come with me and I'll find out if he remembers he asked to see you."

They went inside and the Monsignor helped Steven hang up his heavy coat, hat and scarf. Along the hallway they walked, Steven's army boots clacking on the boards, until they came to large double doors.

The Monsignor knocked and Steven herd Paddy's voice bid them enter.

He stood up from the desk he had been sitting at and with a huge smile on his face, crossed the room, extending his hand for his ring to be kissed. Then he lifted Steven to his feet and held him at arm's length.

"Stevie! It's been a long time!" He held on to Steven and looked him up and down. "Not eating properly Father! We'll must fix that!"

He turned to the Monsignor.

"Joseph. Tell the housekeeper we'll want lunch in thirty minutes and meanwhile ask her to bring two pints of Guinness and some crisps to my study."

"Now Steven. What's happening with the Rovers? I've heard nothing much at all this season!"

The Monsignor left the room amazed while Paddy and Steven walked through the Bishops comfortable study. There was a view of the gardens through the glass doors and the bird feeder set up there had a lot of customers. They sat down and Steven pulled a package from his pocket.

"Your Excellency. I've something for you, now you are a Bishop and all!"

"Stevie, knock of the flattery! Away from formal occasions I'm always Paddy to you."

"Sorry Paddy." He tried to look contrite but failed and Paddy laughed.

He handed over the small package wrapped in simple brown paper and tied with string. Paddy carefully opened it and was rewarded by the sight of a wooden Cross.

"It's not just an ordinary Cross Paddy. It has a history. There's a gravedigger in our Parish, Henry Mosley. Henry has been digging graves there for over fifty years and he told me this story about Robert of Bury. Robert was a young lad, kidnapped and killed in Bury St. Edmonds. Some say it's just legend, and the Church has no evidence to support that he ever existed. However, Mosley says he had heard of a story, passed down over the years that said after his martyr's death they wished to hide the body from his enemies so he was taken to the old Church of St. Mary's and buried in the Churchyard there." He looked at Paddy.

"Henry says there was always a small stone in a quiet corner. The inscription had worn completely off. Legend has it that this was the grave marker of Robert of Bury. Thirty years ago when the new Church was built and no further space in the yard could be found, authorization to dig in the old spaces was given and William said he kept a piece of Robert's coffin that remained and carved it himself. This is what you hold in your hand. I hope it will be your Pectoral Cross. It fits with the ancient tradition that deems these Crosses should contain a relic. Now I trust, you have yours."

There was a silence in the room. Then Paddy unclipped the chain supporting his own gold Pectoral Cross and unthreaded it. He then put the iron loop of the wooden one through the chain and replaced, round his neck.

"Munire me digneris" He said, asking the Lord for strength and protection against all evil and all enemies, and to be mindful of His passion and Cross.

"Thank you Steven. This I will wear for the remainder of my years in the Church. It's priceless!"

The Guinness and crisps arrived, and they toasted each other.

"I have a surprise for you also Steven. St. Mary's is yours. You've been there long enough as Assistant. Now it's Father Steven Blogs, Parish Priest. Tell the sign painters to put it up as soon as you return today. By the way, where did you park? Sometimes there's no space in the forecourt."

"I cycled over Paddy. Keeps me fit for the footie!"

Paddy laughed. "Impossible you are Steven Blogs. Well, you'll not cycle back. We'll get my driver take you. The bike will fit in the trunk of my car, it's huge! Now, how about another Guinness? We have a lot of catching up to do."

It was a happy lunch served with a bottle of Lacryma Christi. Paddy, always the sophisticate, told its tale.

"Lacryma Christi comes from an old myth that Christ, crying over Lucifer's fall from heaven, cried his tears on the land and gave divine inspiration to the vines that grow on the sides of Vesuvius. Its lower slopes are extremely fertile and covered with vineyards. It was a favorite of Cardinal Salazar, a favorite as I also had the honor to be. In his will he left me a dozen bottles a year for twenty years. Octavio Salazar was my mentor. He was a great friend of the Holy Father and he helped my advancement in the Church."

He sat back as his steward poured them another glass and left the room.

"The Church Steven, is a maze. No one person has the map to all of it. You learn this when you first arrive in Rome. Some newcomers believe they can unlock every door. That's not possible. You hope and pray you will attract the attention of someone who knows part of the maze. He will guide you through it. But not all the way. Not even the Pontiff himself knows that! But with a good mentor you can go far. Without one you will always be a Parish Priest, perhaps a good Priest, but you may forget the Purple and should not even dream of the Red. It's a life for the few. Those of us who have been fortunate must help our friends." He paused and sipped his wine.

"You think Steven that because you are a good Priest, you do not need assistance. Believe me, you do. How is it you are at St. Mary's? You are there because I asked that you be sent there when Feldon wanted you transferred elsewhere. Back then some friends close to the Cardinal Archbishop in Westminster, assisted me with that favor. So you see, we all need each other's help."

An hour later, bicycle in the trunk, Steven was driven back to his Church, half a bottle of wine and two Guinness helping make the journey most pleasant.

Chapter 5 – *'The working years.'*

Steven was happy with the independence of being a Parish Priest. He was not immediately assigned an Assistant Pastor so alone, he moved quietly forward with simple reforms that St. Mary's needed. Like most Churches, it required constant upkeep. Diocese help was not always available but Steven, thanks to his being a native of the area, got some of the bigger farm owners to contribute to the various funds he initiated.

He kept the children under his wing even when another young Priest, Father Timothy Peters, fresh from the Seminary, arrived to assist him. The numbers of First Communions and Confirmations continued to grow and the football games after lessons were legend amongst the Parishioners, many who had played themselves when they were kids.

Steven and Paddy met again to attend a Rovers game together one weekend the following winter, but they were both busy and during the next few years only the occasional phone call kept them in contact. During the last of these calls Paddy told him he would soon return to the Vatican. He was, he said, a mere Bishop, but the Holy Father had named him as Acting Head of the Secretariat of the Economy. His talents in that area were sorely needed by the Church.

Four years later Steven had his biggest triumph since joining the Church. After a monumental effort, sufficient funds were collected to repair the leaking roof of St. Mary's. Steven was called to Westminster to receive the Cardinals' personal thanks. That Saturday the Cardinal graciously told him at lunch that he would soon retire and the new Prelate of the United Kingdom would be Patrick Malone. Steven was amazed at the news and it filled his thoughts as he traveled home on the train.

It would hardly affect him he thought, but he looked forward to seeing Paddy again when he arrived. Meanwhile, he had Mass and confessions later that day.

Six months passed and finally a telephone call came. Paddy of course, wishing him a happy Christmas. They talked and Paddy told him he would be down early in the New Year. He wanted an update on how the Rovers were doing!

One Sunday afternoon as the Confirmation class ended, Steven had the opportunity once again, to make the children smile.

It was William Burrows who asked the question. It always seemed to be one of his favorites and usually a dedicated footie player.

"Father. I have a question to ask."

Like dozens before him he looked slyly around at the others making sure he had their approval. They smiled back at him, giving him the confidence to continue with his scheme.

"Go ahead William."

"Well Father. Why is it that when there's a collection the only people that are allowed to take round the offerings baskets are old folks? They never let anyone young do it. It's always Mr. Gorman who limps and Mr. Jones who has a walking stick and coughs all the time. Why is this? You said everyone was equal!"

Having made his point he again looked for approval. Now however, the others didn't commit themselves. They waited for Steven to reply.

"Billy. Ah Billy! Surely you know the answer to that. Don't you?"

"No I don't Father. That's the reason for the question."

"Well Billy. I'll tell you the answer and then what do you say we go have a kick about?"

"OK Father. That's a good idea! Go ahead!"

"Billy. I'm sure you know Mr. Gorman has a bad leg. Now he couldn't have a kick around with us that's for sure. Mr. Jones is quite sick. That's why he coughs."

"So why is it them all the time with the baskets Father?"

"Billy. I see you can't work it out for yourself so I'll tell you. Then it's outside! The ball is just beside the door!" He shook his head.

"All of you come close. I don't want to say this secret in a loud voice." He beckoned them towards him and they huddled up. Speaking quietly he said, "We trust the baskets to the old people Billy because we know they can't run fast and steal the money. That's the reason only the oldies do the collections! Now you know the secret but tell no one!"

Everyone broke into laughter and the boys went outside with Steven, wearing his army boots as usual, for a kick around.

A month later, after Sunday Confirmation lessons and during the kick about, Steven fell over, holding his leg in agony. He called Billy Burrows over.

"Billy, get Father Timothy here right away please. I've hurt my leg and need him."

The Assistant Pastor called for an ambulance and later that evening at the local hospital, they operated and set the broken leg. He would have to spend two days there and then could go home and rest for two weeks before he would be able to walk with a crutch.

Steven slept fitfully that night and on the Monday morning as he was eating a light breakfast, he heard a commotion outside in the corridor. The door of the rom burst open and in walked Paddy Malone in his red Cardinals regalia, followed by the Ward Sister and several Doctors. The visit created a sensation. He walked over to Steven's bed and stretched out his hand. Stevie kissed the ring. Paddy looked down at him.

"Father Blogs! I've told you about playing footie at your age! You're sixty years old! You should be playing chess or doing crossword puzzles." Shaking his head he smiled down at his friend.

"Forgive me Your Grace. If I'd realized the inconvenience it would cause everyone I'd never have played. But then the boys would think I was losing it and we can't let that happen." Paddy laughed.

"You're right Stevie. Have to keep up appearances! Now, if we can get some order in here I'd like a few minutes alone with you." The people in the room, taking the hint, walked quietly out, and the door closed.

"Well Stevie. Apart from this little mishap. How have you been? And no more of 'Your Grace' please!"

"I'm well Paddy. There's a new roof at last!"

"Yes, I know about that Stevie. A great effort that justified my decision to send you here. Well done! I heard very early this morning of the accident. Amazing the speed the Church telegraph works at! Now what happened?"

"Well Billy Burrows sent a pass along the wing and I ran for it but my boot lace tripped me up and over I went."

"Ah Stevie. You'll never change." He leaned over to straighten the pillow and as he did so his Pectoral Cross, the one given to him by Steven, swung across his chest, the black wood contrasting with the bright red of his cassock.

"I see you're looking at the get-up I'm wearing. Well this is Choir Dress, I came straight here from an early service in Westminster. I had no time to change. It's great for circumventing regulations. Visiting hours aren't until ten o'clock but with this lot on they tend to make exceptions! Now, what about the Rovers?"

Paddy stayed another twenty minutes and then a Monsignor knocked and put his head around the door.

"Your Grace. The Bishop is here."

"Stevie. I phoned the Bishop for protocols sake. Now you'll have to entertain him!" He laughed.

"I'll say hello and then I must be on my way. Call me in a week and let me know how it's going."

The Bishop arrived and greetings were exchanged before Paddy left. He was amazed at a Cardinal visiting a Parish Priest and became very solicitous. He wished Stevie well and said prayers would be offered for a quick recovery. Please keep him advised of progress and meanwhile Father Timothy, who had accompanied the Bishop, could stand in for him. During the day he had several other visitors, Henry Mosley the gravedigger and Billy Burrows, the Confirmation pupil amongst them.

Two weeks later he was on crutches and was managing to get about. He called Paddy to let him know. A month after that, apart from a slight limp, he deemed himself back to normal. He found it impossible to give up soccer completely, but he downgraded his playing role to being a goalkeeper where he thought he would be less exposed to any accidents.

The Confirmation classes were nearing their end for the year and it only remained to contact the Bishop to see when the next Ceremony would be. Upon receiving a date two months hence, he submitted the usual paperwork required by the Diocese.

He mentioned this to Paddy when he called a week later and was surprised when told that Paddy was coming to Brentwood for the Easter Vigil Ceremony in two months' time. They would arrange to meet after the event for a talk.

The time passed quickly as the Confirmation pupils were briefed on what they could expect. The requirement for a 'Confirmation name' seemed to be the most exciting thing for the children.

Steven was surprised when he read the submittals that William Burrows had chosen the name 'Steven'.

Chapter 6 – 'A Confirmation.'

The big day arrived at last. The children, their families along with Steven and Father Timothy, made their way the six miles to the Cathedral in Brentwood.

There were many people present for the Easter Vigil Mass and the Cathedral was completely filled. The Cardinal arrived and was greeted by the Bishop. Paddy looked around and saw Steven with his charges. Whispering to the Bishop and accompanied by his Monsignor, Paddy made his way across the Church to embrace him, causing quite a stir amongst his Parishioners who like most people, his little or no knowledge of their past friendship.

When things settled down the Ceremony took place in all its solemnity. The children answered their questions and apart from an occasional hesitation, all went well. Then, as the Bishop stood to address the congregation there was a disturbance. A man burst through the doors of the Cathedral and ran along the aisle to the Altar brandishing a handgun. He seemed distraught. His eyes were red, and he was sweating heavily.

There were screams from the gathering and people dropped to the floor. The man fired two shots into the air and pointed the gun at the nearest group of children. It was the group from St. Mary's.

"These are children of the devil! They must be rescued from his clutches!" he shouted, shooting again into the roof.

Steven, who was standing in front of his contingent, walked towards the man, arms open.

"Stop! Don't shoot any more my son. This is the House of God! We can have no violence here!" The man looked at him and brandished his gun.

"Get away! Get away! The devil is here, and I have been sent to find him. If you stand against me I will shoot you!" He pointed the weapon at Steven.

"No my son. You won't shoot me. I will help you. Lay down the firearm and we will talk together. No one will hurt you." He walked towards the man again. The crowd remained silent, watching what happened but powerless to intervene. The Cardinal's Monsignor slipped quickly away to get help.

"I don't trust you!" said the man stepping back.

"Don't worry. It will be fine. Hand me the gun and we'll talk. You need not fear my son. God understands everything." He walked forward, hand out to take the gun.

"No! No! Step back or I'll kill you," shouted the man. Steven kept coming forward and as he did so the pistol fired. The shot hit Steven in the shoulder but he reached out and embraced the man. Two more shots were fired before they both fell to the floor. Men ran forward, held the man down, and confiscated the gun. Steven lay face up bleeding from three wounds, two of them to the chest.

As he lay on the floor the first to reach him were Father Timothy and Billy Burrows.

"Father. You must lay still. Help is coming," said Timothy.

Steve smiled up at them. "It's fine. Don't worry. Now Billy, put your head close. I can't talk loud. There's one thing I must put in place before I leave. You are to tell Father Timothy that next week you will be a collector at the morning Mass. Is that clear?"

Through his tears, Billy nodded his head. At that moment the Cardinal pushed through the crowds along with an emergency crew. As they lifted him onto the gurney, he saw Paddy.

"What have they done to you Stevie? What have they done?"

He found the strength to answer.

"It's fine Paddy. You mustn't worry about me. I think I'm wanted for a game of footie upstairs!" His feet, enclosed as usual in his old army boots, stuck out from under his cassock. He spoke in a soft voice.

"Behold I see the heavens opened, and the Son of man standing at the right hand of God." Steven had just repeated the dying words of Saint Steven, the first Martyr of Christianity.

His eyes closed. The paramedic looked at the Cardinal and shook his head. Paddy, tears streaming down his face, made the sign of the Cross and started the Act of Contrition.

Other books by Michael J. Merry

The Golden Altar (2003)

The Reluctant Colonel (2008)

El Altar Dorado (Spanish - 2012)

The Education of Santiago O'Grady (2014)

Printed in the United States
By Bookmasters